P9-ASD-771

Table of Contents

Prologue...6
Chapter One: Filo's Friend................................26
Chapter Two: The Fruits of Peddling................34
Chapter Three: Everyone Loves Angels.............47
Chapter Four: The Volunteer.............................67
Chapter Five: A Royal Order.............................80
Chapter Six: Welcome.......................................87
Chapter Seven: General Commander................107
Chapter Eight: Before the Storm.....................120
Chapter Nine: Framed Again?.........................128
Chapter Ten: The Third Wave..........................141
Chapter Eleven: Grow Up................................158
Chapter Twelve: Iron Maiden..........................176
Chapter Thirteen: Parting Ways......................208
Chapter Fourteen: On the Road Again.............219
Chapter Fifteen: The Shield Demon..................229
Chapter Sixteen: Appointment Arrangements....255
Chapter Seventeen: The Princess's True Strength...261
Chapter Eighteen: Persuasion..........................281
Chapter Nineteen: The Tools...........................314
Chapter Twenty: Shadow.................................325
Epilogue: Name...336

Extra Chapter: Before I Met My Best Friend............345

Prologue

"This is going to be a pain. We should have turned it down."

Everything happened because of the villagers' simple request.

They wanted us to do something about the monsters around town.

The Dragon Zombie's rotting corpse had badly polluted the surrounding mountains. Once we took care of that problem, the monsters that had been thriving in the polluted mountains set their sights on the village.

The idea was that once the monsters learned that the village was a dangerous place for them, they would just stay away. So the village hired us as temporary guards to keep the monsters aware of the threat the town posed.

Honestly, I'd wanted to turn the job down, but they'd done so much for us that I ended up accepting it out of a sense of obligation. Considering all they were doing to help Raphtalia with her illness, we couldn't just leave them in the lurch—so we made our way back to the mountains.

"Oh well, let's get this over with."

My name is Naofumi Iwatani, and I am a 20-year-old college student from Japan. I'm also a bit of an otaku.

I was at the library reading an old book called *The Records of the Four Holy Weapons* when I passed out. When I woke up, I found myself in the very world the book had described, and I was tasked with the role of the Shield Hero.

They'd summoned me to their world because they were under threat from a disaster called the waves of destruction. These waves consisted of a rift that opened between dimensions, from which great hordes of monsters appeared. Apparently, they needed the help of the Four Legendary Heroes to overcome the destruction of the waves.

I was forced to assume the role of the Shield Hero, and I had no choice but to stand against the waves when they appeared.

At first it all seemed like a dream—too good to be true. But it turned out that the shield I was forced to carry had other properties as well, some of which were really annoying. I was completely unable to deal damage to monsters.

I put all my strength into my blows, but monsters just brushed them off, like I was nothing but a bothersome insect. I soon discovered that I was unable to attack at all.

However, I made up for it with my defense rating, which was through the roof. You could say that all I could do was defend.

Eventually, I managed to get a party together, and we started traveling the world. Along the way we fought many battles—just then, we were in the middle of one.

". . . ?!"

A huge dragonfly flew at me, brandishing its stinger.

But it bounced off my shield with an ineffectual, hollow clang.

The shield was able to absorb different monsters and materials, which in turn would unlock new shield forms and abilities. You could say that the shield leveled up with me. That was how I learned new abilities.

Anyway, there were a lot of difficulties that went along with it, but it was also proving to be a big help.

It helped me compound difficult medicines, and it improved the quality of my cooking—so I guess it was pretty useful in some ways.

As for the shield, I'd really love to take it off sometime, but it was cursed or something, and I wasn't able to remove the shield at all. It was always there, stuck to my arm. So I needed to rely on the rest of my party a lot. I had to leave all attacking up to them.

"Mr. Naofumi! Are you all right?!"

The girl with the raccoon ears and tail cut down a Poison Fly and turned to me.

Her name was Raphtalia. She was a raccoon-type demi-human. After I was framed and chased out of the castle, I bought her as a slave.

When I first bought her, she looked like she was around 10 years old. But demi-humans' bodies grow as their levels rise.

She matured very quickly as we fought different monsters, and now she looked more like a 17-year-old girl.

She was very pretty. Well, she was cute anyway.

Personality-wise, she was very serious. Watching her, you got the impression that she was constantly evaluating possible routes of action—that she was always trying to determine the "correct" path.

Before I was summoned to this world, there had been a large wave of destruction, and she had lost her family and village in the ensuing chaos. I think that's probably why she was so motivated to fight against the waves with me.

"I'm leaving defense up to you!"

"I know!"

Luckily enough, Raphtalia trusted me.

I had watched her grow up before my eyes, which inspired some parental feelings in me. At only 20 years old, it felt a little weird to nurse those parental instincts, but having seen her grow the way she had, I couldn't deny that I felt responsible for her. I think she probably felt the same way. She'd been with me since she was a kid, so she probably saw me as some kind of father figure.

So she trusted me, and I wanted to take care of her.

That's when it happened. A shadow appeared before me.

"Woah!"

A large bird-monster called a Filolial dashed over to the

approaching Poison Tree, leaned back, then let loose a furious barrage of kicks.

That Filolial was one of my friends, too.

Her name was Filo, and she was a Filolial that had grown attached to me.

Filo had a mysterious power: she could turn into a human. When she's in human form, she is a little girl with blonde hair, blue eyes, and little angel wings on her back.

But her real form . . . Well, she was a Filolial, but not a normal one. Her filolial form was like a mix between an ostrich and a giant owl.

Apparently she was actually a Filolial Queen.

She was strong enough to pull a heavy carriage, and she ate more than enough to compensate for her effort. She was always putting things in her mouth.

Don't let her cuteness fool you. She can really pack a punch.

Her personality was . . . innocent, free, and pure . . . Pure probably sums it up best. She always had a happy look on her face.

The slave trader who had sold me Raphtalia had also been selling eggs, so I found her there. I won her in an egg lottery kind of game. The eggs all looked the same, and a ticket cost 100 pieces of silver. I picked one I liked, and when it hatched, Filo came out.

She was . . . two weeks old now. She didn't look it though— she looked much older. I'd raised her too.

"Looks like we're almost done here, Mr. Naofumi."

"But I want to keep fighting!"

Once we started fighting, the plan worked within an hour. Most of the monsters had fled to the mountains and learned to keep their distance.

"You all right, Raphtalia?"

She was moving slower than normal, thanks to the curse. The curse had been very strong.

The curse that hurt her was from yesterday. We were fighting a Dragon Zombie out here and I . . . I used a curse.

But if you really think about it, it was THEIR fault—the three other heroes. They'd started this mess.

When we were fighting the Dragon Zombie, the Shield of Rage from the "Curse Series" unlocked itself, and I used it. The curse was strong and unwieldy, and it turned its fangs on Raphtalia, my friend.

The curse had swallowed me completely, and she had to sacrifice herself to save me from its grasp. She was seriously hurt in the process.

So even though I couldn't attack on my own, I'd started standing at the front of the battle line to protect Raphtalia.

"As for my wounds, they really aren't so bad, Mr. Naofumi."

"Good."

"Heh, heh . . . It's kind of nice to have you worrying about me."

"I'm really sorry."

"Promise you won't say that anymore."

She smiled to show that she didn't care, but it only made me feel even guiltier.

"Are you okay, Big Sister?"

"Yes, I'm fine. Aren't I, Mr. Naofumi?"

"Yeah, sure . . . but don't overdo it."

"You don't have to . . . Anyway . . . thanks for caring."

Apparently she wasn't hurt too badly, which was good.

"Well, that's the end of our work for the day. Tomorrow we are heading back to the castle in Melromarc so that Raphtalia can get some real treatment."

We set off down the road back to town. When we left the mountains, there was a road that ran over rolling fields back to the village.

"Master! What's that?!"

A wild Filolial A appeared!

A wild Filolial B appeared!

A wild Filolial C appeared!

A blue-haired girl appeared by the Filolials!

Dammit . . . what was a girl doing with wild Filolials?!

I cursed under my breath and watched closely. But she just looked like a normal little girl.

"Hey you! Are you from the village?!"

I thought I'd ask, just to be sure, but the Filolials responded before she did.

"Gah?!"

The Filolials looked at Filo. They were astonished!
Filolials A, B, and C took off running!

"Ahh . . ."

The girl stretched her hand out after the fleeing Filolials.

What was with that girl? Was she playing with the Filolials?

Well, after spending all this time with Filo, I had a pretty good idea of how you could expect Filolials to behave. She was probably feeding them or something, since they liked to eat so much.

At first glance, the girl seemed to be pretty well off. Maybe she was the daughter of a rich merchant.

"What was that?"

The Filolials ran off and left her alone, so I guess she didn't own them.

I guess they were wild.

If the monsters ran away the minute you approached, they might have been the kind of rare monster that leaves behind valuable items and lots of experience points. Still, taking down a random Filolial probably wouldn't yield a ton of experience.

They probably ran because they caught sight of Filo, our Filolial Queen.

"Boy, those birds sure look yummy! I think so every time I pass one of them on the road."

"Those are the same species as you."

Filo was licking her beak in slobbery anticipation.

I guess everything looked like food to her. So she'd go cannibal that quickly, huh? Creepy.

"If we chase them now, we can get them! Master!"

"Leave them alone."

She really knew how to take the tension out of a scene.

As for experience, I guess I hadn't checked our levels after we fought the Dragon Zombie.

Naofumi LV 38 ★
Raphtalia LV 40 ★
Filo LV 40 ★

What was the star?

"Hey, there's a star next to my level indicator. Does anyone know what that means?"

What could it be? I had a bad feeling.

"Um . . ."

"I dunno!"

I decided to check the help screen.

I still didn't get it. The information might have been buried in there somewhere, but I wasn't able to find an explanation for the star.

I guess we'd just have to come back to it later.

Huh? The little girl that had been with the Filolials had noticed us, and now she was walking in our direction.

"Wow, is that a Filolial?"

"You mean Filo?"

"Can she talk?"

The girl and Filo were looking deep into each other's eyes.

"Yes."

"It's always been my dream to talk with Filolials! I hope we can talk a lot!"

The girl, apparently very interested, kept talking to Filo.

She looked around 10 years old. Her hair was blue, but it was all a bit faded. Maybe it was actually navy blue. She had pigtails and gave off an eccentric, powerful impression. You could tell she came from a good family.

"Master, what should we do?"

Good question. What should we do? It almost sounded like this rich girl wanted to take Filo.

If I managed to get along well with her family, then maybe I could steer this in a more profitable direction. That wouldn't be so bad.

I did not introduce myself as the Shield Hero but rather

as a holy man with a bird-god-drawn carriage. People had approached me many times to see if they could buy Filo from us.

Of course, I wasn't planning on selling her. But I used that as a starting point and steered the conversation in such a way that I could usually get the customer to walk away with some new (expensive) accessory.

And because I hid the fact that I was the Shield Hero, most people were very friendly when I approached them. From that perspective, it might be smart to try and arrange my business to keep the public on my side. It couldn't hurt to have some people that owed me favors.

And yet this girl could tell that Filo was a Filolial. She knew it from a single glance!

"A talking Filolial, right? What's your name?"

"Filo."

"Filo, right? My name is Mel!"

"Nice to meet you, Mel."

"Yay! Hey, Filo, want to eat this?"

The girl called Mel pulled some kind of jerky from her pocket and offered it to Filo.

She must have known how much Filolials like to eat.

"Yay! Thanks!"

Filo greedily stuffed the jerky into her mouth.

Heh, heh, heh.

Mel giggled happily at the sight of Filo's puffed cheeks. She started to pet them softly.

She liked Filolials. I could tell that much. I could tell that she was different from those other people that had been interested in Filo—THEY only cared because Filo was rare.

She looked like she actually wanted to be friends with Filo. Honestly it couldn't hurt to network a little, so I'd encourage Filo to be friends with her if I could.

"Filo, we still have some work to do in the village, so you can just hang out here for a while if you want. Have fun."

"Okay! You want to come?"

"Yes!"

So Filo and Mel ran out into the fields to play.

We went back to the village and kept doing all we could to wipe out the sickness there.

I asked the doctor if he needed any help, and he set me to work compounding medicines. Setting out my materials, I got to work. The work went faster than I'd expected, and pretty soon I was finished. There was a part of me that genuinely wished I could ease the villagers' suffering. Hopefully the village would return to its peaceful ways before long.

I looked out at the fields and could see Filo playing with kids out there.

"Um . . . Your Holiness . . . could you . . ."

The village chief appeared at my elbow and handed me a bag of money.

"Your Holiness, thank you for your help. Please accept our thanks."

That reminded me: these people still didn't know who I was. To them, I wasn't the fearsome and criminal Shield Hero. No, I was just a traveling saint with a bird-god companion.

"Um . . ."

I took the bag, opened it, and began to count the contents.

Then I removed half the money and put it into a separate bag.

"What?"

"I didn't do all of this. The doctor did most of it. Give this to him."

"Oh, yes . . ."

If the doctor hadn't been there, we would have been in trouble. Alone, I don't think I could have stopped the spread of the disease. So it was really all thanks to him.

"All right."

To get Raphtalia's wounds properly healed, we'd have to visit a large church, but it was already late in the afternoon.

We'd have to stay one night in town before setting off.

We were relaxing in the village when Filo came running back.

"Hey! I made a new friend!"

"That's great. Was it that girl we met on our way back from the mountains?"

Wait. Did she have any friends to begin with? Shouldn't this girl be her first friend, not her NEW friend?

Raphtalia was less of a friend and more like a mother or at least an older sister.

"Yeah! That girl, you know? She's been traveling to the same places that we have!"

"Really? So she's a traveler, huh? She sure was dressed nicely for a traveler."

Maybe she was a rich merchant's daughter, and she had just been passing through the village when the sickness came upon it.

Anyway, Filo was the type to be popular with kids, I guess. I mean, she was really popular with everyone.

And besides, apparently that girl didn't care so much when Filo turned into a human. So I suppose she was a pretty adaptable girl.

"And you know what? She taught me all kinds of stuff I never knew before! Like what kind of monsters Filolials are and what kind of legends there are!"

"Wow."

I just needed to chime in from time to time to keep her satisfied. Filo wasn't the best conversationalist, so it was hard to get a handle on what she wanted to say sometimes.

Here's an example—when I asked her how to use magic, she said something random, like, "You just pwwwweeeep it out!"

"But when she was playing with the other Filolials, out in the fields, she got separated and lost. That's when we found her!"

"Wow."

"Um . . . Mr. Naofumi? Are you listening to her story?"

"Huh?"

Honestly I hadn't been paying attention. But I could probably remember what she said if I needed to.

Filo became friends with that girl who'd introduced herself as Mel. And that girl had been separated from her companions? It sounded like a creepy story, and so I went to look at Filo, only to see that the girl was there too, standing right next to her.

"I'm sorry to trouble you at this hour. I was . . . I was wondering if you wouldn't mind . . . I'd like to travel with you."

"Wait, just a second. I need to get all of this straight. You were . . . Mel, right? Why did you come here with Filo? If you got separated, why not go look for your friends?"

"Yes, well . . . A Filolial brought me here, but I don't exactly know where I am. I know where I am trying to go, but I was separated from my protectors quite a while ago."

"Protectors? Are you nobility or something? Or a merchant's daughter?"

"I . . . Um . . ."

Mel turned her eyes away for a moment and then nodded to herself.

"You are correct that I am from nobility, but please, call me Mel. I was talking with Filo about the owner of her cart. You're some type of saint? And I also heard that you are going to Melromarc Castle tomorrow. May I accompany you?"

She was very polite as she spoke to me.

I wonder . . . If we brought her back to Melromarc, we'd probably get some money in gratitude. We'd be returning a lost girl to her parents, who were members of the nobility—they'd be sure to show their appreciation.

But still, if the Shield Hero were the one to return her, I'd probably end up accused of kidnapping her. They'd find some way to ruin my life again.

"Well . . ."

"Master, I want her to come with us! She's in trouble!"

"If we help her, we might end up in trouble ourselves."

"Mr. Naofumi, I also think we should take her. We can't leave a lost child to the winds of fate!"

"Thank you very much. May I accompany you on your journey?"

Both Raphtalia and Filo were appealing on her behalf. And we might make some money in the process. Anyway, in a worst-case scenario, I could just jump on Filo and run away.

"We'll have to request payment. Filo will visit your family to receive that payment. Does that sound all right with you?"

"Sure! I'll ask my father, and he will certainly agree."

I guess there was no avoiding it.

Anyway, if her family owned a house in the Melromarc castle town, they must have been pretty well off. Why would a well-off girl like that be playing with wild Filolials? What if we couldn't watch her all the time and she ran off? What if she got herself, and us, into some kind of trouble?

"You better behave yourself, or we will drop you on the side of the road."

"I understand. Thank you very much, Holy Saint."

And that is how we ended up traveling with Filo's friend Mel on our way back to the Melromarc castle town.

We climbed into the cart that Filo was pulling and set off on our journey back to the castle town.

"Thank you for all you've done! Please come back again."

"Later."

The whole village came out to see us off.

On my way out of town I couldn't help but wonder— would they still treat us this way if they knew who I really was? Just thinking of it made me feel strange.

"Mel, I look forward to our travels together. My name is Raphtalia. It won't be a long trip, but I'm sure we'll have a good time."

"Yes. I'm sure we will, Ms. Raphtalia."

I really wanted to make sure that Raphtalia was healthy, so

I was in a hurry to get back to town and get her some of that healing holy water.

"Mel, keep in mind that healing Raphtalia is the highest priority for us."

"What happened to Ms. Raphtalia?" asked Mel.

"We were fighting some evil, vicious monsters up in those mountains, and she ended up cursed."

"So that's what happened . . . right?"

I was making money by compounding medicine and selling it.

But I made up my mind to make Raphtalia my top priority. Honestly, I really wanted to make money so that we could buy good equipment for when the wave came. But if I weighed that against Raphtalia's wounds, Raphtalia was obviously more important.

I mean, I was the one that cursed her, and if the wave was coming, then she needed to be in top condition for it. The equipment could be dealt with later, but Raphtalia had a sickness that needed to be cured now. We needed to get it treated as soon as possible.

"We need holy water from a big church."

"The curse is so strong that you are going to the church in the capital, right?"

"Yeah."

The doctor back in town had told us that we would need strong holy water from a church.

That's why I made up my mind to head back to the capital. It was sure to have the biggest church.

"Filo, we're going to the capital. Quickly now!"

"Roger, Captain!"

"Woohoo!"

Filo took off at such a speed that Mel let out a little shout.

I forgot to mention that Filo tends to shake the carriage a lot when she runs. Most people end up really motion sick.

Would Mel be all right?

"Ahahahahaha! Filo is so faaaaast!"

"Ahahaha! I can go faster!"

Guess she'll be just fine.

"Don't go too crazy now! It's dangerous! Calm down."

Raphtalia reprimanded the sprinting Filo, but Filo gave no indication that she'd been listening.

She was actually running faster than normal. She was probably trying to impress Mel.

But if she kept it up, Raphtalia might get sick.

"Mr. Naofumi, do you mind if I lie down for a bit?"

"Nope."

Were we making it worse?

"This is turning into a real nightmare. I should have turned her down."

I muttered to myself.

We ran into Mel because we'd agreed to chase monsters away from the town. I was starting to regret it, if only a little.

Chapter One: Filo's Friend

The fire was crackling. We'd set up camp for the night.

We were on schedule to arrive at the Melromarc castle town the next day.

"Ahahahaha. Oh Filo! You're so funny!"

"Wait! I got you!"

"You got me!"

Filo was in her human form, and even though we were out in the wilderness, she was so hyperactive she was running in circles.

It was fun to have a sleepover with your good friends. I'd done that before, on summer vacation school trips to the seaside or during lock-ins in the science room. So I understood how fun it could be.

But still, these two liked each other WAY too much.

It only made sense. Filo hadn't ever really had a real friend that was in the same age range as her.

But Mel was from nobility, so they weren't really on equal standing. Mel was more like Filo's owner.

When you looked at them, they looked like close friends. So I guess Mel didn't really care that Filo was a monster.

When we were riding in the carriage, Mel had made a few

fiery speeches about Filolials, about which she seemed to know quite a lot. But she said that she had been on some long trips before, and so she'd probably ridden in Filolial carriages a lot. That was probably how she came to like them.

"Calm down!"

"Okay!"

"Mr. Naofumi, why not let them play? Isn't it good for Filo to have a friend?"

"I guess . . ."

It was almost unbelievable how loud and obnoxious Filo could be with a friend in tow.

"Mel, I'm going to show you my treasure!"

"Yay!"

Filo had a bag that she always kept hidden away in the carriage. She took it out and showed it to Mel.

I wondered what it could be. I kind of wanted to know. What would Filo consider a treasure? I'm sure it was just trash, but if she was filching from my stash, I'd have to lay down the law.

"Master, you want to see too?"

"Sure."

Filo waved her hand to call me over, and I peeked inside the bag.

It was filled with pieces of a broken sword. And some junky-looking jewels from when I failed at an accessory-making attempt. Some glass beads. Connectors.

"It's so sparkly and pretty, isn't it?"

"Yes, it's beautiful."

Mel looked a little confused. In her defense, it was a bag of trash.

She was probably drawn to shiny things because she was a bird. I think I'd heard somewhere that crows liked to steal shiny things. Was Filo doing the same thing?

"What's this?"

There was something else mixed in with the trash. I reached in and took it out.

A brown hairball? It was a large, soft ball, but when I pressed it I could feel a number of smaller, hard objects moving inside. More than anything else, the object smelled terrible.

I had a really bad feeling about this.

"That thing there came out of my mouth!"

It came from out of her mouth. Out of Filo's mouth.

Had she been a cat, the object would have been a hairball. Had she been a human, it would be vomit. But Filo was a bird.

And birds throw up . . . pellets?

In other words, the hard things were pieces of monster bones mixed in with Filo's own feathers and other indigestible materials.

"Gross!"

What was she thinking? And to think—I touched it! I threw the pellet ball away.

"Hey! That's my treasure!"

"That's no treasure! That's excrement! If you put that in a bag again I'll throw all your treasures away!"

"But . . ."

Mel was watching our exchange with a bewildered look on her face.

We finished talking, and I made dinner.

For dinner we had the meat of a monster we met on the road. I skewered it on wooden sticks and roasted it over the fire.

"Master, you're such a good cook!"

"It's true. You're very good at it, and the food is always delicious. Mel, you should have some too."

Raphtalia passed a stick to Mel, who took it gratefully.

"I mean, all he did was stick it over the fire! But it's so GOOD!"

She ate it slowly and thoughtfully. I thought for sure that she would protest eating such barbaric food, but apparently my fears were unfounded.

Was it because of all she'd been through on her travels?

I was judging Mel from her appearance. She was probably just an outspoken, brave girl.

Anyway, we finished eating, and there was nothing left to do but sleep. But it was still a little early for that.

So we were stuck with some free time.

I was pretty used to staying in the wilderness by then, so I thought about taking out the magic book and sitting down to study some more.

A little time went by, and Filo and Mel started to calm down. They probably wore themselves out and fell asleep.

Raphtalia was taking a nap so she'd be fresh for her watch. She still had to cover half the time—I just wasn't comfortable with the idea of leaving Filo and Mel in charge.

"Hm . . ."

Even if it was a book for beginners, it was still filled with many different kinds of magic.

It covered things like "First Guard" and "First Heal."

I still couldn't really use them myself, but those spells seemed to be the powerful end of the beginner's level of magic.

I was reading about spells to raise your attack power and agility. There were so many I wanted to learn, but the grammar was so difficult that following the descriptions proved nearly impossible.

I occasionally threw new logs onto the fire, and time slowly went by.

"Mmmm . . ."

Raphtalia slowly blinked and looked sleepy.

"Did I wake you up?"

"No. Shall I take over?"

"If you want to."

"All right."

I found a good place to pause my studies and then took her up on her offer.

"Um . . . Mr. Naofumi?"

"What is it?"

"Filo and Mel are . . ."

She pointed a shaky finger at the now silent figure of Filo, who was now a giant bird again. Filo was asleep, alone. And the clothes that Mel had been wearing were tossed about the ground around her.

"Um . . ."

Where was Mel? I thought for sure I'd find her, half-naked, asleep on Filo's stomach. But when I looked, she wasn't there.

Even her shoes were lying there. But where was she? "You don't think . . ."

I knew Filo could be a pig, but . . .

"Mr. Naofumi. Remember when you threatened those bandits by telling them that Filo ate people? You don't think that she . . ."

"No way! She wouldn't!"

"But we're talking about Filo here."

"But . . ."

I guess I could believe it. Did she think that friends were people you could eat when you felt like it?

"Raphtalia. Should we pretend we didn't see anything and hide the proof?"

"Wh . . . What are you suggesting?!"

"If Filo ate a person—and a noble's daughter at that—do you think we should take responsibility for that?"

I wanted to avoid that responsibility if I could. I mean, I recognize that it's wrong. But still!

That damn, chubby bird! She really knew how to make a mess.

"Funya?"

Filo's head suddenly shot into the air as she woke up and blinked.

"What happened? Master? Big Sister?"

"Where's Mel?"

"Mel? She's sleeping in my feathers."

"Huh? I don't see her."

I'd just checked a minute ago. I was sure that she wasn't there.

"Mel, wake up."

"Hm???"

The feathers on Filo's back ruffled and stood up before Mel poked her face out of the fluff.

"What the?!"

No way. No matter how you looked at it, Filo couldn't hide an entire person in her feathers. That didn't make any sense. But there she was anyway.

"What is it, Filo?"

"Master was asking where you were. So I woke you up."

"I was just on Filo's back. It's so warm!"

"Why did you take your clothes off?"

"Because it's hot."

They really gave me a scare.

"Anyway, how did you get so deep inside there?"

"Filo's feathers are super fluffy and thick! Stick your hand in here and see."

"Okay."

The time had come. It was time to see what Filo's body was really like.

Mel was calling me over, so I reached out my hand.

"Whoa! It's really deep."

I pushed both my arms in all the way to my shoulder before I finally felt something like skin. It really was very warm in there. If it was that deep, I could understand how Mel was able to sleep in there without anyone noticing.

"I don't understand how there can be that much space."

"I know!"

"Let's take all the feathers off and see what it's like under there. We could sell the feathers too. Might even make some money."

"No!"

"But, Holy Saint, you shouldn't threaten Filo!"

"It was just a joke."

Oh boy, I'd gotten another glimpse of just how weird Filo's body was.

Chapter Two: The Fruits of Peddling

The next morning, we were ready and waiting for the castle town gate to open.

I soon discovered that trying to pull a carriage down the city streets was no easy task. We needed to find a place to stash it.

The only place I could think of was the weapon shop, so we made our way there.

The owner of the weapon shop was a true rarity in the world. He was one of the only people who believed in me and tried to help me.

Even after I'd been framed for a terrible crime, he sold me weapons at a fair price—I knew that I could trust him.

"Hey, old man! Sell us some weapons and armor, would you?"

I hadn't seen him in a while. He was leaning on the counter, his brow knit in concentration.

"Come on, kid, give me some warning next time!"

"What's business if not a series of unexpected developments?"

"I guess you're right. How's your budget looking?"

"Good question."

I pulled out my three and a half weeks of profits and dropped them heavily on the counter before him.

There were three bags stuffed full of money.

"I haven't counted it, but that's all silver."

"Come on, kid! Count it for me!"

"Pretty good, huh? That's from my traveling merchant life."

"This must be a hobby of yours—trying to give me a heart attack, that is."

"Unfortunately for you."

"Fine then. Let's get to counting, shall we?"

"Sure."

The old guy and I started counting coins. Raphtalia joined in too.

"Hey, Princess, what's wrong with you? Are you hurt? You're moving differently than you used to."

"Yes. Unfortunately, I was cursed quite badly in a recent battle."

Without meaning to, I stopped counting and looked over at Raphtalia.

"Ah . . . A curse? Those can be real trouble. Guess you're in recovery?"

"Yes. Once we leave your shop we're heading for a church to get some holy water."

"I see."

Did we fool him? No, he had no reason to suspect me in the first place.

It seemed like a lot of money, but when I started counting I realized that there was actually a lot of bronze mixed in. Calculating the actual value, it wasn't as much as I had been hoping.

"This is all worth almost 50 pieces of gold! You sure know what you're doing there, kid."

"You don't have to tell me twice."

I'd always prided myself on my business acumen.

Still, I'd made all this money off the misery of others. It didn't put me in a great mood.

"We have some stuff to sell too—some equipment we lifted off of some bandits we met."

Filo had been wandering around the shop, looking at products. I snapped at her, and she quickly ran out the door and pulled in different items from the cart outside.

"Can I bring Mel back home?" asked Filo.

"Sure, but get back here before noon. And make sure that her parents show their gratitude."

"Okay!"

"Holy Saint, thank you for all your help. I'll see to it that you get what you are owed. Thank you again for your assistance."

Filo finished dragging in our loot, and then she left to bring Mel back to her family.

That was fine. She had only come with us so that we would bring her home, and I couldn't see there being any further complications. We'd only spent a day together, but still—I felt like I'd started to get a handle on just what kind of girl Mel was.

She had been very polite, and getting in her parents' good graces certainly couldn't hurt. When Filo was on her way out, I told her to run away at the first sign of any trouble.

"All right, so you want to trade this stuff in?"

I turned back to the weapon shop owner and returned to our negotiations.

There was a pile of equipment between us. We had managed to steal it from some violent bandits we had encountered.

"Kid, you've got your hands in all sorts of honeypots, don't you?"

"With that, plus all the money, how's our budget looking?"

"Let's see here . . . You're talking weapons and armor for her and then armor for yourself, right?"

He crossed his arms and started mentally tabulating.

"Don't get me wrong—I'm glad that you bring me all your business. But you can try some other shops too, you know?"

"What's that supposed to mean?"

"Nothing in particular. The other heroes have stopped coming around, so it made me think that there must be some other shop out there—a better shop."

"Hmmm . . ."

It wasn't impossible. The other guys already knew all about the world from their games. So there was a good chance that they knew a different store, one with better prices and equipment.

But his shop was supposed to be the best in the castle town. So if there were a better place, it would have to be in another country. Right?

"You have any ideas?"

"Maybe if you went to our neighboring country, there might be a shop with better equipment than mine."

"If I have to gamble on a hunch, I'd just as soon take my chances with you."

"There you go, kid! I won't let you down!"

"Worst-case scenario, I'll just have you make me whatever I need. Those look like skilled hands you've got."

"Good eyes! When I was younger I was the apprentice of a famous blacksmith to the east."

"That's what I'm talking about. That's why I like working with you—for your skill and your efficiency."

"I'm on it, kid. I won't let you down!"

The old guy jumped over the counter and started pacing his shop, considering all the products there.

"Hmm . . . For the little lass, I'd think that a magic silver sword would serve her well. Of course I'd include a Blood Clean coating also."

After some discussion we agreed on a price of 10 pieces of gold.

The Blood Clean coating he referenced was a way of making swords so that blood and guts wouldn't stick to the blades and ruin them.

If you don't get the guts off your sword quickly enough, the blade will rust and lose its edge. The coating was really important if you planned on using the blade for long.

"As for armor, I think magic silver armor that's been manufactured with magic defense properties. Yes, that should do it."

"Magic defense manufacturing?"

"The wearer of the armor will absorb magic from the enemy. It increases the wearer's defense proportionately."

"Sounds great."

If I wasn't able to perfectly protect her, that armor would help her escape battles unscathed—if I made a mistake, that is. It would be important going forward.

The old guy was still thinking of equipment we could make for 10 pieces of gold. That was a pretty expensive piece of equipment.

"Hey, we have more money. If we went all out here, what could we get?"

"Kid, you gotta think about the girl. It will cost money to get that curse lifted. Besides, what if the equipment doesn't work for you? You'll lose money trading it in and all that."

"Hmm . . ."

"Right. Also, that's about the best I can do with the materials I have on hand right now."

"Fair enough."

If it was the best equipment he could make, then I guess it was good enough for me.

"If you want to push for something different, I'll have to make it custom. I can do that, but it will take a little time."

"Yeah, I guess you'd need time to make it."

"Right. I have a bunch of different materials now, but still not enough. Mostly, I'd need ore."

"I thought that maybe we could use the skin from that dead dragon."

"Put that aside for a second. What about you, kid?"

"What about me?"

"If we are talking about your armor, I could make a heavy armor with the Air Wake processing. That way it would be lighter. Or I could make something new from all the stuff you brought in."

"What would be better?"

"It would probably be about the same."

"Hey, I remember you said that you could improve the Barbarian Armor if you added some bones."

"You're right. I was about to suggest that. Chimera and dragon bones are really great materials. Then we could cover it with dragon skin and fix the dragon's core into the center. That would be perfect!"

The dragon core he was referring to was a crystal-like core that had reanimated the dragon after it died. It was like the heart of an undead dragon. Filo had eaten most of it, but we still had what I'd set aside.

I bet that items like that, *rare* items, would make great equipment.

"Awesome. Sounds good to me, old man. Let's do it."

"Thanks! I'll add the bones for free, which means that you just need to cover the manufacturing and material costs."

He took 5 gold pieces and a pile of materials and took them all back behind the counter with him.

"Hey, kid, you better leave your Barbarian Armor with me when you leave."

"Sure."

I went to a changing room and slipped out of the armor, and then I set it on the counter.

"All right, I should have this all done in two days or so. So come back then! I'll have good stuff for you."

"Thanks. Oh hey, old dude."

"What?"

"There's a star next to my level now. Any idea what that means?"

"Oh yeah? Guess you guys are about ready to change class."

"Class?"

"What? You don't know? Class-up. You are going to

advance into the next class. Once you break through your class, you can reach even higher levels—plus, you get a huge power boost for breaking into a new class."

Say what? What now?! So it was like a game where you could change jobs at a certain level?

"Normally only knights, wizards, and adventurers with special permission from the Crown are permitted to go through the class-up process. But you're a hero, aren't you, kid? You should be able to."

Thinking back on it, it would explain why the bandits were so much weaker than I would have expected. They weren't able to break through level 40! So adventurers and villagers that weren't trusted were kept under a certain level—that's how they were able to keep the peace. They controlled everyone's power.

That reminds me—when we'd been fighting the bandits, I think the bodyguard had said something similar.

"When you go through a class-up, you have to decide what direction you want to take your growth. It sure worried me when my time came. Once you get that star, your options really open up. It's a big deal."

"Where can I do it? Where can I class up?"

"Haven't you already been there? The room with the dragon hourglass."

So that's where it happened. Thinking back on it, it did seem important and well protected.

The dragon hourglass was a giant hourglass that counted down to the arrival of the waves of destruction.

A while back I'd met up with the rest of the heroes there.

Could it be that I'd met them there because they'd gone to class up?

Just what level were they at, anyway? I felt myself getting flustered.

"Anyway, the immediate priority is getting Raphtalia's curse lifted. Filo's busy too—so I'll worry about it once we're all back together again."

If I could, it would be better to class up as soon as possible.

"Okay, old dude, you mind if we all meet up here?"

"If that's what you want, I'm fine with it."

The guy really did treat me well. I wanted to give him all the business I could.

We finished up at the shop, and Raphtalia and I left for the church.

There was a large church in the center of town, looming over everything and immediately visible.

It was huge. There was a symbol over the door; it looked like a sword, spear, and bow combined.

I didn't like the look of that. There was no shield.

"Sh . . . Shield Hero?!"

We walked into the building, and one of the sisters there

shot me a cold glare. Putting aside what they thought of me, is that how they behaved in their church? Or were those accused of rape not even allowed to enter the church at all?

"Do not let it upset you."

A man, some type of church patriarch by the look of him, admonished the sister.

Something about it made me uncomfortable, but whatever it was, I let it go.

"Father!"

"What brings you to our holy space today?"

"My friend here has been hit with a powerful curse. We've come in search of a powerful holy water so that we might cure her."

They hadn't done anything rude to me yet, so I saw no need to be combative right off the bat.

"We will require a financial offering."

The wall was plastered with various items and their prices, but I decided to ask anyway.

"How much?"

"Holy water is not very expensive, but it is available in different potencies. Starting with 5 pieces of silver, 10 pieces of silver, 50 pieces of silver, and up to 1 gold piece."

Well at least they weren't out to get whatever they could.

Had they tried to wring money from us, I'd been prepared to show them how I felt about it.

"Well, I certainly wouldn't want to start debating over money here in the house of God. We'd like the holy water for 1 piece of gold, please."

"We can't, Mr. Naofumi. I can't accept such an expensive item."

"It's fine. We already went over this. You're important to me. What's a piece of gold if it will save you?"

"Th . . . Thank you so much! You won't regret it!"

I took out a piece of gold and passed it to the priest.

"Thank you."

He pointed to a sister, who immediately came over with a bottle in her hand.

I remembered my appraisal skill and used it on the holy water.

Low-level holy water: quality: poor

I glared at the priest. He looked taken aback, then took the bottle from me. The color left his cheeks.

"Why did you bring this cheap holy water?"

"But I . . ."

"The Lord is merciful. If you have done this to appease your own sense of justice, then you must repent immediately."

"I . . . I'm so sorry!"

"I beg your pardon. A member of our church has behaved rudely to you."

"If I get what I paid for, I'll have nothing to complain about."

"Thank you for your understanding."

The priest left to retrieve the water himself, then returned with a bottle. I used my appraisal skill on it again.

Curse-lifting holy water: quality: excellent

"Looks good to me."

I took the bottle of holy water from him.

"Please thank the Lord for his guidance. All is delivered through the mercy of the Lord."

Religions sure did have an air of self-righteousness. He spoke as if it were to be assumed that I was evil and that I should be grateful for his forgiveness.

Raphtalia and I left the church. I was ruminating about their behavior as we left the building behind.

Chapter Three: Everyone Loves Angels

"OOOH! Shield Hero!"

We were leaving the church when I heard a shout I couldn't ignore.

I turned to see a young boy of 14 or 15, dressed like a soldier, running in our direction. He was nearly out of breath.

We were in the castle town, so when I saw soldiers running in my direction, I was prepared for bad news.

I didn't think. I turned and started running. Raphtalia was right behind me. There were too many ways for this to go bad.

The king who had framed me, the guy I secretly called Trash, was a moody man. Who knows what he had decided to frame me for this time?

"Wait!"

Yeah right. Why should I? I knew that nothing good was waiting for me. Who would wait for a soldier who was shouting for them to wait? Only a fool.

So I took off running. But then I realized Filo wasn't with us. I couldn't let us get captured, but I also couldn't escape town with our carriage if Filo wasn't there with us.

"Wait!"

"Damn this kid! Raphtalia, you get Filo and bring her here.

We need to finish our shopping and get out of town."

"Roger!"

Raphtalia and I split up and ran from the soldier.

The soldier followed me.

"Damn, I can't lose him."

The soldier was very persistent. I crawled down a small ally and came out into a crowded main street where I was finally able to lose him in the crowds. Now I just needed to get out of town before he caught me.

But how would I meet up with Raphtalia and Filo? If I could make it to the weapon shop, I'd be able to meet them there.

Or so I was thinking, when . . .

"AHHHHHH!"

What the . . . ?

I turned to see a crowd led by Motoyasu. He was pointing at me and running. The crowd parted for him.

Damn! If they saw me now, what good was it that I'd escaped?

"Naofumi! I found you!"

That was Motoyasu Kitamura. He was the Spear Hero, summoned to the world just like I'd been, but from a different Japan. He was the favorite of that Bitch, the princess who'd framed me, and he was really living it up here, doing whatever the hell he wanted.

He was probably the most attractive of us heroes. He was light-hearted, always hitting on girls. His head was as empty as you'd expect.

He'd really made my life here into a nightmare.

"You! What are you doing?!"

"What the hell? Don't try to pin anything on me!"

"Playing dumb? Good luck! We already know! We know that you're the owner of that fat bird."

Fat bird . . . Filo?

"Give us the bird—we'll kill it!"

"Ha! What are you talking about? That was all your fault. You should have been more careful before you approached her!"

Once, a little while ago, Filo had given Motoyasu a hard kick to the crotch—sent him flying. It had felt good to watch him flip through the air.

"Still playing dumb? That fat bird of yours was after me the second it saw me!"

Hm? What was he talking about? Was he imagining things?

"What are you talking about?"

"Like I said, that fat, stupid bird of yours tried to run me down!"

I looked at Motoyasu. His armor was as nice and shiny as ever, but the crotch was missing and covered with a cup.

This was hilarious! Ha! The guy was traumatized! Ha!

Oh boy, this just kept getting better and better. I'd have to give Filo a treat later on. She'd known what I really wanted and taken the day to give me this present.

"What are you laughing at?!"

"Ahahaha!"

"You bastard . . ."

Seriously, what was he so mad about? This was great.

Motoyasu apparently realized that his current conversation tactics weren't getting through to me. He changed the subject.

"And hey, let that girl go! You slaver!"

"Not again! You really don't know how to give up, do you?"

There had been a time, in the past, that Motoyasu had tried to "save" Raphtalia from me. That she was beautiful must have been a motivating factor. He challenged me to a duel I had no hope of winning, and he was right. I lost—but only because Bitch cheated and attacked me from behind.

And now he was at it again! He hadn't changed at all.

"Raphtalia already turned you down."

Once Raphtalia figured out what was going on, she turned him down and that was the end of that.

"I'm not talking about Raphtalia!"

His hand curled into a fist.

"I know all about it! You've found yourself a new slave, haven't you? I saw her leaving the weapon shop!"

What was he talking about? I had no idea.

The only people that traveled with me were Raphtalia and Filo.

Motoyasu had been upset about Filo this whole time—but now he was calling her a slave and demanding her release?

"Who are you talking about? Not Mel? She's not a slave."

"I don't know her name! The girl with the blonde hair!"

Blonde hair?

"If her hair was blue, that's Mel. If it was blonde, that's Filo."

"Exactly! That girl with the little wings on her back! You know who I'm talking about! You call her Filo?"

He was practically screaming now, suddenly impassioned.

He'd just said he wanted to kill her, but now he wanted her set free? The guy was crazy!

"You . . . As long as she's a girl, you want her—is that it?"

"No!"

He shouted again.

"I've never seen such an ideal girl . . . I . . ."

"What?"

"Who would think it? There really is a girl out there that's just like Fleon of the magical lands!"

Who was he talking about now? Must have been a character from some game he played.

That reminded me of something though. I guess Filo was similar to characters from games I knew too. The pure, angelic girl character—a classic archetype.

"I can't help it. I REALLY like angels . . ."

"Shut up! I don't want to hear about your sexual preferences!"

"This world is the BEST! My heart was fluttering the second I laid eyes on her!"

Motoyasu was very excited. From the look on his face, you'd never know he was the same person that had just been screaming about a giant bird. His eyes were shining now—he was enraptured.

The other members of his party were looking annoyed. That must be why they were standing there silent.

"I know that you own that girl somehow! Let her go!"

"God, you're annoying!"

Okay, okay, so he was saying that I needed to hand Filo over just because she happened to be his type?

I wished he'd keep his jokes to himself.

"You think I'm just going to go along with that request?"

"If you won't, we'll fight until you agree!"

He readied his spear and pointed it at me.

"What? You want to fight here?! Stop that! Think about your surroundings!"

"Chaos Spear!"

Before I could finish my sentence, Motoyasu had already called a skill and sent an attack flying in my direction. I lightly lifted my shield to stop the barrage, but the flying spear tips that missed me flew on down the street before burying themselves in a storefront and bringing the wall down with a crash.

There was a crowd of people in the street, and now they were all screaming because of Motoyasu's violent outburst.

"Hey!"

"Air Strike Javelin!"

He pointed his spear again and sent it flying in my direction.

Damn! I dodged it, but it could've hit the crowd of people. I might not have known much about this country and its people, but I knew the difference between a good place to fight and a bad place to fight. Could Motoyasu think about anything but himself?

"Let her go!"

"Who would?!"

He wants me to let that ravenous bird loose? Was he crazy?!

I almost considered it, just so he'd understand what a bad idea it was to let that crazy bird loose.

"So you won't listen?"

The surrounding townsfolk were on the verge of panic.

"Come on! Control yourself!"

"I don't care if you are heroes. Don't fight here!"

Shouts of protest from the townsfolk grew more and more frequent.

This was not good. No matter how much damage Motoyasu caused, I was sure to take the fall for all of it.

"Motoyasu! Calm down!"

It was time. Should I switch to the Shield of Rage, like I did with the Zombie Dragon, and counter his attack?

No. That would burn everything around us. And that was how Raphtalia got hurt. I shouldn't use it when there are people around. Even still, it wasn't like I could just run away.

"Hey! You guys stop too!"

I yelled to Motoyasu's little posse of Bitch and her friends. They needed to know that they were pissing off a hero.

They only looked over at me and laughed.

I was getting a bad feeling about this. She never missed an opportunity to piss me off. She'd do anything.

"Everyone please calm down! This is a duel between the Spear Hero and the Shield Hero. It is a legitimate duel, recognized by the Crown, whom I represent here today!"

Bitch was pretending to go by the name Myne, but even though she pretended to be someone else she still felt entitled to issue commands as the Crown. She flashed a certificate that supposedly empowered her to speak for the royal family.

"Give me a break!"

The first person to express their discontent was the owner of a shop behind me. Soon others in the street joined in his shouts of protest. I didn't find anything about it surprising in the least. Anyone watching would have seen Motoyasu start the fight all on his own—and now she called it a "duel." Give ME a break!

"You would speak against the command of the Crown? You scoundrel!"

Scoundrel? Look who's talking—Bitch Princess!

A glance at the gathering crowd and it was clear that supporters were mixed in with the pedestrians who wanted the duel stopped. The confusion was growing, and the whole scene looked ready to collapse into a riot.

"Damn . . ."

This was not looking good.

The worst part was that I had just finished escaping my pursuers. They were probably still around here, and if a big duel started they were sure to find me.

"Second Javelin!"

Motoyasu produced two glowing spears and sent them flying in my direction.

I stopped one with my shield, protecting a shop behind me in the process—but the second one grazed my arm and left me scratched.

"First Heal!"

I could heal myself with magic—but I couldn't hope to win a duel by only defending.

What should I do? Without Raphtalia or Filo I didn't stand a chance of winning.

And Motoyasu KNEW that I couldn't attack. He was doing this on purpose to humiliate me.

Did he only start duels that he knew he would win? The jerk.

If it was going to be an unfair fight from the start, I wouldn't have any choice but to run.

Unlike last time, they didn't have Raphtalia as a hostage, so I didn't have anything forcing me to fight him.

Or so I thought . . .

"Please stop that! Spear Hero!"

The soldiers I'd been running from appeared from the crowd and positioned themselves between Motoyasu and me.

"This area is heavily trafficked by our citizens. We cannot permit you to duel here."

"Yes, we can."

Bitch immediately snapped at the soldiers. She flashed the certificate and continued. "Your assistance is not necessary here. This is a duel between HEROES, and the interference of a mere soldier will not be tolerated."

That Bitch . . . she was rotten to the core.

"Uh . . ."

The soldier's eyes swam with confusion. Even if she was hiding out, she WAS the princess, after all. Certainly they didn't care about protecting me.

"Even still, the country and its people . . . I'm a soldier to protect them. If the personal affairs of someone—even if they are heroes—threatens the people of our country, I must put a stop to it!"

What's that? It felt like a cool breeze blowing through—things might be different this time.

"And so, because the Shield Hero is unable to fight, I will take his place—I will be his sword!"

"Wh . . . ?"

"Huh?"

Motoyasu and I both fell speechless.

A mere soldier wanted to cover for me as my sword? He was going to challenge Motoyasu?

"I will too . . ."

A kid who looked like some kind of wizard appeared from the crowd, walked up behind me, and leveled his wand.

He seemed to be some kind of soldier as well.

"Imbecilic fools. You would challenge me? Do you understand my position?"

What Bitch really wanted to say was that even if they survived the duel, she would make sure they were taken care of later.

"Your position is irrelevant. We are merely carrying out our orders."

Bitch's face turned red at the answer.

"Insolence! You think you can ignore the will of the Crown?!"

"I will not permit the personal disputes of heroes to be settled here."

A soft voice came from the crowd, followed by its owner.

Everyone reacted as though someone with the proper authority had finally arrived. I'd never seen people act that way since I'd come to this world, so I was surprised as well.

All the authority figures I'd met since I came here were scoundrels—rather than stopping a duel, they were more likely to instigate and enjoy it, like Myne, who was second in command.

Who would speak out against her? I turned to see.

It looked like a mere child. Wait, no . . . It was Mel!

She was flanked on both sides by Raphtalia and Filo, who both looked unsettled. They were walking in my direction.

"What are you doing here?!"

"It's been forever, Sister."

SISTER?!

Mel reached into her pocket and pulled out a certificate.

"That's . . ."

Everyone was speechless when they saw the paper, and they let their heads droop.

What was it? Who had more authority than Bitch?

"Spear Hero, please try to understand. I would appreciate it if you can put your disagreements to rest today."

"But! But!"

"Please look around you! You would fight in a crowded town square? Are those the actions of a hero?"

"Ugh . . ."

Motoyasu sighed and slowly calmed down. He seemed to understand the situation.

"Mr. Naofumi!"

Raphtalia came running to my side.

"Are you all right?"

"Yeah. But what's up with Mel? She's that thing's sister?"

"Holy Saint . . . But that's not who you are, is it? Allow me to reintroduce myself. My name is Melty. Thank you for bringing me back to the castle town. It was a very enjoyable trip we had together."

Mel gave a curtsy.

"Shield Hero, what happened here?"

"I don't know. Motoyasu once again challenged me to a duel—he wants to steal my party members away."

"AGAIN?"

Raphtalia knit her eyebrows in disbelief and shot Motoyasu an annoyed look.

Motoyasu ignored her and looked over at Filo.

"What's your name, Miss?"

"Um . . . Filo!"

"Don't tell him the truth!"

I had to jump in to save her.

"This guy is making you pull heavy carriages around, isn't he? Let me save you."

"Well that's true. She is pulling a heavy carriage for me—pretty much every day."

I couldn't lie about that. I mean, that is the kind of monster she was.

If I don't let her pull it, she throws a fit. She cries like a baby.

"You bastard! You'd treat this poor little girl like she was one of your fat birds?"

He sure did have a big mouth. What I did with Filo was my business.

"Let Filo go!"

"Shut up already!"

Why did he think everyone in town was trying to calm him down? But he was angry again; he pointed his spear at me.

"I believe I just said that you were not to duel here."

Mel once again had to order him to stop, but he completely ignored her. Was he just going to ignore her? He was the kind of guy to lose all of his senses when a woman was around.

"Ladies! You must escape! I'm telling you, this guy is very dangerous!"

Motoyasu turned to Filo and tried really hard to look like the good guy.

Didn't he know that he was fighting so hard to save the "fat bird" that he was screaming about wanting to kill just a little while ago?

Or . . . I guess she was in human form right now. She just looked like your standard, pretty little girl. What a Motoyasu kind of mistake to make.

"Huh? Why? Master isn't dangerous!"

"MASTER? You bastard! Air Strike Javelin!"

Motoyasu ignored Mel's order and performed a skill. I immediately blocked it.

"What are you doing to Master?!"

"It's okay, Filo! I'm going to save you!"

Why didn't he listen? We weren't allowed to fight here!

"I suppose there is no getting around it . . ."

Mel closed her eyes and raised her hands.

"Filo, I have a request of you. Please stop the Spear Hero."

"Okay! I will protect Master!"

Filo stood before Motoyasu.

"Filo, please move. I can't take care of him with you right there."

But Filo didn't move. She stayed where she was and opened her arms.

"Filo, he called you a fat bird."

"Naofumi! You bastard! How could you say that to a little girl?"

"I didn't. You did. You just said it like five minutes ago. You said you wanted to kill her."

"Yeah, and the last time I met you, you laughed at me. I hate you, Spear Guy!"

"Laugh? When did I ever laugh at you?"

With a puff of smoke, Filo returned to her bird form. Yes, the Filolial Queen form.

"Huh? What?"

Motoyasu looked shocked at Filo's transformation. He was leaning over a little, as if to protect his crotch.

Filo watched him, watched the confused look spread over his face, then charged up her powerful leg and delivered a quick kick to his crotch.

"Aaaaahhhh!"

I saw it happen. His face froze in shock, and his body snapped into a tailspin, flying ten meters through the air.

The cup he was wearing shattered into dust and came raining down from above on our heads.

"Ugh!"

"Filo wins!"

Filo threw one of her wings in the air and struck a victorious pose for the crowd.

Was that enough to keep him down? Nah, he was probably just fine. He'd been wearing a cup.

Raphtalia was pale and whispering to herself, but I'm sure she was fine.

For whatever reason, his party didn't run to help him either. I suppose there wasn't much anyone could do.

The crowd erupted in applause. It was immediately clear who they'd hoped would win.

My bad mood was feeling better already.

"Please take the Spear Hero to get some medical care."

The soldiers that had challenged him now picked him up and carried him off.

"All right, Sister? I have to say that it seems you've really behaved poorly here. May I ask what the problem is? I might have to report to Mother on this."

"I . . . I am simply doing what I must to support the heroes, as requested."

"It certainly didn't look that way."

"You cannot judge by this single, isolated event, Melty."

"Can't I? Your barbarous behavior stands out on the reports."

"You would turn on me? Your superior? Your older sister?"

"I could ask the same of you, Sister."

"Pfft . . ."

Bitch shot us all hateful looks.

What kind of relationship did they have? From where I was standing, it sure looked like Melty held more authority than Bitch did.

Bitch noticed that Motoyasu and his party members had slunk off, and she quickly followed them—a good excuse as any to run away.

"Master! Didn't I do good?"

Filo came running over to me, expecting some kind of praise.

There was no getting around it. I reached over and rubbed her head.

"There, there. That's the second good kick you've given Motoyasu now. Good work. That was one of the best moments of my life."

"Yeah! I kick him every time I see him!"

"Yes, you do! You're great!"

Eh, heh, heh . . .

"Why are you congratulating her?!"

Raphtalia was angry.

But I wouldn't back-peddle on this—Filo really HAD done a good job, after all.

"I swear . . . These heroes . . ."

Melty held a hand against her forehead and sighed.

"I sure wish they'd stop causing a fuss—at least here in the middle of the castle town."

"Oh, I . . . I suppose I should thank you . . ."

"Sure, but not here. Let's find a quieter place to chat."

I looked around for a good spot, and sure enough, the crowd was watching us closely.

That only made sense. We shouldn't talk where everyone and anyone could overhear us.

"Okay."

"Shield Hero . . ."

The soldier that had stood up to cover me was now giving me a pleading look.

"Yeah, yeah . . . You guys are coming too, aren't you? Not that I know what you are up to . . ."

"We were never trying to capture you, Shield Hero. I hope you will believe me."

Considering the way they'd chased me and their obedience to orders, I wasn't really sure if I could trust them. But I suppose it couldn't hurt to hear them out . . .

Chapter Four: The Volunteer

"So yeah, this weapon shop is one of my favorite places in town—I give the guy all my business. You remember it, right?"

"Yes."

"Hey, kid, think I could trouble you for an explanation?"

"A bunch of stuff happened, and I'd like to borrow your shop for a meeting."

"I don't really care what happened. But this is my place, not yours. Do me a favor and find another place for your meeting."

The weapon shop was the only place I could think of where we could speak undisturbed, so after all the drama in town I marched everyone straight there.

"There aren't really any other places. Like what else? The monster trainer tent?"

"C'mon, kid. The monster trainer is really . . ."

The old guy knew. He knew what really went on in that tent.

"If you're going to take a bunch of kids to a place like that, then I guess I have no choice but to let you hang out here."

"And so there we have it: the owner's permission. Now then, who are you? Your name was Melty, right?"

"Yes, I am the first heir to the throne of Melromarc, the

second daughter of the royal family, Melty Melromarc."

"Huh?"

Let's see, Bitch is the oldest child, right? So why would the second daughter be the heir to the throne?

"My older sister has had personality . . . issues . . . for many years now. After she caused problem after problem, it was decided that I would be the heir to the kingdom."

Normally that would sound crazy, but when I thought about just how awful Bitch really was, it started to make sense. Even still, something seemed off.

Could Melty really share blood with that crazy Bitch? How did the Trash king produce a daughter like her? It was hard to believe.

"Filo."

"What?"

"You can't hang out with this girl anymore."

"Mr. Naofumi. Why are you acting like her father yet saying such awful things?!"

C'mon, she's Bitch's sister! If she'd managed to become the heiress before her sister, she must have been good at manipulating people. At that young age, she might be even more manipulative than her Bitch sister.

Was she after Filo? Or even worse, was she working for Motoyasu?!

Had she coordinated this whole run-in just so that she

could swoop in and earn my trust? She could have!

She might have had her eyes on us since that eastern village with the epidemic. She earned our trust and infiltrated our group, and she'd been planning on capturing us when we delivered her to the castle. If Raphtalia hadn't caught up, who knows what might have happened?

"And . . ."

"Sorry, but I think that's enough talking for now. I simply cannot trust you. Or I should say that I can't trust you ANYMORE—now that I know who you really are."

"Please listen to what I have to say!"

"Have you heard the things your own father and sister have said? I'm sorry, but there is no way we can talk. I can't trust you."

Even if I told her the truth, there was no guarantee that she'd believe me.

Just think about it—she was the Trash king's daughter! I couldn't just tell her to believe me.

"I'll accept the help you just provided us in the street as payment for bringing you back to the castle town. Now get out!"

"But you . . ."

Before the second princess could get angry, a knight opened the door to the shop and poked his head in.

"Ms. Melty. The king has summoned you. Please come with us."

"All right."

I thought she'd throw a tantrum, as children do, but the younger princess instead gripped the frills of her dress, took a deep breath, composed herself, and followed the knight out the door.

"Bye then, Filo."

"Okay. Later!"

There would be no "later" though. I wasn't going to give Filo away to some princess or to Motoyasu.

I swear! Everyone in this whole damn kingdom drove me nuts.

"Mr. Naofumi, shouldn't you have at least heard what she had to say?"

"Yeah, kid, she's right."

"Sorry, but I just can't trust the royal family."

"Shield Hero . . ."

"What? Oh, you guys are still here?"

I thought they'd left with the young princess, but I turned to see that the soldiers who'd chased me through the streets were still there.

Just how many tricks would I have to put up with? These soldiers were in on it too, no doubt!

I waved them away, but they didn't budge.

"Get out of here! We don't have anything to talk about!"

"I'm not moving until you hear what I have to say!"

Oh, come ON . . . All they were going to say was "give Filo to the princess" or something like that.

"Fine. Spit it out."

If I didn't let them talk, they'd never leave.

"Um . . . When the waves come . . . When the wave is here, I'd like to fight with you."

"What?"

What was he saying? I stuttered in disbelief and stared at the young soldier.

"Myself, and many other lower-ranking soldiers, were very impressed by the way you conducted yourself during the last wave. Also, I come from Riyute, and I feel the need to repay all that you've done for my family and friends there."

"Is that so?"

"Yes. And, well . . . A number of us were impressed with your actions that day. We came to realize that if anyone fought to protect others, it was you, the Shield Hero. We formed a group—we want to fight with you."

"With me? I don't think your commanding officers will be too excited about that."

The knights and leaders of the kingdom had never shown any desire to cooperate with me on anything. Once, during the first wave, I'd been fighting off a horde of monsters when they decided to rain fire down on me from afar.

"You're right. They won't be happy about it. But you

protected us when we needed it. We want to follow your example and help others."

"And so you came looking for me?"

"The guards posted around town are all in agreement. We've all talked it out, and we agreed that whoever found you first needed to stop you and tell you how we all feel."

"You don't say."

"We aren't supposed to fight against the wave directly. That's not our role in the battle. Even still, we believe our number-one priority should be protecting our citizens from harm."

What a refined philosophy to have. If only the other stupid heroes shared it . . .

"So please, Shield Hero. When the next wave comes, let us fight with you."

"If you just want to fight against waves, I don't see why you need to fight with me."

There had to be some other reason they were offering me their services.

There was probably some system of advancement within their military so that soldiers that proved themselves in battle would earn promotions quicker than their compatriots. If that was true, then battling side by side with a hero against the wave was sure to improve their standing.

And even if we were heroes, no one could hope to face down a wave by themselves. They knew that I needed whatever help I could get.

In the status magic bar there was a category under "party members" called "Battle Formations." It probably referred to something we could use during the wave.

It would make sense if we used it when battling the wave. It seemed like the proper way to go about it. It was probably something similar to online MMORPGs, where guilds and clans could fight one another. In this situation the enemy wouldn't be another guild, but it seemed like they were talking about a similar setup.

If not, how were one person and their immediate party supposed to face down a whole wave of enemies? That would be about as reckless as a person could be.

Sure, when we got to the boss monster, the high-level ace players—in this case that would be us heroes—would have to step up and defeat that monster. But what about the rest of the other, weaker monsters? You'd think that plenty of normal people and soldiers could take care of them easily enough.

The last wave pretty much proved my theory.

The last wave occurred near a village named Riyute, and the knights and soldiers were able to arrive quickly. That settled it easily enough.

But the country was big. If the wave occurred somewhere far away, the damage would be incalculable.

If that happened, there would only be a few of us there to protect people.

Whatever. Setting aside the actual battle formations and strategy for a second, I wanted to know why these young soldiers wanted to fight by MY side. Was it because I was the weakest of the heroes? If there was a lot of competition to get in with a hero during battle, it only made sense for them to come to me first.

Either that or it was all a big lie. Maybe they just wanted to arrest me when the wave arrived and I was transported to the area it was occurring. Or they'd make me count on their participation and then leave me there when the time came just to spite me. That could have been it.

"We simply want to fight with you to protect our citizens."

Of course, he could say whatever he wanted—that didn't make it true.

"Are you trying to get a promotion or something?"

"Not at all."

He shook his head in response so quickly it was clear he expected the question. Then he turned and waved to someone standing behind me. It was a young boy in robes like a wizard. I say "like a wizard," but his robes were nothing like the purple robes I'd seen at the magic shop. They seemed cheaper, shoddier. They were yellow. The two young soldiers lined up before me and bowed deeply.

"I . . . I am from Riyute. You saved my family, so I . . . I want to help you if I can."

"Ah, I get it now."

So he felt obligated to me because I'd saved his family. If he really was from Riyute, I could probably trust him.

"I'm sure you're right—that there are plenty of people that would use you to secure a promotion. But I just want to help you."

"Huh, I guess there are some curious people in your group."

"Um . . . Shield Hero?"

The young boy dressed like a wizard raised his face.

Looking closely, I saw that the boy was a demi-human.

Melromarc was very obvious about its preference for humans over demi-humans, so how could this young demi-human survive, much less become a soldier for the Crown?

His robes were much shabbier than the those of wizards I'd seen during the last wave battle. Could it be that there was a reason for that besides his age and rank?

"This little guy is a real fan of the Shield Hero. Long ago, in a different country, there were legends of other heroes appearing. This one as always looked up to the Shield Hero."

"Huh . . ."

It seemed like there really was a small group of people that believed in me and wanted to help. This kid hadn't mentioned it directly, but it seemed like all the while I'd been peddling my wares and saving villages, there were people gathering to support me.

I could give it a try.

There was a bag in the back of my carriage that was filled with accessories I'd yet to sell. I pulled it out.

"One hundred fifty pieces of silver. If you can pay for that, I'll think about your offer."

"Huh?"

"What's wrong? If you guys buy this off me, I'll trust you."

"Mr. Naofumi . . ."

Raphtalia sighed and looked a little worn out. I suppose it did sound like I was demanding money when all they wanted was to help. Normally it would be the opposite. It was just my nature. If they were after promotions or money, then they'd turn their noses up at this.

My real concern was that they might be connected with the younger princess, in which case I couldn't trust them.

"Very well. We will go meet with everyone and collect the money you require. Please wait for us."

The young soldier I'd been talking with made the declaration and ran off.

"Kid, I tell you—you're awful."

"If something sounds too good to be true, it is. I have to make sure they aren't lying."

The young, wizard-looking boy was still there, just standing around.

"You disappointed in me?"

The young wizard boy shook his head.

"I believe in you."

"Heh."

Curious little kid. I was mulling it over when the soldier came running back. He was out of breath.

"Huff . . . Huff . . . everyone chipped in. Here you go."

"That was fast."

"I was just going to run around to the knights, but I stopped by the dormitories on the way. Everyone chipped in."

Hmm . . . So I guess he'd asked quite a few people.

I had purposefully asked for a lot of money. He passed me a heavy pouch, and I looked inside.

"Each person could only give a little bit, but it should all be there. Please believe us."

"Sure. Okay. How many people are you representing?"

"Let me think. Including me . . . five."

"Huh."

I took five items from the bag and gave them to the boy—along with all the money.

One of those items was a necklace that would absorb a certain level of damage. It was imbued with a special effect, making it a very convenient piece of equipment to have around.

I was thinking of testing it, and I'd just made it by accident, so I felt like I could give it away.

During the wave battles, you never knew when you were

going to die. If they were going to fight with me, it seemed fine to let them have it.

"Um . . . This . . ."

"I asked you to get the money—I didn't say I was going to take it. I just wanted to get a feel for your sincerity. Because of this little test, it must have made it easier, even among your own group, to tell who was in this for real—and who just wanted to get their hands on money or on a better position."

Granted, the money was minted by the Crown, so there was a limit on how much you could trust it. But they'd been polite enough. So I'd trust them for now.

From the battle formation menu, I chose a formation leader and set it to the young soldier in front of me.

The party status was set so that I was the leader, followed by Raphtalia and Filo. Underneath that, I was able to set the formation leader authority to the soldier.

What it meant was that the soldier had authority to give commands, but that authority was subject to my judgment. Basically, it meant that I could decide whether or not he would receive experience from our battles.

"This is . . ."

"You understand?"

"Sure."

"If you don't want to be the leader, then give the authority to that guy. You just need to get together a group that wants to participate. But don't misunderstand me. If you try to use us, or try to pull something sneaky, that authority will crumble, and the whole formation will break."

"Understood! Thank you!"

The two of them lined up and bowed deeply before leaving the room.

There were plenty of holes I could poke in this situation, but it seemed like, just maybe, people around here were actually starting to believe in me.

Except that, just like I'd warned them, if they crossed me I'd show no mercy.

"All right then, let's go do the class-up thing."

"Hey, kid. You don't have the nicest methods, but you are starting to act like a real hero."

"So you really were just trying to see if they were lying or not?"

"It's like I said: they could have been in it for profit. I had to see that they were willing to sacrifice."

We left the weapon shop and went on our way.

We might have run into some trouble, but now I could return to my immediate goal: class up.

Chapter Five: A Royal Order

To class up, we had to make our way to the Dragon Hourglass.

"That reminds me. I heard that classing up will open up a bunch of new opportunities. What do you want to do, Raphtalia?"

"I want to do whatever you ask of me."

"Stop that. Raphtalia, you should decide on what you want for yourself."

I'd played a game once that let you choose the path of light or the path of darkness after a certain class change. The whole point of that mechanic was that the player would pick whatever they wanted for themselves.

"When the waves are over and I go back to my own world, you'll still be here without me. I need you to become strong enough to survive without me."

"What? Are you going to leave me, Mr. Naofumi?"

"Yeah."

I didn't feel any particular connection to this world. I'd helped some people and gotten a party of friends, but did that really make it worth it to save the world? If I didn't like it there, I couldn't think of any reason to stay.

"You wouldn't take me with you?"

"Where?"

What was she saying? If a girl like Raphtalia came to my world, people would stare at her.

"Filo could take me there. Where are we going?"

"I don't think Filo could take you there."

"Really?"

"Let's change the subject. Filo, what do you want to do when you class up?"

"I want to . . . Um . . . I want to learn to spit poison!"

". . ."

Now there's a phrase for the history books. What did this stupid bird want now?

Was it because we'd fought a lot of poison-type monsters lately? Did that make Filo think that it was cool or something?

Like the BioPlant and the Dragon Zombie?

"You're already spitting poison."

I just meant that she had a sharp tongue. She just babbled whatever she wanted without thinking about her surroundings.

"Really?!"

She narrowed her mouth to a slit and exhaled sharply.

"Did I do it?"

"That's not what I meant. Anyway, let's get going."

We thought about the impending class-up and made our way to the Dragon Hourglass, our hearts leaping in our chests.

The Dragon Hourglass was situated very prominently in the center of Melromarc's castle town. There was a great view from the grounds. It was a very sunny spot too, and there was usually a crowd of people lounging around in the afternoon sun.

I was thinking over the location on our way there, and soon enough we arrived at the Dragon Hourglass.

Just like always, it stood silent in the building, a heavy and important atmosphere floating over the hush.

"You must be the Shield Hero."

Just like the last time, I was greeted by a grumbling sister of the faith.

"Yeah."

"And to what do we owe the pleasure?"

"We'd like to class up."

"In that case, we will need 15 pieces of gold from each of you."

Fifteen pieces of gold? Was she crazy? What could possibly justify a price that high?!

The sister remained calm and unmoved, though her eyes seemed to be laughing at us.

Was she waiting for us to say that we couldn't afford it so that she could laugh in our faces?

"You said 15 pieces of gold each?"

With both Raphtalia and Filo, we wouldn't have enough money to cover it.

But there was still time until the next wave came, so I guess we would just have to focus on making money with the time we had left.

"Raphtalia, you class up first."

"What? Just Big Sister?!"

"We don't have enough money, so there isn't much we can do about that. You can class up the next time we come here, so just relax. I'll get you a treat on the way home."

She sighed in exaggerated discontent.

I'd been meaning to treat her to something anyway, ever since she delivered that good kick to Motoyasu, so it was good timing.

I took a bag filled with 15 pieces of gold, Raphtalia's portion, and showed it to the sister.

The sister's face suddenly flushed, and she ran to retrieve some documents from the desk at the front of the room.

"The Shield Hero is prohibited from classing up."

"What?! What's that supposed to mean!?"

"It is a royal order. The Shield Hero and his party are prohibited from classing up."

That Trash king! He sure did know how to piss me off!

First, they set an illegal price, and then when I show that I can still afford it, they say that I'm prohibited from even trying! Give me a break! If I couldn't class up, what could I do?!

Why would I have to fight on without a job change? Was

this some kind of "new game +" playing strategy for hardcore gamers?

"Give me a break!"

"It is the rule. And besides, the Shield Hero has, right from the very start . . . oh . . . Never mind."

"From the very start WHAT?"

When I jumped to my feet, some knights that had been milling about the back wall all snapped to attention.

"Geez! Fine . . ."

I put all my strength into my legs and pounded my feet loudly as we walked out of the room.

I should have spent longer with the younger princess. What if she had really wanted to help me?

She was in line to inherit the throne, and if she really did want to be on my side, she might have been able to do something about this stupid rule.

And besides, if they were putting the brakes on my ability to class up, that was a good enough reason to go see her anyway.

"What are we supposed to do?"

Raphtalia whispered. She looked upset. She was right. This was a major problem.

"Hey! What's that big hourglass? I wanna look at it more!"

"Calm down."

I decided to look at the help menu.

I found the section on class-up. I'd better read up.

Class-up is a ceremony to increase the possibilities for party members of a hero.

The ceremony is performed at the Dragon Hourglass.

We suggest you wait until there is a star by your name before attempting to class up.

There are no limitations on the growth potential of a hero.

There were no limitations on a hero's growth potential? That must mean that I, and only I, was able to level past 40?

But . . . But that was no good at all!

If there was no way to class up Raphtalia and Filo, then they'd be in a tough spot when it came time to battle, and that would leave us without any way to attack.

"There's nothing we can do. Let's come back to this later."

It would be fine. I hadn't planned on doing much more leveling until the wave had passed anyway. We could worry about all this after that.

Maybe we'd meet an adventurer or two that had a certificate allowing the bearer to class up. We could get Raphtalia to team up with them to get to class up—or something like that.

We had some cash to throw around. Certainly we could come up with something.

But that reminded me—the slave trader had slaves that were over level 40. I didn't really want to spend more time with him than I had to, but I guess I didn't have a choice.

"All right, let's go see the slave trader."

Filo suddenly looked very scared.

"Are you going to sell me?"

"I'm not going to sell you, so just calm down."

She was sniffling, but she seemed to relax, and we all made for the slave trader's tent. Even still, I was in a terrible mood. Whenever I felt myself getting grumpy, I closed my eyes and tried to recall Motoyasu's face after Filo had kicked him. That made me feel a little better.

"Mr. Naofumi, that's quite a smile you've got there!"

Raphtalia never knew when to shut up. What was wrong with laughing a little to myself?

Chapter Six: Welcome

We went to see the slave trader.

"Ah, if it isn't the hero. What can I do for you today?"

"Before we get into that . . ."

I couldn't help but focus on what he was wearing.

He seemed suddenly very rich. His clothes and jewelry looked much more refined than they had before.

"You look like you've run into some success recently."

"All thanks to you, Hero. Yes sir."

"Huh?"

"Since you've been out on the road selling your wares, I've used the opportunity to make some money myself."

"What's that supposed to mean?"

I had a few theories on what he might be talking about, but I didn't have the confidence to accuse him of any of them.

"First of all, there was the Filolial Queen excitement. Many nobles and wealthy families have stopped by to inquire where they might find such a creature."

So just seeing Filo in the streets, pulling my cart, had helped advertise his store. It only made sense—considering what a rare creature she was, people would look into where she came from, and then they'd find the "monster trainer" pretty quickly.

I'd met plenty of wealthy people who'd tried to buy her off of me directly.

Come to think of it, that was probably why the younger princess had tried to get close to us in the first place.

Not only was she a big help in battle, but she was a useful business tool also. Too bad for them, I wasn't planning on selling her.

"Well, I've gained a reputation because of that, and now many people come to purchase monsters from me. Yes sir."

"Good for you."

Of course, as for what makes a Filolial become a queen, no one actually knew—and we weren't any closer to an answer. So of course I couldn't sell her.

Maybe if the Filolial was raised by a hero she'd become a queen. It was hard enough taking care of Filo that I couldn't even think about trying to manage two of them.

"Aside from the monsters, people have also seen your slave and come to learn that the slaves I supply are of superlative quality. That's led to some handsome profits. Yes sir."

He was talking about Raphtalia. And he was right. Even I couldn't help but notice that she had a beautiful face and body. If people caught sight of her, they were sure to consider this slave trader to be trustworthy.

But I suppose this meant that I was largely responsible for his new business and profits.

"Now then, why have you come in today? Are you looking for a slave? Or are you looking to assist with my Filolial experiments?"

"Slave trader, what do you know about classing up?"

"Classing up?"

"Yeah. Trash has declared that no one in my party is allowed to class up. It's becoming a real headache. Then I remembered that you were selling slaves over level 40. I thought there might be a certificate or some way around the rule."

The slave trader turned to me and tenderly rubbed his chin in an impression of deep thought.

"I regret to inform you that I will be unable to assist you regarding your problem. I do not have any certificates."

"You don't? Oh well, guess I came to the wrong place . . ."

So I guess he wasn't able to level those slaves up through any sort of special authority he had.

"If you want to class up, why not go over to our neighboring country? If you can gain their trust, then you should be able to use their Dragon Hourglass to class up."

"What?"

Did that mean that there were dragon hourglasses in countries besides this one?

"You mean there are other dragon hourglasses outside of Melromarc?"

"Yes, but it can take a very long time to earn their trust."

Time was the one thing I didn't have. I wanted to class up as soon as possible.

I wondered if my poor reputation had already spread to the neighboring country. If it had, then I might as well not even bother.

"If you are looking for a country that will be relatively easy to win over, may I suggest the mercenary kingdom of Zeltoble? You could also give some thought to the demi-human kingdoms of Siltvelt or Shieldfreeden. Yes. Other kingdoms will not be so easy."

"I didn't know there were so many."

"There are. For you, Hero, I'd recommend you try Siltvelt or Shieldfreeden. They should let you over their borders without much trouble."

"Hmm . . . How long would it take to get there from here?"

"They are all about the same distance. About a month on foot or two weeks by boat."

The slave trader pulled out a map and showed me what roads I would need to take.

He was right. If you calculated backward from the average daily distance we could cover, the borders were all very far away. Filo could probably cover the distance in two weeks or so. Just to be safe, I decided to call it three weeks.

"If you had a flying dragon you could get there faster, but considering the modes of transport available to you right now, these are pretty much your only options."

"They're so far . . ."

But if I wanted my party to get stronger, it looked like I didn't have any other options.

I'd just have to make up for lost time later. If I couldn't get Raphtalia and Filo's levels up any higher, then there was no point. It was pretty much inevitable: we'd have to make for the nearest demi-human country. It was our only real option.

"Once the next wave passes, let's go."

I swear, Trash would do anything to drive me crazy. It was his singular passion in life.

"Hero, was that the only reason for your visit today?"

The slave trader was wringing his hands. It was starting to look like he wasn't going to let me leave so easily.

"Have you given any consideration to getting some weapons for your Filolial Queen there?"

"A weapon for Filo?"

"A weeeeeapon?"

I guess I really hadn't purchased anything for her but those clothes.

She really did already have a pretty great attack power, but with the wave coming it might not be a bad idea to try and get her some equipment. If I did, I'd talk to the weapon shop guy first. He made the best stuff. Some claws for her made from dragon bone or something would be good.

"Just so you know, monster equipment is only dealt with

by monster trainers. So a normal weapon shop won't carry the things you are looking for. A normal shop might be able to do a custom order for you, but the cost would be through the roof."

Damn, he knew exactly what I'd been thinking.

"Can you do it?"

I'd promised Filo some kind of treat. This could be it. Just thinking of her kicking Motoyasu with some claws equipped put a smile on my face.

The slave trader's eyes moved over Filo.

Filo, in her human form, had been humming a song to herself, but when she noticed him looking at her she quickly ducked behind me to hide. She really didn't like him.

"A weapon for her would be either a horn for her head or some kind of spiked horseshoe for her feet. If you are looking for armor, they make some for Filolials . . ."

Thinking about Filo's body shape though, I doubted there was any armor made that would fit her.

We could get a piece of armor custom-made for her unique body type. But Filo transformed into human form a lot, and if the armor couldn't change shape with her, then changing in and out of it would be a real pain.

"What do you have in mind when you say 'horn?'"

"It's a type of helmet that fits over the head and is spiked. It turns a head-butt into a deadly attack."

"Hmm . . ."

The horseshoes he mentioned must have been some kind of hard shoe.

"Finally, there are claws."

"Well, well. Filo, what do you think?"

"Hm?"

Filo still looked nervous. Was she so afraid of the slave trader that she had stopped listening to the conversation?

"There's a helmet for your head or shoes for your feet. Then there is armor."

"But I like to transform, and I don't want the armor to pinch me, so no thanks!"

I wonder if that thread the tailor had given her in the past was still working for her.

We had a tailor make Filo some clothes for when she was in her human form. They were made from magical fabric that turned into a simple ribbon when she was in her Filolial Queen form.

The helmet would work fine when she was a bird, but it would be way too big and heavy for her human form. The horseshoes would hurt her feet, and the armor would never fit. What else was left? We could go back to the tailor and see if there was some kind of metal version of the clothes we made— but that was sure to cost a small fortune, and the defense rating would probably be a joke.

"If you're looking for something that can easily be taken on and off, may I suggest the claws? Yes sir."

"Sure. What do you think, Filo?"

"Okay!"

"I'll just get your measurements then. Can you transform into your monster form for me?"

"Hear that, Filo?"

"Okay!"

There was a puff of smoke, and Filo was back in her monster form. She held out her foot so that the slave trader could measure it.

But the slave trader did not move. A subordinate of his emerged from the shadows and measured Filo's foot.

"Hmm . . . She's much larger than an average Filolial."

"How long will it take?"

"Luckily enough, I think we have this size in stock. Will iron claws work for you?"

I didn't know how to answer that because I didn't know what sort of attack power I could expect from different materials.

Is it more important for them to be hard? Or is it better that they are sharp?

"I have a little spare cash, so give me the best you have."

"Right away, sir. The best I can do at the moment is magic iron."

"And how much will that cost me?"

"Well you are a loyal customer, so I think we can offer you

a special price. How does 5 gold pieces sound? It's half the market price."

"Can I haggle you down?"

"Your parsimony never fails to impress me, hero. Very well, I will accept 4 pieces."

"That'll do it. Throw in some reins too."

"Absolutely!"

The slave trader was looking very excited. He was easy enough to manipulate, but I was getting the feeling that I was being used too. In that sense, he was very skilled at business. I'd have to be on my guard.

He brought out a pair of large claws from the back. They were made of metal and were just large enough to fit Filo's feet.

"I can't believe you keep claws that big in stock."

"They are actually designed for flying dragons. It's the largest size we carry."

So they weren't for Filolials.

"They go on my feet?"

"Yeah, those are your weapons."

The claws were lined up on the floor. Filo stepped into them.

"They look like a perfect fit."

They really did. All you had to do was tie the strings over her feet to keep them on.

Filo raised one of her feet into the air and wiggled it to get a feel for the claws.

"They feel so weeeeird!"

"Get used to it. With those on, your attack power will be way higher than it used to be."

Her legs were already really strong. If her attack power went up even higher . . .

I found myself mentally replaying the scene of Filo kicking Motoyasu.

It was such a funny thing to see, but if she kicked him with these on, she'd probably rip him in half. It was funny to think about, but if it really happened, he'd be in real danger.

"Filo, from now on, when you see that guy with the spear, you can only kick him if you are not wearing those claws, okay?"

"But why?"

"Because he wouldn't get out of it with just a pair of smashed balls."

Sure, he was a jerk, but he was still a hero. Who knew what would happen if we killed him? Maybe it was even too late to try and restrain Filo.

"Hmmm . . ."

It looked like she was focused on exploring her new claws and was only half-listening to me.

Was she really listening?

I gave four 4 gold pieces to the slave trader.

"Thanks for your help."

"If you'd like to express your gratitude, you may."

"No thanks, but that reminds me of something. Is there anything she can practice using those claws on?"

"Do I get to kick something?"

"Unfortunately, I would be in a tough position if you were to kill any of the monsters I have here. Yes sir."

So I guess he was saying he didn't have anything that would survive a kick with those claws.

And yet, if we tested them in the field and it turned out that they were of poor quality, that would put US in a tough position.

I guess we could go just outside the town gates and try them there—but the balloons were too weak to really try them out on.

"I'd like to try them on some strong monsters, but where am I supposed to find any?"

"If you head for the coliseum in Zeltoble, you should be able to fight whatever you like."

"But it's really far, right?"

"Yes."

That wouldn't work. We didn't have that much time before the wave came.

We'd just have to try our luck out on the plains. I could have tried them out on the slave trader, but that would probably come back to bite me.

"Well, now that you mention it, I have something that

might be just perfect for someone in your situation."

The slave trader's subordinate stepped forward and spoke.

"Yeah, what's that?"

"The nobility of Melromarc has been using the sewers to raise a monster in secret, but it grew too large for them to control it."

"So it's under their control with a monster control spell?"

"It had been acting on its own for so long that it found ways to get around being controlled."

That didn't sound good at all . . .

"And the monster has gotten so big that the spell stopped being strong enough to control it quite a long time ago."

How could they allow a monster like that free rein in the sewers? If a kid or something went inside to play, just think what could happen.

It was like some kind of movie—the idea that there was a monster hiding out in the sewers.

I couldn't explain why, but I was picturing some kind of alligator.

"No one has gotten hurt yet, but people are talking about hiring an adventurer to go down there and take care of it."

"I assume there is some kind of reward?"

"Naturally. Yes sir."

I nodded along, deciding that taking the job would be a good idea.

"Very well then, this way please."

The slave trader led me to the back of the tent.

Soon we left the tent all together and were at the entrance to some kind of large tunnel, which apparently was an entrance to the sewers.

". . ."

So he'd already been prepared to bring us here. What was that supposed to mean?

"This is a map of the sewer system."

The slave trader handed me a map that had apparently had a spell cast on it. The target area was glowing.

"This will tell you where the monster you are hunting is at the moment. Yes sir."

"Good. By the way, what level is this thing at?"

"The owners stopped keeping track at level 50. Yes sir. As for its current level, no one knows."

So it was over level 50. Guess that meant that even monsters could class up before we could.

But at the very least, it seems that owned monsters can't level up on their own in quite the same way that monsters in the wild can. So its growth would have to be limited to how big it could grow on the food it could find in the sewers . . . maybe.

The sewers stunk as badly as you'd think. I pinched my nose as we walked.

"It stinks!"

"Yes, it does."

"Both of you just deal with it. We're almost there!"

We had walked a long way into the sewers without running into any dangerous monsters.

The slave trader's subordinate had given us some instruction to get through the tricky parts, and so we were able to arrive without much trouble at all.

And when we got there, the monster we found was . . . yup—an alligator.

Its body was a yellowish-white, and its eyes were shining red. It looked really creepy down in the sewers.

Altogether it was probably around six meters long, which is huge. I mean it wasn't a dragon, but it looked very strong.

"Grrrrrrr . . ."

"Are we fighting that thing?"

"Yes. Hey, Raphtalia, give that new sword of yours a practice swing."

"Okay!"

We all turned and readied ourselves for the fight against the monster, the Cream Alligator.

"Let's do it!"

The Alligator came running at us with its jaws open wide, trying to eat us. I jumped out of the way, and once I saw its jaws snap shut I leapt onto its head to keep it from opening its mouth again.

I'd read a book once about how to fight off an alligator. Of course, that book was about alligators back in my world.

Even still, it seemed to be working.

"Grr?!"

I kept my weight on the top of its head, but it was trying so hard to open its jaws that its eyes were spinning.

But probably because of how much weight I was throwing at it, it wasn't having much luck.

"Now!"

"Argh!"

Raphtalia ran at the Cream Alligator's thrashing tail and swung her new sword.

With a swift and satisfying thwack the sword slid through the tail, slicing it off clean and leaving a stump. The rest of the tail went flying through the air.

". . . ?!"

"Big Sister, you're so strong! I won't let you show me up!"

Filo dropped her weight to charge up, then turned to the Cream Alligator's exposed belly and kicked it with all her might.

The alligator flew into the air.

"Finish it!"

The spinning gator crashed into the floor headfirst.

Then . . . Well, its skull was completely crushed, so the Cream Alligator just lay there, dead. I had been standing near where it landed though, and now I was drenched in its blood.

"Wow! Wow! These claws are awesome! That would have been a little harder without them!"

"Um . . ."

Filo was so excited about her victory that she was jumping up and down in place and cheering.

And the monster was apparently over level 50, so I guess our new weapons were working really well.

And so our test of Raphtalia's new sword and Filo's new claws was a resounding success.

We hurried back to the slave trader's tent, though of course I cleaned the blood off of myself before we got there.

By the way, I did go ahead and let the shield absorb the Cream Alligator's body, but it only unlocked a shield that wasn't as strong as the Chimera Viper Shield. As for equip effects, there was only one. It was an ability that raised your fighting ability at night—apparently by improving your vision in the dark.

"Well, well . . . I must say I'm very impressed that you were able to defeat the monster in such a short amount of time. Very impressed indeed. Yes sir."

The slave trader was obviously excited by what had just happened. His eyes flashed when he gave me the reward money. That money more than covered the price of the claws.

I was ready to leave, thinking we had nothing else we need-ed to do there, but then I remembered something.

Back when we'd fought those bandits in the woods, I thought about selling some of them into slavery, but it would have been a pain, so I never did.

"In this country humans are not allowed as slaves. If you looked really hard though, I'm sure you could find a buyer. They'll want high-quality specimens though, and it will be risky."

So I guess demi-humans were as far as you could push it here. They were human supremacists after all.

"Okay then. Later."

We turned and left the tent. Filo turned back into a human and carried her claws. Our shopping was finished for the time being, so we went back to the weapon shop.

"Hey, kid, that carriage isn't looking so good these days."

"It has gotten a lot of use."

Filo loved the carriage so much that we hadn't even parted with it long enough to make repairs. I'd done what I could on my own, but I wasn't a professional.

"Want me to make you a new one?"

"Really?"

Filo's eyes were flashing in anticipation.

"C'mon, Filo . . . I just bought you those claws."

"But . . ."

It had been rattling more than normal lately, so I'd thought about getting it fixed. As for buying a new one, I wasn't so sure about that.

"I'd make it as cheaply as I could."

He was right. If we wanted to keep traveling, I needed to consider the durability of my carriage. I didn't want to spoil Filo, but at the same time, if we were going to have to keep making repairs to our rickety wood cart, it would be better, in the long run, to just have a higher-quality one built.

"I'd like a durable one that can fit a lot of materials in it. My budget is around 10 pieces of gold."

"With 10 pieces of gold, you can make a really nice carriage. You don't care about how it's decorated, do you?"

"Of course not. Focus on the practical details. Filo doesn't mind if it's heavy."

Sometimes Filo even pulled the carriage with one hand. We could make it much heavier and she wouldn't complain.

"Gotcha, kid. Leave it to me. The bird-girl is fine with it, right?"

"Um . . . Yeah! I want a big one—like a house!"

"That'd be pretty big, lass."

That would have put us over budget. I was about to mention it when the owner gave me a sign that he knew what I was thinking.

"Thanks."

"Now, lass—it's good to have dreams and ambitions, but why not wait until you are bigger and stronger before you make one that big?"

"But . . ."

"Wouldn't you be embarrassed if I made one that big and you couldn't pull it?"

"Yeah . . ."

"Excellent. Well, I don't know how much you can pull, so I'll just make something that looks good to me. Okay?"

Yeah, and it would be custom anyway. It would be different from the sorts of carriages that the nobility used, so it was a new project altogether. That made it important to set priorities.

"Fine. I'd like a new carriage then."

"Good thinking, kid."

Okay then—we still had some time before the wave came.

It would be a little while before the weapons and carriage were ready, so I decided to get back to our traveling merchant work.

Chapter Seven: General Commander

I was thinking that we could probably move our stock faster. So we went to a village in the southwest and purchased cheaper materials.

You see, I'd heard that there was a famine in the north, which meant I could sell my stock for more money and make a good profit.

The village in the southwest was the very same village we'd already visited, where the BioPlant monster had caused a big ruckus.

We cleaned up their mess for them the last time we were there, but before we left, we gave them the improved BioPlant seed.

That's why I figured they'd be willing to sell us some food at a cheap price. And just like I'd expected, the villagers were happy to see us. They sold us food at a huge discount.

From the look of things, the improved BioPlant seed I'd given them had been planted. The fields of that southwestern village were covered in vines that hung with plump, red tomato-like fruit.

We loaded up the carriage and headed north. Then something happened in a little town on the way there.

"Huh? Some kind of traveling merchant certificate?"

We were stopped on our way into town by a guard on duty who demanded a tariff and taxes for his governor.

So I showed him the certificate from Riyute, but . . .

"That means nothing here! Pay your dues!"

"But . . ."

The guard ignored Raphtalia's protest and continued to demand money.

I stepped forward to start negotiating with him, but he wouldn't back down.

"You brute!"

Hm . . . For them to get so angry, something must have been going on.

Since I started this whole traveling merchant gig, I'd learned a thing or two about how to get your way.

The first of which was threats. If you had power, you could use it to force people to agree to things they normally wouldn't. You had to identify their weakness and use it to sell things at a higher price. This strategy worked the best on haughty customers. But looking at the way this guard was acting, he was taking us seriously. The next was negotiation. We form our relationships with people based on the ebb and flow of conversation. It works the best on people who aren't antagonistic. This guy was not exactly antagonistic. He was in a hurry.

THE RISING OF THE SHIELD HERO 3

If neither of these methods would work on him, it must mean that . . .

"Sounds like your governor is a pretty crazy guy."

I looked around the town and muttered to myself. The guard noticed, and his expression changed slightly.

"Do not speak ill of our governor! You'll have charges brought against you!"

Things were starting to make sense. The guard apparently had bigger problems that just dealing with us—in which case, neither of my strategies would work.

If I pushed too hard, we'd end up paying for it.

If I wanted him to budge, I'd have to create a big stink and get him flustered or cause enough of a fuss to get the governor to come talk to me. But I had no way of knowing if the merits of the outcome would compensate for the risk of the undertaking.

"Fine then. I can see you have your own problems to deal with."

I gave him the amount of money that he asked for. When I did, the guard suddenly looked very disappointed.

"Here you go."

He leaned forward and whispered.

"Sorry . . ."

"No problem."

He must have been under orders from Trash. There was obviously some kind of problem with the governor here.

We entered the town to find taxes levied on nearly everything: from food and equipment to handicrafts and rooms at the inn. And the tax rate was invariably high.

It looked like the town had plunged into some sort of depression. The markets were nearly empty. The businesses must have been under the burden of heavy taxes.

"I'm going to go look for some food and try and figure out what's going on."

"Okay."

"Yay! Bring me back a souvenir!"

"You have enough already. Don't tell me you still want more!"

Didn't Filo realize how overpriced everything was here?

I left Raphtalia and Filo, who was in human form, in the inn and went out to a bar to figure out what was going on.

Also, I turned my shield into the Book Shield and roughed up my appearance a little before I entered the bar.

And there was someone I knew there. Someone I didn't want to run into.

Or so it seemed.

He carried a bow but for some reason also had a sword at his waist. He was dressed simply and carried shabby equipment. And he was holding a small bow that could change shapes, like my Book Shield. If it were my first time meeting him, I could be forgiven for thinking he was a vagabond.

He had some people with him, one of whom was wearing brightly colored armor—the guy with the bow hid in the shadows.

That's right, Itsuki, the Bow Hero, was hiding out in the corner of a bar, deeply involved in conversation.

Like Motoyasu, this one had also arrived from some alternate Japan.

He was 17 years old and had the face of a quiet piano player. He kind of looked mild-tempered.

He hadn't noticed me yet.

I wondered what he was talking about, so I slunk over without letting him see me and tried to eavesdrop.

"The governor is . . ."

It sounded like he and his party were gathering information on the local governor.

From what I could gather, it sounded like the guy had set his taxes higher than what the Crown demanded and accepted bribes from some merchants in the area. He used the money to hire a bodyguard and would severely punish anyone who spoke out against him. Everything he did, he did to line his own pockets. All in all, he sounded like your standard corrupt official.

"Sounds like we'll have to teach him a lesson."

Whoa! I was so surprised by Itsuki's words that I nearly lost my footing.

But how should I go about joining the conversation?

Here he was hiding out for no reason, and, putting aside whatever his plan was—just what kind of a general commander did he think he was?

Did he think he was traveling the world to save it?

Even accounting for lies and elaboration, I still hadn't heard a peep about what the Bow Hero was up to.

Although, to be fair, I was traveling around as a holy man with a bird-god, so I couldn't exactly deride him for hiding his identity.

But in my case, I had a good reason—people had been lied to about the Shield Hero, and there was a terrible reputation I had to escape. Even now, if people found out who I was, they would be on guard, so it was in my interests to let them think I was a saint. People still whispered about the Shield Demon!

Anyway, as far as I knew, there was no compelling reason for Itsuki the Bow Hero to keep his identity secret.

Was it some kind of order from the Crown? Even if it was, I never heard anything about the Bow Hero. So he was purposely lying about who he was . . .

"Very well then. Everyone, let's go."

They finished their conversation, and Itsuki led his party out of the bar.

My best guess was that they were planning on heading over to the governor's mansion and causing a ruckus before revealing Itsuki's identity and telling the corrupt guy off. There were similar storylines in my own world in period dramas on TV. They always feature the archetypal traveling warrior who rights the wrongs of the world.

It was easy enough to picture. The king would find out that the corrupt politician had been deposed, and he'd appoint someone new. It all made sense.

Was he an idiot? Why go out of your way to get further involved?

I carried out what I'd come there to do: look for information on where I could buy foodstuffs for a reasonable price. Then I went back to the inn for the night.

Filo's souvenir? Like I would buy souvenirs in a town where the cost of living is through the roof.

Of course Filo had some choice words to say about that, but I didn't bother listening.

The next morning the whole town was talking. Adventurers had infiltrated the town in the night and had removed the governor from office.

Among the throngs of pedestrians moving up and down the street, Itsuki was standing around chatting up a beautiful girl.

"Oh woooow! No, really, thank you so muuuuuch!"

"Oh, it's really no trouble at all. But it is a secret, all right?"

A secret? I don't think so! My suspicions had been confirmed. I figured out why I hadn't heard anything about Itsuki this whole time.

He was the kind of guy that liked to hide his real abilities so that he could pull them out when necessary and drive everyone wild.

If he really was able to enjoy that kind of game, he had pretty poor taste as far as I could tell.

He was going out of his way to hide his identity just so he could revel in the joy of exposing himself. If that's not what he was after, why would he be standing there in the middle of the street? Or at the very least I'd figured out that he didn't have to run from anything like I did, so he wasn't doing it to protect himself.

I could picture it all now. The evil governor demanded taxes they couldn't pay, so he took this girl away from her poor geriatric father as payment. I'd seen a period drama like that on TV once.

Give me a break. I got out of town as fast as I could.

We traveled for half a day or so before we came to a town near the border with a neighboring country.

We were able to sell all the food that we hadn't sold off the day before, and it sold out very quickly. I guessed we were getting into areas affected by the famine.

But there were a lot of people around that didn't seem to be locals.

Maybe it was the way they dressed. I don't know. I can't put my finger on it exactly, but I could tell they were from somewhere far away.

"Hey, you guys . . ."

I'd heard rumors of a nearby country ruled by a despot, but the tyrant had recently been ousted from power. I felt like I was probably getting close. Were these people citizens of that country, here for business?

Some of them walked by, and a passing glance into my carriage excited them so much that they immediately ran over and started talking business with me.

But they didn't want to use money. They wanted to barter with me. I could use medicinal herbs and stuff, sure—but I didn't have much use for lumber or wooden handicrafts. I climbed down from the carriage and started talking with them.

"I'd really prefer money."

If they foisted their bundles of straw and twine and stacks of charcoal on me, I'd have no way to get rid of it. On the other hand, I could take a lot of medicinal herbs and process it all into medicine.

"I'm sorry, but we don't have money . . ."

The person speaking was all skin and bones. He looked like he might keel over at any moment.

"I'll get some food for you all. Eat it and be on your way."

There was no getting around it, so I borrowed a large pot from some villagers. It looked like the villagers were also on the verge of starvation, so they were more than willing to help.

"Thank you so much!"

Everyone gathered around the giant pot and ravenously scarfed the food down.

While everyone was eating, I took the opportunity to ask just what was going on in these parts.

They said that everything was fine until the despot was ousted. The tax burden was eased, and everyone's lives started getting better.

But soon enough, things went back to how they had been.

The worst part was the leaders of the resistance had started raising taxes again as soon as they were in power.

"But why? After all they went through to oust the bad king?"

"Well, they needed funds to manage the country, and to secure enough money for the military, they had to raise taxes."

I was starting to understand. It wasn't just that the king was a bad guy. It was that he needed to raise funds to secure their military strength in order to protect the country.

If your country lost its citizens, then you wouldn't have a country—so you would lose your country if you didn't protect its citizens.

In the midst of all that, if you only listened to the negative rumors about the king, well, of course you'd want to oust him from power.

I didn't know anything about that king, but I couldn't help feeling an affinity for him—to be hated and ousted by your own people.

Certainly there were times in life when you had to do things because you had no choice, whether or not your actions would be viewed in a positive light or not.

But that doesn't apply to the Trash king. That guy was an evil idiot from day one.

"Even if the leadership changes, we still can't support ourselves. So we've brought all our valuables across the border, here to Melromarc, to see if we won't have better luck in this more prosperous land."

"The poor king! He really was thinking of his citizens first! Whose fault is it that I'm this hungry?!"

"Shut up! You would doubt me?"

"Yeah!"

Filo knew just what to say to piss him off, so I had to control her.

She'd started to learn a little bit about how the world works, and she'd developed a dirty mouth in the process.

"I thought he looked . . ."

Raphtalia was whispering to herself and looking over at us with a strange look on her face.

"Maybe . . . Mr. Naofumi?"

"Huh?"

"Oh, it's nothing."

Filo was running her mouth off, but if I had to make a guess from the rumors I'd heard, it sounded like Itsuki had been assisting the resistance. Maybe his heart wasn't as pure as he wanted everyone to think it was. As for these refugees, were they sneaking across the border to buy stuff on the black market?

By the way, it looked like market prices in the area were soaring. That was good for me. Itsuki, the little general that he thought he was, traveling around righting the world's wrongs, you'd think he would stick around to give some support. He was only using these people to satisfy his own little sense of personal justice!

"With how things are now, our country is at great risk of invasion! Anyone could rush in and take over, but we can't even afford to eat."

"Really."

Maybe it was due to the waves, but it seemed like famines were breaking out everywhere.

"Oh well."

I found the leader of the ragged group and gave him one of my improved BioPlant seeds.

"What's this?"

"If you plant it, it grows food very quickly. It actually caused a big problem down in the south, but I was able to fix it with a special technique of mine. It should be fine now, but you should still keep a close eye on it. If you don't manage it well, it could turn into a real headache."

"Oh, wow!"

"I'll come back through here in a while. I'll accept your gratitude then."

The next time I came through the area, I was sure to get a warm greeting.

They all obviously knew who I really was. Later, I heard that the citizens of that small country, suffering from famine, finally had some food to fill their bellies.

Chapter Eight: Before the Storm

The sun was setting, so we went back to the inn for that day and focused on treating Raphtalia's wounds.

I poured the holy water into a different bottle so I could use it to soak bandages. And then I wrapped those around her body.

There was a soft hiss, and black smoke slowly snaked from the bandages. Her skin was looking much better, but apparently the root of the curse was still in there somewhere. If we kept up with her treatment, the wounds were sure to heal though.

"Are you okay?"

"Oh, yes. It's like . . . it's like . . . itchy, and my muscles relax. It feels strange."

"Oh . . ."

I wanted her to get better as soon as possible, especially considering that I was the one who had hurt her.

"The places that you've treated feel much better than they did, Mr. Naofumi."

"That's good to hear."

I wanted her to be completely healed. How much longer would that take?

"Hey, no fair! Big Sister gets to cuddle Master all by herself!"

Filo knew that we were trying to treat Raphtalia's curse, but she never missed a chance to yell something annoying.

"We are not CUDDLING!"

"She's right. We are trying to heal Raphtalia's wounds."

Cuddling? Is that what she thought? Oh well. Where did she even learn a word like that? Regardless, we weren't cuddling. Raphtalia and I did not have that kind of relationship.

"Oh . . . Because Raphtalia is all black?"

"I wouldn't phrase it that way."

They were becoming good friends.

"Well, the next wave will be here soon. Why don't we head back to the castle town, pick up the new stuff from the weapons guy, and then take it easy?"

"Okaaaay!"

"That is a good idea. We've been very busy lately. A little break would be wonderful."

"Yeah, that's what I was thinking."

"Master, are you going to make food for us?"

"Sure. Maybe we can borrow that metal plate from the weapon shop guy again."

"Yay!"

We spent the rest of the night tending to Raphtalia's wounds, and then we went to bed.

After a few days of meticulous holy water application, Raphtalia was completely cured. I was so relieved that worked so quickly.

We decided to stop our traveling sales activities for the moment and went back to the castle town to see what kind of things the weapon shop owner had prepared for us.

The wave would be here soon enough, so it was high time we got prepared in earnest.

We arrived at the weapon shop just as he was opening his doors for the day.

"Hey, kid, you're out bright and early."

"I guess. Well? How'd it go?"

"Check it out."

The old guy went into the back of the shop and came out with his arms full of my new equipment.

It was made from bits of chimera and dragon bones: Bone Mail . . . Except that it looked almost exactly like the equipment I already had.

It looked like something an apocalyptic gang member might wear.

Honestly, from a distance it looked the exact same as my current armor except that it had some glossy parts and some color here and there.

"Old dude, are you trying to turn me into the boss of a bandit team?"

I guess it was because he'd made it from parts of the bandits' armor, but it would have been nice if he had taken it in a different direction.

"Huh? What are you talking about, kid?"

Was I supposed to wear that? I know it was a fantasy world, but it was starting to feel like all of my clothes had a villainous look to them.

"What do you call that armor?"

"Well, it's all custom, so I don't even know. How about Barbarian Armor +1?"

"I don't think the +1 really captures all you've done."

The armor had been held together with a denim-like fabric before, and that had been replaced by dragon skin, which looked like glossy black rubber.

Around the chest was a plate of metal. It really didn't look any different.

Barbarian Armor +1: defense up: attack endurance (medium): fire resistance (strong): shadow resistance (strong): HP restore (weak): magic up (medium), magic defense processing: automatic recovery function

The armor came with a whole list of resistances.

Automatic recovery—I think that was pretty much self-explanatory. It would probably repair itself if it broke.

If the armor came with so many different functions, I'd probably never take it off.

"What is it, kid?"

"I thought maybe you were holding out hopes for me."

There had to be some reasons that he made the clothes the way he did. Did he want people to think I was a criminal?

"Master, are you going to ride on me dressed like that? I hope so! Guess what? I found some black glasses. I think it would be fun to run if we were wearing these."

Filo was staring at me, her eyes shining. What was she up to?

"Kid. When that bird-girl is in her human form and she yells 'ride me,' there are bound to be some misinterpretations."

"Shut up! You know we don't mean it like that!"

I wondered, did he just think of armor making as a way to piss me off? Was this some kind of joke to him?

"What is it, kid?"

I guess not. He didn't seem to have anything but good intentions.

"Oh, um . . . Nothing. I'll take it."

Raphtalia was standing off to the side, saying how cool I looked. Whatever.

If I walked around town dressed like this, I was going to stick out like a sore thumb.

"All right, what should we do?"

If we wanted to get any stronger, we'd have to find some way to class up Raphtalia and Filo.

When the wave came, we'd be automatically summoned. If so, why not use our time on a trip to the neighboring country where we could make some money and level up a bit?

"We still have some time before the wave comes. Raphtalia, Filo, do you guys want any accessories?"

"Accessories?"

"Yeah, to compliment your equipment. I think we could get some made up easily enough."

I'd made up my mind to try and get them some kind of present for their efforts. This was a good time to do it.

"Raphtalia, you're getting to the age where you probably have started to care about that kind of stuff, right?"

"I . . . Uh . . ."

"Me tooo!"

"I know. That's why I asked you both if you wanted anything."

Raphtalia looked like she was a little stunned. Was what I was saying really all that surprising?

"Hey! You know what I want? A hairpin!"

So Filo wanted a hairpin? That was a shock . . . I thought for sure she would ask for a saddle or something.

"A hairpin? Why?"

"It won't pinch me when I transform!"

I guess she was still worried about that. Whatever, if she put it on her head, she would be just fine.

And considering how young she looked when she was in human form, it actually wasn't inappropriate at all.

"Raphtalia, what do you want?"

"Me? Hmm . . ."

She thought about it for a moment before looking at me and answering.

"I'd like a bangle. But I would like it to be imbued with equip effects."

"What?"

"I would like something that will contribute to my abilities, Mr. Naofumi."

What was she hinting at? She had responded differently than I'd expected, and I couldn't quite follow along.

I thought she would want a ring or earrings or a necklace, but she wanted a bangle—and it had to have equip effects. I'm sure it was my fault for raising her this way.

"Oh, um. Okay then. I'll see what I can do."

"Me tooooo!"

"Okay, okay."

Chapter Nine: Framed Again?

"Oh! There he is!"

We left the weapon shop to find, for whatever reason, Itsuki, Ren, and their parties all running in our direction.

Ren was like me. No, actually, he came from some sci-fi version of Japan where people could actually enter virtual worlds online.

And he was summoned to this world as the Sword Hero. Like Motoyasu, he had a handsome face, attractive. There was something almost womanly about him. His black hair had a shiny quality to it, and he was silent—cool.

What did it mean? They were all together here in the town at the same time?

Itsuki, unlike the last time I saw him in shabby dress, was clad in good equipment.

They must have noticed the miserable look on my face. Itsuki stepped forward and called out in a loud voice.

"It was YOU. I fulfilled an official request, and you swept in to steal my reward!"

"What?!"

Why did I have to steal his petty reward?

"Me too. You stole my rewards as well."

Ren looked like he could kill me with his eyes.

I had an idea of what he was getting at. Who was it that caused all the trouble in the mountain town? Who let everyone get infected by that horrible disease?

"Ren, okay, you're right about that. But I don't know what Itsuki is talking about."

"You're going to play dumb?!"

"I don't know what I don't know."

"Okay, hold on. We need to talk it out first. If we don't, what will Naofumi confess to?"

"You're going to assume I'm guilty before we even talk?"

"Did Master do something?"

"Nothing I can remember."

I tried to comfort Filo and Raphtalia while glaring at Ren and Itsuki.

"Anyway. Why don't you at least tell me what you are talking about?"

Itsuki started explaining what exactly his qualm with me was.

"It happened in a northern territory. I'd been charged with investigating the actions of a local despot, and then I was charged with removing him from office—which I did."

After that, he apparently did what he always did, which was send one of his party members (who was always dressed in gaudy armor) to receive his reward payment from the guild that divided out these requests. But when he went to receive payment, he was told that the payment had already been accepted, and the only person Itsuki could think of that would do such a thing was me.

"Um, excuse me for speaking out of turn, General Commander, but have you ever considered that if a hero goes out of his way to hide his real identity, he might not get recognition for his actions?"

"General commander?! What's that supposed to mean?"

"You were walking around with a sword on your belt, pretending to be a generic adventurer. Weren't you, General?"

Itsuki, perhaps thrown off guard, started yelling at me. His attitude of secrecy toward his quests was clearly becoming a problem.

No one had any way of knowing what the Bow Hero looked like or what he was doing.

So the people of Melromarc would obviously think that all the good being done in the world was the work of the Sword and Spear Heroes.

He could swear up and down that he was really doing lots of awesome stuff, but that wasn't going to affect his reputation at all.

Sure, it was a cool idea to sneak around saving people, to be a secret hero, but that wasn't going to gain him any recognition.

I was still a student, but I knew enough about the world

to know that once I went out in the world I was going to be responsible for my own reputation.

As for Itsuki, if he was still dressed as the Bow Hero and someone else was screaming to take responsibility for his actions, then he wouldn't be able to get anyone to believe him with his normal taciturn demeanor.

But it's not like a hero who behaved like that would also be the kind of person to chase after money and fame by doing evil things in secret.

I did feel a little self-conscious listening to him speak though, considering that people were calling me the saint of the bird-god.

"When you complete a quest, is it counted as being completed by the Bow Hero? As far as I know, the only quest we can confirm you carried out was what you did up in the town with the taxes. And that's because I saw you there."

"But that's because I am acting in secret."

"Then let me confirm. There was a bow-carrying adventurer who helped support a resistance effort in the northern country. Was that you?"

"Y . . . Yes! I fought with the resistance to out the evil king who was ruling as a despot. We ousted him."

"And do you know what ended up happening in that country after you left?"

"Well the evil king is gone, so I'm sure they are prospering."

"They are NOT prospering. They are starving, and things are so bad they are sneaking over the border to barter for food."

"No! That can't be true! Why?"

"Well, think about it. The king might have been a bad guy, but the whole country was also in the midst of a famine. Just switching out the king isn't going to make that go away."

"That doesn't have anything to do with me. Stop changing the subject."

Ugh . . . Irresponsible brat . . . Couldn't he care even a little?

"Okay, back to the topic at hand then. You send a party member to go receive your payment? Can your party member explain all this?"

"Y . . . Yes! Of course! Of course!"

"At the guild, right? And this friend of yours has some way to prove that he is your party member to whoever is in charge of dolling out payment?"

"Yes, well. There is a certificate! A certificate bearing the royal seal!"

Itsuki's face displayed his confidence. What was he even saying?

"It's a special certificate made with special technology! It would be very difficult to fake!"

"That's all well and fine, but since I don't have such a certificate, how was I supposed to pick up your payment?"

"Dammit . . ."

Itsuki swore in annoyance. He knew I was right.

"Then . . . What about this weapon?"

Now he was really reaching for excuses. I guess he was desperate to make this my fault somehow.

"You can change the shape of your shield, so you could have made it look like my Legendary Bow and taken my payment without the certificate!"

"You think? Look around you. There must be plenty of people that could pull off a scheme like that."

"Can you prove that?"

"Filo."

"What?"

"Turn back into your real form."

"Okay."

Filo turned back into her real form. When she did, her clothes disappeared and reformed as a ribbon that wrapped around her neck. I pointed to the ribbon.

"What?!"

"Get it? Transforming equipment exists in this world. There might be tons of different kinds of equipment that can change to look like a bow. And besides, when it comes to heroes, I'm not the only one with a transforming weapon. I'm sure you see where I am going with this . . ."

"But . . ."

"Itsuki, give up already. You don't have enough evidence to accuse Naofumi."

Itsuki was desperate to pin his troubles on me, but Ren stepped forward and told him to back off.

"Besides, did you even ask what they looked like? This person that pretended to be you?"

"Um . . . No . . . but . . ."

Ren's questions were pointed enough that Itsuki was losing his confidence.

"You just have to give up. If you want recognition for your actions, you're going to have to be more open about them. Okay, I'm next . . ."

"I assume you're talking about the eastern territory epidemic?"

"At least we are on the same page. You stole my reward."

"Only because I was there. Don't you know? You killed a dragon, but its corpse started to rot and it spread disease over the whole area."

"What?!"

Ren was suddenly speechless. He stood in temporary silence.

What was he thinking? I thought he was crueler than this.

"A lot of people ended up dying. They had to start a new graveyard out behind their main hall. If I hadn't been passing by, they'd all be dead by now."

"That can't be true . . ."

He looked unsteady on his feet and tottered off vaguely to the east.

"Wait, wait! You don't have enough time to get there. What about the wave?"

"But . . . If it's my fault . . ."

"I took care of the dragon corpse. The sick people are all getting treatment from a local doctor. If you want to call that 'stealing your reward,' then go ahead."

All the color had left Ren's face.

"Are you going to believe him?!"

Itsuki turned and shouted at Ren.

"He doesn't have a reason to lie. The quest was completed, and so the reward was canceled. That's not incorrect."

"When the dragon corpse reanimated and became a Zombie Dragon, I have to say—I was pretty surprised. Raphtalia here ended up cursed after that fight. We were able to get her healed, but it was a hard time going."

I wasn't lying. But I didn't mention that the curse was my fault.

"So that's what happened. I'm sorry."

Ren turned to Raphtalia and bowed his head to her.

I couldn't believe my eyes. I'd thought that Ren was cold and heartless. Apparently he was weak when he thought about any troubles that he'd directly caused. Honestly, I thought he'd say something like, "It's their fault for being weak."

"Why did you leave the dragon corpse there to rot?"

"One of my party members suggested leaving it there so

that other adventurers could use it for materials. I thought it sounded like a good idea."

That reminded me, I'd heard that the village had experienced a short moment of prosperity.

"We decided to leave it up to the villagers and any passing adventurers, but . . ."

"Well, next time you had better clean up after yourself. Corpses rot. Rotting corpses breed disease. At the very least, you need to do something about the organs and meat."

"Yeah . . ."

His response was disappointing. Even if he was upset, he still hadn't said anything about the village or what happened there. I guess they didn't want to admit that there was a darker underbelly to their activities. Well, you reap what you sow, I guess.

"Well, I still don't believe you."

Itsuki was more persistent than Ren.

"I'll find a way to prove that you did it."

"Go right ahead. I'll be waiting. But don't you dare fake it. If you find out who did it, don't ask them if the Shield Hero had forced their hand. With my reputation, anyone would pin their crimes on me."

"What's that supposed to mean?"

"We were attacked by a group of bandits, but we beat them off. Apparently they were planning on going to town and telling everyone that they were attacked by the Shield Hero."

"But that's . . ."

"Exactly what you are doing, general commander. You should work on that—learn to see through the lies."

I don't know if Itsuki suddenly discovered stores of sympathy for me over my ruined reputation, but he was looking at me with an oddly sympathetic gaze. It drove me nuts.

Why did I have to be the victim of his sympathy?

"I'll put the case on hold for the time being . . ."

"I didn't do it."

I swear, how many crimes did I have to have pinned on me? Was I supposed to be the fall guy for the entire world?

"But I'll get you, and I'll prove it too."

Full of haughty arrogance, Itsuki turned and left. Ren, a little on edge, followed him.

"Let's go."

I should have known that nothing good was waiting for me in this town, considering how it was stuck under the nose of Trash. We decided to go back to the inn for the night.

"Good evening, Shield Hero."

I was relaxing in my room when five of the soldiers from before stopped by to say hello. The two I had spoken to directly were representing their group and spoke on its behalf.

"What is it?"

"We thought it would be a good idea to have a meeting concerning the impending arrival of the next wave."

They sure were a serious group. Whatever—I guess that was good for me.

"Raphtalia has experience with the waves. Filo, you join in on this too."

"Hmmmm?"

"Everyone keep in mind that I'm not exactly an expert on any of this stuff. But I don't really have a choice, so when the wave comes, you'll be transported to the site with me. So I'll try to explain how I plan on fighting and what you can do to assist, all right?"

"Yes! In order to protect the innocent people of the world, we want to work with you."

I had my doubts about whether or not to take what they said at face value, but I decided to go along with it for now.

"Let's go over what happened in the last battle. The last time a wave came, the monsters pouring from the rift all went to attack a nearby village. So I had to stand at the front of the line to protect the people there."

Yes, it had been an intense battle. There was a giant rift through the sky, and hordes of monsters poured from it. Monsters with names that almost invariably began with "interdimensional."

There were some giant monsters mixed in with the hordes, and they all set their sights on Riyute. Everyone was confused and panicking. There were groups of people under immediate threat from the monsters, but I was able to save them with my Air Strike Shield and my Shield Prison skills.

Raphtalia helped me evacuate the villagers, and then we turned our sights on a nearby giant. We defeated it.

Honestly, it was similar to a player versus monster war.

"The highest priority is the safety of bystanders. Do all that you can to ensure their safe evacuation from the area."

"Yes, sir."

"Well, considering all the things they have to be repentant about, I'm sure that the other heroes will enlist some knights to help out."

There must have been soldiers besides those who I was directly speaking with who placed some value on the lives of the country's innocent civilians.

"About that . . ."

"What?"

"We thought that other soldiers would come forward and ask to join your ranks, but that hasn't happened yet."

What was that supposed to mean?

The only idea I had was that maybe these soldiers were low-level and there was a cutoff point set for participating in the wave battles. Either that or higher-ranked positions attracted the selfish and power-hungry, clearing those ranks of decent people. That was about it. The higher-ranked officials might have all just been terrible managers. I wonder if the other heroes cared about this kind of thing.

"What should I dooooo?"

"We will be evacuating people, so whenever a monster gets close to us, you should take them out. Raphtalia, you help with the evacuations, and help these soldiers."

"Okaaay!"

"Understood."

"Honestly, unlike the other heroes, I don't know very much about the waves. So I'm honestly a little worried about all this. I'll need your help."

"Yes, sir!"

Everyone nodded. I guess I could count on them.

Chapter Ten: The Third Wave

I finished making Raphtalia and Filo's new accessories just in time.

"Check it out, the accessories you asked for. Raphtalia, you go first."

I had made a jade bracelet for Raphtalia. I gave it to her.

"Thank you."

"The equip effect is Magic Up (medium). Your armor uses a little magic power to up your magic defense. This should balance that out. Thanks to you, I was able to make something nice."

A little while back, Raphtalia and Filo were able to save up a bunch of money at that hot-spring town we'd passed through. Because of that I was able to buy good materials that would have previously been out of my reach. That was what enabled me to make these good accessories.

"I'll treasure it."

"Are you sure that's what you really want? I could make one a little more . . . fashionable."

"What are you saying? Do you think we are powerful enough to focus on fashion?"

Well, well. If that's what she said, then I had no choice but to believe her.

"Okay, Filo, you're next."

I gave her an amber hairpin. I'd focused on the details when I made it so that it would look good on her even when she was in her bird form. When it was clipped to her down feathers, they would fan out and look like a feathered hair ornament.

"The equip effect is Agility Up (medium)."

"Thank you, Master!"

"That's the best I could do with the materials we had on-hand. I might be able to make better ones later, but that's the best I can do for now."

"It's no problem at all. I only hope that I can put this accessory to its best use."

"Yeah! I'll try hard too!"

"I know you will. Both of you."

We'd finished our planning meeting with the support soldiers too, so I guess we were as prepared as we were going to get.

Filo had shown some hesitation at first, having no idea what to expect and no idea what the wave even was. But I convinced her that all we could do was tackle problems when they presented themselves, and she understood.

We had plenty of medicine. As for the carriage . . . Our new one wasn't ready yet, so Filo was pulling a luggage cart instead.

That was fine. Unlike the other heroes, I would be spending most of my time in nearby villages, protecting the people there.

I'm not sure my participation was even necessary, but I could only imagine what people would say about me if I tried to sit this battle out.

00:05

There were five minutes left. Once we were transported to the wave, I'd have to figure out where I was and find some way to tell the soldiers.

I changed my shield to the Chimera Viper Shield . . .

00:00

The time had come! The whole world filled with an echoing sound, like glass shattering.

In the next second, our surroundings completely changed. We calmly surveyed our new surroundings.

"Where are we?"

Yup, we were near that village where the old lady had been sick. It would take one and a half days, at the very least, to get here from the castle town.

I looked up at the sky, and just like last time, it was wine-red and covered in cracks like a tortoise shell.

"Shield Hero!"

The soldiers had been transported along with us, and

they were running in our direction. Then I saw the other three heroes and . . .

"Filo! See those guys running toward the cracks? Kick the spear and knock the other ones over. Don't overdo it!"

"Okaaaay!"

Just as I'd asked, Filo removed her claws and ran for the heroes!

She quickly caught up with sword, bow, and spear.

"What the?!"

Spear turned around to see, and just as he did, Filo kicked him, and he flew into the others, knocking them down.

"AAAAAHHHHH!"

They all fell like bowling pins, giving us time to catch up with them. Having seen Bitch fly through the air, I was in a good mood.

Filo really had held back, like I'd asked, and no one had suffered any serious damage from her kick.

"What are you doing?!"

Spear was in a fluster, shouting at us all. I ignored him and shot a cold glare at sword and bow.

"That's what I want to ask you, you idiots!"

"What do you want?!"

"Yeah! We have to destroy the monsters that are surging from the rift!"

I was beyond being angry with these foolish heroes. I was just annoyed.

"First, you need to listen. We can take out the enemies later."

I ordered my support soldiers to head for the nearby village. They nodded and followed my orders, running for the village.

"You are getting in the way of our mission!"

"No, I'm not!"

Itsuki jumped back when I barked at him, shocked. He blinked.

"Everyone calm down. Let's think this through. I didn't receive any funding, so I'm not fighting against the wave directly. The best I can do is protect the neighboring village—so that's my job. Do you all understand this?"

"Yeah."

"Sort of disqualifies you as a hero."

The group of heroes was glaring at me, but I ignored them and kept talking.

"Okay, Ren, Itsuki, Motoyasu, your job is to take out the monsters that are coming from the rift. You can either take out the major enemies to do it or you might have to attack the rift directly—I haven't done it, so I don't know."

"The rift is linked with the boss!"

Linked. That was gamer-talk. Itsuki wasn't taking this as seriously as he should, but whatever.

"But you understand that my job is really important too, right?"

"What?"

Ren didn't seem to understand. But hey, this world was basically the exact same as some game that he knew, right? He should understand everything about it.

"And hey, where are the knights?!"

The three heroes all shut their eyes when I shouted.

"They'll come later."

Maybe it was to help them find us, but there was a magic beacon of some sort glowing over us in the sky. They'd probably set their sights on that.

"We're a day and a half from the castle town. They'll never make it in time, you idiots!"

"Then what do you want us to do about it?!"

"You're asking ME? I thought you knew everything!"

I pointed to the soldiers that had come with me, who were now running for the village.

"Speaking of which, how did you get those soldiers to teleport here with you?"

"Are you really asking me that? Don't you know about battle formation functions?"

"You mean party members? How did you trick all of them into joining you?"

"That's not it. You can appoint someone as a leader and then make your party with that person subject to your leadership. If you do, they all get transported with you."

Could it be? Were there things they didn't know about the waves?

The soldiers had said that none of their superiors had sent out orders to join any of the heroes' parties, but could it be because the heroes just didn't know about the ability to do so? I was stunned into silence. That would explain why there were no knights here.

"Well, let's check up front. Who here looked into their help menus to learn about how to fight in the wave?"

Nobody raised their hand.

"I guess if you already know everything there is to know about this place, then there's no need for you to read the help menus or tutorials, is that it?"

"Yeah, we already know everything."

"Exactly. Can we please focus on battling the wave now?"

"Fine then. So what do other games call these battles against the waves?"

"Huh?"

"What are you asking?"

"Shut up already. We need to go!"

Itsuki ignored my question, turned, and started to run.

"Motoyasu, you can see what I'm getting at, can't you?"

"Uh . . . sure . . . an instant dungeon?"

"That's not it. It was a Time Attack Wave."

Ren . . . That's not it either. I said "other games," didn't I?

The game that he knew all about was called Brave Star Online, wasn't it?

"Guild wars, team battles, either that or large-scale battles!"

In the game that I used to play, there were major events every week or so when the players fought against each other. If you were to use the support troop system, then the game would make sure there were more enemies appearing than you could manage on your own. So during the last wave, had the knights not made it in time, I'm not sure we would have been able to keep the damage down to the level we did.

"Look, even if you all have experience with the game system, you don't have any experience managing a large guild, do you?"

In large-scale battles, you had to prioritize cooperation, though of course, the ace players, the heroes, would lead the charge. But in order to keep the destruction to a minimum, we were going to need the cooperation of the locals.

If they couldn't understand something that simple, then they were idiots.

"I've managed a team before."

Motoyasu spoke up but kept his eyes on Filo in her bird form. He probably didn't want to get kicked.

"Then why don't you understand this?"

"There's no need to."

"What?!"

"It'll work itself out."

Jeez . . . and I thought this guy couldn't get any more obnoxious—any more irresponsible.

Bitch, that's your job. That stupid rotten princess—as if she was intelligent enough to deal with responsibility like that.

"I never had any interest in that kind of stuff."

Ren, the jerk. But I knew his type well enough. There were always one or two of them before a guild war, and I never enjoyed trying to talk to them.

If someone like that was supposed to have been a guild master, I actually can't think of any way that would be possible. How would the guild even function?

"Anyway, we can only work with what we've got this time. But next time make sure that you link up with the knights!"

I brushed them away with my hands, motioning for them to scurry off toward the wave. Ren and Motoyasu made no effort to hide their annoyance with me when they ran off.

"All right, guys, let's head for the village. Raphtalia, Filo— you're with us!"

"Okaaaay!"

"Understood!"

We jumped in the cart and headed for the village as fast as we could. The soldiers with us had their own cart, and they managed to keep up with us.

By the time we made it to the village, it was already overrun with monsters from the wave.

There were black condor-like monsters, black wolves, goblins, and lizard-men.

But the lizard-man didn't look like a demi-human, not quite. It looked more . . . sinister.

When I got closer I was able to see their names: Dark Condor, Black Shadow Wolf, Goblin Assault Shadow, Lizard-Man Shadow. Next to all their names, unmistakably, were the words "inter-dimensional."

Like demi-humans, these shadow monsters disappeared like ghosts when you defeated them.

They were a creepy lot of thugs. And the monsters were completely different than they were in the last wave. Weren't there rules governing this sort of thing?

Whatever, just leave it up to the heroes. They'll take care of everything.

And yet? There!

"Hiyaaa!"

The battle cry that had been splitting through the scene was coming from the old lady I'd given medicine to back when I was traveling through here.

She was swinging a hoe with one hand and fighting with all her strength. The soldiers were all stunned.

"Ah! Holy Saint! You were a big help! Hiyyaa!"

She yelled a phrase of thanks to me just as a group of monsters surged from the wave. She swung her hoe at them.

She was pretty strong, actually, and her surroundings were littered with monster bodies.

"Hey, you thank him too!"

The lady's son quickly bowed to me, like he had to do it all the time.

"More and more monsters are coming out of the waves. You had better evacuate."

The soldiers with me were helping evacuate the villagers. Among the chaos, we were fighting and killing monsters, but they kept on coming. It was going to be a hard fight, and we were going to have to focus on killing monsters.

"Hiyaa!"

The old lady was taking out enemies left and right. It was hard to believe that, only a month ago, she was sick in bed, on the verge of death.

"I've got my old strength back, thanks to you, Holy Saint! Hiyaa!"

I looked for her son and spotted him across the street, fighting monsters with all his might—but he wasn't as strong as his mother. Some soldiers joined him, and together they were able to hold off the enemy. He wasn't anywhere near as strong as his mother.

"I might look old, but back in the day, I was pretty famous

as an adventurer. My level and my age are almost the same! Hiyaaa!"

"Don't overdo it, lady!"

I wouldn't go so far as to call her an unmatched warrior or anything, but she was definitely one of the strongest fighters I'd seen.

I held off the enemy's attacks while Filo reeled back to kick them. They went down fast.

It looked like I could count on the lady in battle, but I was afraid she'd keel over once the battle was done.

"What medicine did I give you, anyway?"

"Who knows?"

Raphtalia was staring at the old lady, her mouth agape. We'd have to get the full story from her son later.

Regardless, we needed to focus on getting treatment to the wounded.

"Get all the injured people over by the cart! Keep them safe and away from the line!"

I would call out commands and treat people whenever I had a spare second.

"Hiyaa! Holy Saint! There are some weird ones showing up!"

I looked in the direction she was pointing. There was a huge crowd of inter-dimensional Lizard-Man Shadows, but I could just make out something else among them—something large. It looked to be at least double the size of anyone else.

"I'm going!"

The leader of my soldier supporters ran in the direction of the large monster.

"You idiot! Hold back!"

The giant inter-dimensional Lizard-Man Shadow turned to the running soldier and tried to crush him with his giant sword.

He dodged and tried to fix the defensive line, but there was no time!

But then, without warning, the soldier's necklace started glowing, activating some sort of instant effect before shattering. Then the inter-dimensional Lizard-Man Shadow's sword rattled back in shock from the strike.

"What?"

"What are you doing? Retreat!"

"O . . . Okay!"

Damn. The burden on the volunteer troops was too much. One attack shattered his defense necklace. The giant must have had an enormous attack rating. I would have to use my shield to stop its sword and rely on support to take the monster out.

"Raphtalia, Filo. Come with me—we're taking that thing down."

"Okay!"

"Okaaaaay!"

The three of us ran toward the giant monster.

The inter-dimensional Lizard-Man Shadow swung its large black sword at us.

I ran ahead of the girls and readied my shield. There was a loud clang, and sparks rained down around me.

Poison Snake Fang (medium) activated and poisoned the enemy. But it wasn't very effective.

I suppose it only made sense that poison would be weak against these reptile-like monsters. But it was never my plan to poison the thing.

"Hiyyyyaaaaahhh!"

Raphtalia thrust her sword into the belly of the inter-dimensional Lizard-Man Shadow and stopped him in his tracks.

"AAAAHHHRRRH!"

Filo's clawed foot flew in a tight arc, connecting with the inter-dimensional Lizard-Man Shadow's face. A portion of his head went spinning through the air.

The giant fell forward and hit the ground with a deafening crash.

"Whoa . . ."

The soldiers whispered in amazement.

"Thank you! If you hadn't given us those items, Shield Hero, we would already be dead!"

"Well, you made it out alive."

If I'd managed to save a life, then all that time I spent learning to craft items hadn't been a waste.

I felt enlivened.

"All right! You all run to the next town and do whatever you can to protect it."

We should be able to protect the village we were in now with six soldiers, that old lady, and the adventurers that had happened to be in town when the wave hit.

But there was another village close by. If we didn't hurry over there, who knew what would happen to it?

"I'm leaving some medicine with you all. This won't be a smooth ride, but let's get to the next village over!"

The soldiers climbed into the cart I was pointing at.

"Go!"

"Hiya!"

Filo got a grip on the ropes and ran off at full speed.

By the time we made it to the next village, the soldiers wobbled out of the cart, having gotten motion sick on the way. I didn't have time to comfort them.

There were houses on fire and injured villagers. This village looked worse off than the last one.

"Hurry and help those villagers!"

"Y . . . Yes, sir!"

We slaughtered monsters left and right and waited for the wave to end.

"Too late!"

Three hours had passed.

In that time, we had managed to secure the safety of most of the villagers, and we were now focusing our energies on cutting through the hordes of monsters that continued to descend on the village.

Most of the villagers had been evacuated, and we kept casualties relatively low. But I didn't know how long we could keep their shelter safe from the hordes. We kept fighting.

But everything was taking too long. What were those stupid heroes up to?

"Hero, why not leave this village to us. You should find the other heroes and assist them."

It was the young soldier who had originally approached me.

"I don't think I can do much to help them."

It was their job to fight the wave directly, and I'm sure they would just complain if I showed up.

"But, sir . . ."

He wasn't looking so good. His face was pale.

He'd been fighting monsters for three solid hours. His stamina was going to give out soon.

I was exhausted too. I could tell that Raphtalia and Filo were worn out too.

"Hiya! Take that!"

Filo kicked an inter-dimensional Goblin Assault Shadow, and it crumpled to the ground. She still had enough energy to keep going.

Yeah, Filo would be fine. The girl was like a giant ball of stamina.

"Can you handle it?"

"Leave it to me!"

I guess they had enough energy to keep going.

"All right. Then I'm going to see what's going on. I leave the village to you."

"Yes, sir!"

"Raphtalia, Filo, let's go!"

"Understood."

"Okaaaay!"

We left the village to the soldiers and adventurers, climbed onto Filo's back, and ran toward the wave itself.

Chapter Eleven: Grow Up

"This . . . This should be it."

"I think so too."

"Yup."

The wave was made up of giant rifts in the sky, and they extended to the ground. The ground was splitting open too.

"Huh? Wh . . . What?!"

There, among the cracks in the sky hung a giant . . . ship. Ghost-like, it floated in the air. Monsters were pouring from it.

The ragged masts were hung with tattered sails. Veins of lightning lit the sky around it. The ship seemed to be made of wood and was littered with holes.

I had no idea how the thing managed to stay afloat in the air, but this was another world, and I figured that anything could happen during the wave. If I wondered about every odd occurrence, I'd get nothing done.

There was mist everywhere, and to be honest, I didn't really want to go out of my way to get on board that thing.

I guess the monsters from this wave were pirates?

"They've been fighting this thing?"

The other three heroes and their parties were fighting against the ghost ship.

I could tell that Ren and Motoyasu were aboard because I could see their skills flashing through the mist. Itsuki was firing volleys at the ship from a distance. The fight looked a little reckless to me.

Just then, a cannon appeared on the side of the ship, and it shot a giant ball.

It was heavy and flying straight at us.

"Air Strike Shield!"

"Hiya!"

I was able to deflect the cannonball with my skill, and Filo jumped up to kick the ball away.

"How long are you guys planning on hanging out here?"

I yelled at Itsuki, who was sluggishly firing arrows.

"N . . . Naofumi?! What are you doing here? I thought you said you weren't going to fight."

"You all are taking your sweet time over here! We finished evacuating the villagers a long time ago, so I came to see what was taking you so long, and this is what I find? I thought you knew everything about this from your games?!"

"We have to destroy the ship, but for some reason Ren and Motoyasu insisted on boarding it."

They split up under conditions like this?

Putting that aside for a second, why would they all have different ideas on how to take down the boss?

"Damn . . ."

The ghost ship thing looked pretty ragged. What was going on with these waves?

I thought it over for a while as I watched Itsuki and his party fight.

It looked like they had based their tactics around Itsuki's skills. The rest of his party was fighting with different weapons.

"Even if you are attacking the ship directly, shouldn't you be cooperating with the other heroes?!"

"I don't have time to go over all this with you!"

His answer annoyed me. The stupid general commander!

"Well it looks like this fight could go on forever. You can keep throwing your skills at it, but it doesn't look like it's going to collapse any time soon. Try something else!"

What was Itsuki thinking? Were his attacks even effective? If it were a game, he'd be dead already.

"Besides, the other two set boarding the ship as their highest priority, didn't they?"

I suppose it could have been a giant monster that just happened to look like a ghost ship. Wouldn't that be something?

There were monsters that looked like houses, after all. They would start spinning and thumping when you got close to them.

"Maybe the ship has a weak spot on its interior. There might be a way to kill it that you couldn't do in your game!"

"There's nothing like that in the Dimension Wave I know!"

"Get a handle on yourself, Itsuki! This isn't a game!"

Did he have any idea just how much damage these waves were doing?

Seriously, monsters were coming from the rifts this whole time, so the longer they took to defeat the wave, the more monsters appeared and the worse the damage got.

"Let's get on the ship, find the weak spot, and bring that thing down!"

"Damn! Again! You're always stealing from me!"

"If it bothers you so much, come with me! Let's go, Filo!"

"Okaaay!"

Filo ran and sprang into the air. I quickly released an Air Strike Shield that she could use as a step. She landed on it and jumped again, and we landed on the deck of the ship.

"Ah! Wait!"

Itsuki and his party were chasing after us.

Good. If it was going to take this long to defeat the wave, then they had to be doing it wrong.

Ugh. It's good that we made it to the deck, but the whole ship was littered with bones. The floorboards were rotted through and filled with holes. There were dead fish everywhere, and the ropes and lifesavers were rotten. We'd really have to watch where we put our feet.

We made it to the deck, but there was . . . huh? At the back end of the ship there was a giant tentacle, and Motoyasu was fighting it with his party.

"Shooting Star Spear!"

Motoyasu let out a triumphant shout, and his spear began to glow before splitting into hundreds of energy-spears, which rained down on the giant tentacle. The tentacle died but quickly regenerated and resumed its position.

What was going on? Was there a kraken-like monster clinging to the ship like a hermit crab?

"Filo, don't tell me you want to eat that thing."

"Why . . . I can't eat it?"

That would be tough, even for Filo.

I looked down to the other end of the deck, and there was Ren, fighting something like a skeleton captain.

The skeleton captain looked like a pirate straight from the Caribbean, dressed in ornate robes and a hook where his left hand should have been.

He looked like . . . a skeleton version of Captain Hook from *Peter Pan*.

"Shooting Star Sword!"

Ren's sword flashed, and the flashing light turned into a stream of stars that slammed into the skeleton captain.

"Damn . . . he's tough."

"Ren!"

One of Ren's party members ran forward and attacked the skeleton captain. The skeleton captain swung his sword in response. Ren and his group attacked again, and the captain stumbled back. Then Ren swung what looked like the final strike, and the captain fell apart.

"Whew . . . was it dead?"

But before he could catch his breath, the pile of bones rose into the air and reformed the skeleton captain.

"What?!"

And the captain, his skull wrapped in a bandana, rushed to attack again.

I turned back to Motoyasu and the kraken.

"Filo, can you get us to the back of the ship?"

"Sure!"

"Raphtalia, hold on tight!"

"All right!"

She wrapped her arms around me to keep from falling, and Filo dashed across the ship.

From the stern to the bow, the deck was covered in tentacles, but Filo kicked them off, and we moved on.

We made it to the stern and discovered the source of the monstrous tentacles.

". . . !"

I was right; the kraken was holding on to the ship like some kind of hermit crab.

Did it have . . . one head? More than that? It was hard to tell.

Over where Motoyasu was fighting, there was a head, but the eyes were rotten . . . clouded.

It didn't seem to be breathing.

Filo had no problem eating rotting things, but could she not eat this because it was already completely rotten?

Itsuki had been attacking the ship directly, but it hadn't fallen.

Motoyasu was trying to kill the kraken.

Ren was fighting with the skeleton captain.

They were split up. They were all over the place.

Sure, they could have said that they didn't have a chance—but still. This was reckless.

And it didn't seem like they were making any progress at all.

What did all these enemies have in common? The only thing I could think of was that the real enemy was somewhere else.

Why couldn't the other heroes, with their supposedly perfect knowledge of the game, figure out something that simple?

Thinking back on all they'd said up until now, it seemed like they were operating under the assumption that what had made them successful in their games was going to work here. But they were all fighting differently.

"Ren!"

"What? N . . . Naofumi? What are you doing here?!"

"You're taking too long, so I came to find out what the problem was. Why do you keep on fighting that thing?"

"If I can defeat this, the real boss—the Soul Eater—will appear."

"And?"

"You have to defeat him a few times and then the boss will show up."

"Huh . . ."

Apparently he actually was thinking about his strategy. But why was it taking so long?

"Motoyasu!"

"Wh . . . What are you doing here, Naofumi?!"

He saw that I was sitting on Filo and covered his crotch when he turned toward us.

He must have thought that he would be kicked again. Ha! If Filo kicked him with her claws on, he'd be dead in an instant.

"Mr. Motoyasu, don't listen to him!"

Bitch looked at me like I was garbage, and she warned Motoyasu to ignore us.

"You need to shut up!"

"Do you have any idea who you're talking to? You can't speak to me that way!"

"I don't care! Motoyasu, what are you going to do after you kill the kraken?"

"The Soul Eater will show up, and then I'll take him out."

So that's what Motoyasu thought too. Itsuki must have been thinking the same thing.

But it didn't look like their attacks were doing any good.

If this were a game, it would mean that the Soul Eater was hiding out somewhere, waiting for his chance to appear.

Ren was attacking the skeleton captain, Motoyasu the kraken, and Itsuki the ship itself. Yeah, that would take a while.

"Finally, I caught up with you, Naofumi."

Itsuki climbed up onto the deck. That meant all the heroes were now aboard.

And yet . . . Soul Eater?

I had never seen one, so I didn't know what kind of monster it was, but based on everything else, it was probably a safe bet to assume it was some kind of ghost.

So it was hiding somewhere, and it could control the undead. That was why we'd have to destroy whatever medium was carrying it, I guess.

"Can't we use light magic to get the thing to show its face?"

"Want to try it?"

Raphtalia spoke up. Oh yeah, I'd almost forgotten that Raphtalia had the power to use light and shadow magic.

Then we might as well give it a try.

"Can you?"

"Leave it to me."

Raphtalia took a deep breath and focused on her magic spell.

"I am the source of power, and I command you to heed my words. Light spring forth!"

"First Light!"

When she finished speaking the spell, a ball of light appeared in the air over us.

The ball was filled with a shining, intense light, and the whole deck was illuminated by it.

Huh? The skeleton captain that Ren was locked in battle with looked different—his shadow had changed somehow. That strange shadow was . . . There were more of them, all around the ship.

They certainly weren't normal shadows, and they seemed to be grinning.

"There!"

"I got it! Shooting Star Sword!"

Ren turned and directed his attack at the captain's shadow.

"YAAAAAAAAAAAAAAAA!"

Something emerged from the shadow. It was like a ghostly fish draped in white cloth. It had a dark, evil-looking face with red eyes and long fangs.

It must have been the Soul Eater.

Once everyone realized what was happening, Motoyasu and Itsuki all began to direct their attacks toward the shadows, and Soul Eaters started appearing left and right.

"So THAT'S where they were!"

"Logically, our attacks shouldn't affect them!"

They were like ghosts. So I don't think our physical attacks were going to be able to hurt them. We were going to have to rely on magic.

"What?!"

The Soul Eaters all gathered in one place and merged to form a single, giant Soul Eater.

Similar things were known to happen back in my world. Fish did that—they would swim in schools to look like a larger, more dangerous fish.

Yeah, anchovies did that. The Soul Eaters seemed to be the souls of fish or something—so that might explain their behavior. And yet they really had formed one giant monster, and it was MUCH larger than the individual Soul Eaters had been.

Inter-dimensional Soul Eater.

"Mr. Naofumi, it's coming our way!"

The inter-dimensional Soul Eater had set its sights on Raphtalia because she had performed the light magic. But Raphtalia was sitting with me on Filo, and the Soul Eater was charging straight at us!

"Air Strike Shield!"

There was a loud clang, and we were able to deflect the Soul Eater's charge, but it kept on charging in a new direction— straight at Ren and his party.

"Look, we found it. Now you have to kill it!"

Motoyasu, Itsuki, and Ren all shot me looks of displeasure

before they turned to the Soul Eater and let loose a rain of battle skills. Their party members were all working to support them, but their physical attacks weren't going to work on this boss!

We weren't prepared to fight something like this, but Raphtalia could support them with her light magic.

"Filo, use your magic."

"Okaaay!"

Filo cast First Tornado and was able to deal some damage to the inter-dimensional Soul Eater.

But I wasn't able to use Hate Control, so I wasn't going to be any use to anyone.

It happened the second I let myself think about it. The inter-dimensional Soul Eater started preparing for some kind of major attack.

The beast opened its large slit of a mouth, and a black ball of magic appeared there, slowly growing larger and rising into the air.

The magic ball acted like a small black hole, sucking all the light from its surroundings and warping the air around it like a lens.

"Crimson Sword!"

Ren leaped into the air and sliced at the Soul Eater with his sword.

Huh? There was an explosion of sparks.

"It's harder than I thought it would be."

Hey, these damn game experts. I found the monster for them, and they still couldn't take it down?

If it got away and hid again, we'd be in a tough spot.

"Wind Arrow!"

Itsuki performed a skill.

"Lightning Spear!"

Motoyasu's skill wasn't going to be enough to kill the monster.

Did it have to do with the monster's weaknesses? Sometimes it took forever to figure out what worked against ghost-type monsters.

It looked like light magic should be effective on it though.

The ball of black magic the Soul Eater had released looked like it was nearly charged and ready to release its attack.

"Hurry! That evil skill is almost ready!"

"Oh!"

Ren shouted and Motoyasu turned, ready to attack.

"YAAAAAAAAAAAAA!"

With a reverberating thwack, the Soul Eater spit the large black ball of magic. It flew like a cannonball and slammed into the deck.

There was a large black explosion. The entire ship shook violently.

This wasn't good at all! The enemy was powerful enough

that all the fighting up until that point was starting to look like little more than a warmup.

Had we finally lured the snake from the grass? It didn't matter. If we wanted to end the wave, this was the only way.

I jumped down from Filo, ran in front of everyone, and readied my shield.

"AAAARRRRHHHHHHHH!"

Ren, Motoyasu, Itsuki, and their parties were all caught up in the blast.

I felt the force of the explosion through my shield.

"Ugh . . ."

It actually really hurt. The thing was strong enough to break through my defense, and over a really wide area.

Ren and the others hadn't been killed by the blast, but they were tottering, unsteady on their feet.

The inter-dimensional Soul Eater had apparently noticed how effective its attack had been, as it was already producing another ball of black magic.

That powerful attack AGAIN?! Give us some time before you fire off another one! It was annoying, but I suppose that was the only way to fight. You had to do what your enemy didn't want you to do. In games, the makers knew what would anger players, so they made it so monsters wouldn't behave that way. But that was the difference between games and reality.

"Filo!"

"Yeah! I know!"

She was already running, full-speed, at the Soul Eater. She leapt through the air and kicked it hard. I heard the kick connect, but the inter-dimensional Soul Eater just laughed it off.

"Haikuiku!"

Filo spun away from a second kick, landed on the deck, and started casting a spell.

For a second, Filo looked somehow blurred.

There was a series of quick clanging sounds, and the Soul Eater fell back. A second later and it was back up and preparing to launch a black ball at Filo. Apparently she'd found a way to bother it.

"You can't hit me!"

Filo shouted a taunt at the thing and ran behind me. That's it, Filo. That's how we'll fight it.

I readied my shield and cast a healing spell just as the black ball exploded before us. I blocked it with my shield, and Filo dashed to fit in another attack.

Raphtalia was casting light magic spells the whole time. If she didn't, the Soul Eater would be able to hide from us again.

"Hiyaaa!"

Filo was dashing here and there, fitting in attacks when she could and slowly dealing more and more damage. This thing was tough. That's why it was the boss, right?

If this were a game, a monster like this would only appear at the end of a large group battle.

As far as the Internet games I was familiar with, a boss like this was about as strong as they got. It was the kind that required a bunch of strong players to team up and take down within an hour.

What options did we have?

We could keep making small attacks and hope that they wore the monster down enough for us to win. But would they?

The longer we spent fighting the boss, the more damage the surrounding villages would incur.

Even now, monsters continued to pour from the rift.

We didn't have the time to spend chipping away at it. If only there were some kind of powerful skill we could . . .

There was a way. Only one way, but it might turn the tides.

My shield had a power that, maybe, the other heroes didn't have. We didn't really have any other choice.

"Raphtalia."

Raphtalia had fallen back. I took her hand.

"What is it?"

"Help me."

She quickly guessed my intention.

"Okay. I am your sword. I'll follow you—even to the pits of hell."

"I'm doing it. Back away."

I had gotten really irritated, and even though I didn't want to use it, I was curious to see how much power there really was.

"Filo, if something happens, stick with Raphtalia and keep away."

"Okay!"

I looked over at Raphtalia once more.

"Mr. Naofumi!"

She believed in me.

But if I lost, Raphtalia and Filo would . . . die.

More than anything, I couldn't let that happen. I wanted to protect them. I really did.

I wouldn't let myself be swallowed by anger. I couldn't . . . I swear.

I readied my shield.

"Shield of Rage!"

The dragon core stone has caused you to grow up!
Curse Series: Shield of Rage abilities increased!

Shield of Rage II: ability locked: equip bonus: skill: "Change Shield (attack)" and "Iron Maiden"
Special effect: self curse burning: strength up: dragon's rage: roar: kindred ruckus

Wh . . .

The dragon's final memories were playing before my eyes, as I'd used the core stone as material for the shield.

A hero with a sword had stabbed it deep in the chest and forehead, and the dragon had lost consciousness then. The anger it had felt was like something I'd never imagined.

It was the anger at having lost to a human.

I was able to understand how wretched, how terrible that was for a dragon.

Grow up? What did that mean?

My shield melted and reformed. It looked like it was made of glowing embers with a giant blood-red dragon in the center.

My Barbarian Armor +1 also changed form to match the shield.

Was all of this because of the dragon core?

The armor looked different now, and it was covered in a dark black dragon pattern.

The anger was so strong my vision was turning black. Everything was filled with hatred, anger, and the desire for destruction.

This anger, this hate, it wasn't all coming from me! I could see all the rage there before me, glowing red, erasing everything but itself. It took all of me.

No! Not here, not now! I had to fight for the people that believed in me! Not now!

Chapter Twelve: Iron Maiden

Red dragon flame . . . The Shield of Rage II had grown into something else altogether. I turned it on the black shadow.

"Aaaaaarrrhhhhhhhh!"

When I screamed, the air around us seemed to crawl and tear—like it was screaming with me.

"Yaaaaaaaaaaaaaa!"

The inter-dimensional Soul Eater took its eyes from Filo and turned them on me.

This wasn't good. Compared to the last time I used the Shield of Rage, the emotion was much stronger. I felt like I was losing myself.

Was it because of the shield's growth? This "grow up" that had been mentioned?

Ugh . . . My vision was wavering.

"Mr. Naofumi."

Suddenly, a kind touch. It must have been Raphtalia.

I couldn't . . . I couldn't lose her here.

There were people out there—people depending on us to stop the wave. I couldn't let myself be swallowed by rage and hate. I couldn't let them down!

I threw off the dark shadow and shook my head to steady my vision.

The enemy was there before me. I stared at it and readied myself.

"U . . . Uaaaahhhhhhh!"

Ugh?!

I turned, and for whatever reason, Filo was engulfed in dark flames.

"Gaaaaaaah!"

Her eyes were sharp like a bird of prey. She ran at the enemy and kicked it hard.

It might have been because she'd eaten the dragon core that I'd used on my shield.

Filo turned on the Soul Eater and kicked it again.

"Yaaaaaa?!"

It looked like her attacks were successful.

But it also looked like she was unable to distinguish the real enemy. She turned on another random monster in the area and started to attack it instead.

"Ugh . . ."

The shield was threatening to absorb me.

I ran at the inter-dimensional Soul Eater and pressed it back with my shield.

It gnashed its teeth at me, scratching my shield—but I wasn't taking any damage.

Perfect.

The Shield of Rage II had self curse burning. It was a

counter-attack that answered an enemy's attack with a powerful curse, one that would burn the enemy to ash.

I felt the cursed flames rising within me. They roared throughout my body and engulfed the Soul Eater.

"Yaaaaaaaa!"

The inter-dimensional Soul Eater screamed in pain, but the self curse burning wasn't powerful enough to completely burn it.

The skeleton captain, kraken, and ship's cannon all turned to focus their attacks on me.

"I don't think so! Shooting Star Sword!"

"Shooting Star Spear!"

"Shooting Star Bow!"

Ren, Motoyasu, and Itsuki had recovered their footing, and they all unleashed a barrage of skills at the enemies before them. Then they turned to the inter-dimensional Soul Eater.

They were trying, and their attacks connected and worked— but none were powerful enough to defeat their targets. The enemies healed themselves too quickly.

Wasn't there some other way?

I remembered that there was another skill. One I hadn't tried yet.

Change Shield (attack) and Iron Maiden.

Both of them were skills from the Shield of Rage II. I didn't know what they did, but it was worth the risk to find out.

I'm pretty sure it was Shield Prison to Change Shield (Attack) to Iron Maiden.

It might have meant that performing the skills in order would lead to some kind of chain reaction. Could it be some kind of combo skill?

"Shield Prison!"

I turned to see the enemy encased in a cage made of shields. Luckily enough, maybe because Ren and the others had drawn its attention, the Soul Eater had left itself wide open.

Now it was caught in the Shield Prison.

The monster was now attacking the cage directly, and it seemed ready to crumble at any moment.

I wouldn't let it escape. I couldn't let my chance slip away.

"Change Shield (attack)!"

The command was the same as my normal Change Shield skill.

I was presented with a number of new shields to choose from.

A needle-covered shield seemed like the obvious choice. There was the Animal Needle Shield and the Bee Needle Shield to choose from.

I chose the Bee Needle Shield.

"!"

The shields that made up the Shield Prison all suddenly turned into Bee Needle Shields, their needles facing the interior of the cage, and the monster took damage.

The walls were pressing in on the monster inside.

Iron Maiden!

I was ready to use the skill when a paragraph appeared in my head.

"The punishment I have chosen to inflict on the foolish criminal before me is called the Iron Maiden. They will be pierced through from every direction, enveloped in their own screams, and will taste true pain!"

"Iron Maiden!"

I shouted to activate the skill, and a giant iron torture device appeared in the air. Its door swung open, and the entire Shield Prison was pulled inside.

With the door open, I could see the interior was filled with large spikes, and the victim inside would have to prepare himself to be stuck through by them.

When the door closed, whoever was inside would be impaled in every direction.

The Shield Prison disintegrated, the door slammed shut, and the enemy was impaled before it was even able to scream.

There was a loud clang, and the door of the Iron Maiden swung open. The Soul Eater inside was stuck through so many times it looked like a honeycomb. Weakened, it turned to escape.

But . . .

The door slammed shut again, and the Soul Eater was once again impaled on the spikes.

At the same time, my SP meter dropped to zero.

The skill used up all of my SP?

The Iron Maiden either ran out of time or power or whatever. The torture device vanished.

"Huff . . . Huff . . ."

"Whoa . . ."

Everyone was whispering, breathless.

The inter-dimensional Soul Eater was riddled with holes and clearly dead.

"We won!"

I tried to control my ragged breath and changed my shield back to the Chimera Viper Shield. I would have to find some way to control Filo. She was running around violently.

With the shield powered up, I apparently wasn't able to use it for very long.

"Huh? Whew . . ."

Probably because the Shield of Rage II had disappeared, Filo slowly came back to normal. She sat down, exhausted.

"Whew . . ."

"You did it."

"I guess."

"Oh boy! What happened?!"

I turned around in time to see Raphtalia run up to me and Filo collapse in exhaustion.

"Did we stop the wave?"

"I'm tired!"

Ren, Motoyasu, and Itsuki were all glaring at me. They looked envious.

"We lost this time, but things will be different next time."

"What was that? After all you said about not knowing anything about the world, that was some fighting you did."

"You didn't join the fight for so long that you still had all your energy."

Itsuki had the nerve to say something like that? He traveled the world and tried to not stand out, doing all his adventures in secret, and he had the nerve to call me lazy?

"Regardless, now we've . . . ?!"

Wh . . . What the hell? I suddenly had the worst feeling. Every muscle in my body was tense.

It looked like Ren, Motoyasu, and Itsuki felt it too. They were feverishly looking around the ship.

One of Itsuki's party members was overcome by fear. He fell to the ground. There was an overpowering sense of dread. It was so powerful that the Soul Eater we'd defeated was nothing in comparison.

What was going on?

There was a shuffle, and a person's shadow fell over us all.

Was it another enemy? This was getting ridiculous. I didn't have any energy left!

"Are you all so threatened by these little monsters? It seems there is but one true hero among you."

She was wearing a deep black kimono that was embroidered with silver. In my own world, it looked like the kind of clothing a wealthy relative might wear to a funeral.

This whole world had seemed to be like the European Middle Ages, so it was weird enough to see someone in a kimono.

Her hair was long and jet-black.

She looked Japanese but also somehow ghostly.

It was like . . . It's hard to describe, but she occasionally shimmered, like she was semi-transparent.

She held a fan-like weapon. Without warning, a stream of light burst forth from it, flying over our heads.

We all turned to see what was happening, only to see the light collide with another inter-dimensional Soul Eater that had been creeping up behind us.

"I would prefer to fight without your interference. The approaching battle is of sublime importance."

"Wh . . ."

The Soul Eater fell to the deck, dead, from her single attack.

It couldn't be true. We'd spent all our energy and time on a Soul Eater, and she'd just killed one with a single attack!?

The girl narrowed her eyes and looked directly at me before she spoke again.

"Well, from what I saw of the last fight, it seems that you are a hero. The others seemed unable to fight at all, but you are different."

"Maybe."

"And what is your name?"

"You'd ask my name without giving your own?"

"Pardon me. My name is Glass. If I must elaborate, it wouldn't be wrong to consider me your enemy."

I wasn't about to consider her my friend.

"Naofumi."

"Naofumi then. Shall we begin the real battle of the wave?!"

The girl named Glass opened her fan and rushed at me.

Dammit! I'd just used the Iron Maiden, and I wasn't in any position to start a new fight!

If I used the Shield of Rage II, I would have to contend with its poison. I was barely able to hang on. Thanks to Raphtalia, I'd been able to control the poisonous emotions from the shield, but I felt my limit approaching.

"I won't let you!"

Ren, Motoyasu, and Itsuki all readied their weapons and aimed their skills at Glass.

"Shooting Star Sword!"

"Shooting Star Spear!"

"Shooting Star Bow!"

The three skills were flying at Glass when she looked down and let her lips curl, ever so slightly, into a smile.

"How cute . . . Circle Dance Zero! Reverse Snow Moon Flower!"

It was the middle of the day, but the wine-red sky began to glow and pulse.

There was an attack coming. I ran to Raphtalia and Filo and readied my shield to protect them.

We looked to the sky to see a blood-red moon hanging there, silent and powerful, like it had absorbed the shouts of its enemies.

There was a flash of red, circular light, and the other heroes and their parties all fell.

"GAAAAHHHHH!"

Something like a tornado lifted them from where they'd fallen, then flung them all through the air.

"Ugh!"

They fell to the deck again.

Damn. They knew a lot about the world, and they were all at a high level. How could they fall so easily?

But if she was so powerful that she could defeat the Soul Eater with one hit, then how could we ever hope to stand against her?

We'd used all our power against it, but it was looking like that fight had been nothing more than a warmup.

I'd thought that this wasn't a game, but the difference in our strength was so apparent that we really stood no chance.

If this WERE a game, I would assume it was a battle that you were forced to lose, that losing would trigger an event of some kind. But this was reality.

If we lost, there wouldn't be a secret event to save us. Life wasn't that simple.

Besides, the people who already knew all about the game and used that knowledge to efficiently level up had just been defeated—just like that.

I'd spent my time trying to make money. What hope did I have of standing against her?

Still, I couldn't lose. I had to win for Raphtalia. For Filo.

"What a pathetic little bunch. I feel bad for your Holy Weapons. They must be crying."

Her weapon was an Iron Fan. She held it open with both hands, and her fighting looked like a dance.

"This is certainly unexpected."

"Master, that girl is super strong!"

Filo's feathers were all standing on end.

"It's true. I can feel her power from way over here. She's much stronger than we are."

Raphtalia's tail was erect and puffy. She was obviously trying to control herself.

I ran over to the fallen heroes and looked down at the fainted Bitch.

Those heroes she had depended on were like toys to Glass.

But what were we supposed to do?

Honestly, the Iron Maiden had used up all of my SP. At the very least, I'd need a way to recover that.

That's it. Motoyasu spoiled Bitch. Maybe she had some kind of tool that would prove to be useful. Or maybe she'd have a good item or two.

There. She had Magic Water and Soul-Healing Water. The selfish Bitch.

The first item would replenish any magic that you used when casting spells, and the other would recover any SP you used when you used a skill.

Well, Soul-Healing Water was so expensive that I'd never had a chance to try it. But I had heard that it would increase your concentration, and that would make your magic more powerful.

I decided to try drinking the Soul-Healing Water. It tasted a little like the nutritional drinks I'd made, but as I drank it I could see my SP meter being replenished.

Yes, so it really did restore SP. Thinking back on it, Ren and the others had been using one skill after the other, so they must have had a way of replenishing their own SP.

"Mr. Naofumi!"

Raphtalia saw me rummaging through Bitch's pockets and yelled at me.

But seriously, they weren't fighting, and I didn't really have any other option.

"How cheap. And you call yourself a hero?"

"I'm fine with cheap. This woman has done much worse than 'cheap.' I'm not very fond of her."

"Master, you look like a bad guy!"

"Shut up."

"The enemy speaks truthfully. I don't know what to say."

Raphtalia sighed to herself. The enemy seemed to be growing annoyed with us.

"She is not on our side, but she is not incorrect."

"Whatever."

I stepped ahead of the other heroes, and Glass readied herself for a fight.

They weren't capable of fighting for themselves, so there wasn't anything I could do to further involve them in the battle. Glass seemed to understand that too. She had a samurai-like stoic character to her too. She probably only wanted to fight those who would challenge her.

"Very well then. I think our chat has gone on long enough!"

She opened her fan and rushed at me.

She was fast! I immediately raised my shield. Just in time—I caught her attack with the shield, and it reverberated with a dull clang.

Damn! It was so heavy. She'd only attacked once, but the shock had shaken my shield arm until it went numb.

Her attack was stronger, much stronger, than even the

Zombie Dragon's attack had been. If she could manage such a powerful attack with her fan, then Raphtalia and Filo were in real trouble.

"Raphtalia! Filo! Watch out! This one is strong."

"Understood!"

"Okay!"

"I am the source of power. Hear my words and heed them. Protect them!"

"First Guard!"

I cast supportive magic on both of them, and the battle began in earnest.

"If we fight here, the fallen heroes will be in the way. My aesthetics do not tolerate unnecessary interventions in our noble struggle. Let us go somewhere else."

As if she had understood my real intentions, she leapt from the ship. We followed her.

"This seems like a place where we may battle undisturbed. Here I come!"

If the fan's attack hit anywhere I couldn't manage to cover with my shield, it was strong enough to overcome my defenses, causing pain and leaving a wound. If I had the chance, I would cast First Heal to cover the damage I was receiving. But there was very little time.

Her attacks came quickly and powerfully. More than anything else, she was intelligent. It was nothing like fighting a monster. She realized that her attacks were not as effective on me, and so she set her sights on Raphtalia and Filo.

"I won't let you!"

I used Shield Prison. I sent it over to where Glass was standing.

"Ha! Pathetic."

Glass destroyed the Shield Prison with a wave of her hand. But that wasn't my real plan.

The real reason I used Shield Prison was . . .

"Hiyaaa!"

"Take that!"

So that she wouldn't be able to see Raphtalia and Filo's attacks coming.

"Ugh!"

Raphtalia and Filo's attacks covered a larger range than Glass could defend with her fan, and where they connected they produced a shower of sparks.

"So you are using a similar battle tactic. This is much more interesting than those other heroes."

She was quick with her counter-attack. Her fan opened and sliced at Raphtalia.

I wouldn't let that happen!

I jumped ahead of Raphtalia just in time and covered her. I took the attack with my shield, which activated the counter-attack skill Snake Fang (medium), and the shield bit deep into the enemy.

"Do you think a simple attack like that will defeat me?"

It didn't look like the poison worked on her. After taking the Snake Fang attack, she didn't appear fazed.

Of course, I knew her defense from when I saw her parrying Raphtalia and Filo's attacks with her Iron Fan.

Regardless, she was too powerful. Her attacks were so strong.

The fact that she had defeated the other heroes so quickly proved how powerful she really was.

Honestly, I couldn't picture a version of this fight that ended in victory for us. Even if I could keep us healed, I didn't see a way to defeat Glass. We just weren't powerful enough.

"Master, watch my magic!"

Filo entwined her hands and ran straight for Glass.

"Haikuikku!"

She had used that back when she was fighting the inter-dimensional Soul Eater. It was a powerful technique that made her move faster.

For a second, just a second, Filo was nothing but a blur.

When she hit the enemy, the attack was so strong it sent the air vibrating, and I felt the shock through my shield.

"Ugh . . . That person is so hard! She took my attack and didn't go flying!"

"Yes, you were able to kick me eight times in that second. Unfortunately you simply aren't powerful enough."

What? Did she mean that she was able to follow Filo's attacks?

Glass turned quickly, like a pirouette, and opened her fan, slicing at Filo. She was our enemy, but I couldn't help but admire her graceful movement. She took the brunt of Filo's attacks without even batting an eye.

"Filo! One more time!"

"I can't! I don't have any more magic, and I need time before I can attack again!"

So that was her secret, her ultimate attack? I guess she hadn't been able to use it in quick succession during the last fight either.

It wasn't looking good. We were running out of options.

While Filo kept Glass occupied, Raphtalia had maneuvered behind her and sprung a surprise attack. She appeared out of nowhere, so she must have used magic to hide herself.

"Now! Filo!"

She'd waited for the perfect moment—for Glass to expose a weakness. Glass would surely take heavy damage if she were attacked from the rear.

And yet . . .

"What are you doing?"

No! Raphtalia had snuck behind Glass and aimed an attack straight at her back, but Glass had stopped it without even turning.

"There's no point."

Glass looked a little disappointed. She sighed and then flicked her fan, parrying Raphtalia's sword. She seemed to move as lightly as a breeze, but the clang of her fan against the sword spoke to the strength she concealed.

Clang!

"Wha . . ."

Raphtalia's sword . . . broke?!

How strong was this girl? Sure, Iron Fans had long been known to be capable of breaking a sword—but to think that she could do it so easily? I'd cast First Guard on myself and switched to my hardest shield, but even at that I could barely stop her attacks.

Now only Filo had a chance of defeating her. But she wasn't strong enough.

"Ugh . . ."

Raphtalia jumped back to put some distance between herself and the enemy. Then she pulled out another small sword she'd had stashed away. Did she stand a chance?

"Is this really your true ability? To be honest, I'd expected more of a fight from you."

"That's what you get for assuming. We've been giving this our all the whole time!"

"What a shame."

Glass's whole body started to emit a light.

No! That was the attack that had defeated the other heroes!

"Raphtalia, Filo!"

Glass began to spin, as if she were dancing. There was only a second—we could barely move in time! Raphtalia and Filo leapt behind me.

"Shield Prison!"

I set myself as the target, and we are immediately enveloped in a magical cage of shields.

This was the other way to use Shield Prison. It wasn't only for stopping the enemy. I could use it to protect us too.

The wall of shields would protect us while we were inside.

Among all my skills, the Shield Prison had the highest defense rating.

"Dancing Circle Zero! Reverse Snow Moon Flower!"

There was a powerful wind, and a barrage of clattering Iron Fans destroyed the Shield Prison.

"Ugh . . ."

The attack was incredibly strong. If it destroyed the Shield Prison and injured us, then it only seemed natural that it had decimated the other heroes.

"Are you two all right?"

"Yes . . ."

"It hurts!"

I turned to find both of them suffering from the attack.

I quickly applied healing ointment to my own wounds. They were within the effective range of the skill, so the ointment worked on them too, healing their wounds.

"Impressive. That you might stand after my attack speaks to your defensive capabilities."

The tornado vanished, and the enemy walked in our direction.

"So glad we've won your approval."

We were tattered and tired, but we hadn't lost yet.

"What's next? Aren't you going to use that shield of flame from before?"

Did she think I was holding back?

Or not quite . . . It's like she was waiting for me to use the Shield of Rage II.

What should I do? Keep fighting a losing battle? Send Filo running away and use the Shield of Rage II, knowing that it would consume me?

If we were going to lose anyway, should I accept the regret of using it?

"Fine. But you don't know what you're getting into!"

I switched to the Shield of Rage II.

"Gaaaaahhhhh!"

Filo ran at Glass again and unleashed a fury of kicks.

"Your attacks are stronger than they were, but unfortunately . . ."

Glass didn't even change her footing.

All of Filo's kicks were connecting, but Glass was completely unfazed.

"What's the point?"

She used her fan to lightly brush Filo away.

"Gah!"

She'd barely touched her, but Filo flew five meters through the air.

"Ugh . . ."

How strong was this girl? If this were a game, I'd have expected the inevitable "losing event" to have started by now.

"Ugh . . ."

But I was still standing.

I'd be okay. No matter how powerful the hatred that might overtake me, it would never be able to stand up to the feeling I had for those who believed in me.

But if I let it go on for too long, it would be dangerous.

Cold sweat dripped down my face, but I stepped forward anyway, signaling for Raphtalia to get away.

"Mr. Naofumi . . . Are you sure?"

"Yeah, I can control it."

I kept walking until I was close to Glass. There was still some Soul-Healing Water in the bottle I'd taken from Bitch. I drank it and recovered my SP.

I felt like I could concentrate suddenly. I felt fresh. I felt like I could keep the shield from consuming me entirely.

"Please show me what you've got."

"I sure as hell will!"

Her fan flicked open and slashed at me.

Yes, this attack was much stronger than the Chimera Viper Shield. I readied the shield.

Self curse burning activated, centered on me.

The flames burned with an intensity proportionate to my anger. But I had managed to control my anger, so that was probably limiting the power of the counter-attack.

But the flame was still cursed. Raphtalia backed away at the sight of the flames.

A moment later the Shield of Rage II exploded in black flame, spiraling toward the sky. Glass was knocked back.

"What?!"

But she wasn't concerned. She stood there, placid, like the winds were massaging her.

Could it be? The self curse burning was the strongest counter-attack I'd seen. Could she really let it batter her without worrying at all?

How tough was this girl?!

"Why are you still playing around?"

Dammit! She was too strong! Not even the Shield of Rage II could stand against her!

"Is that all you've got? Circle Dance Rupture, Tortoise Shell Crack!"

She pulled her Iron Fan back and then thrust it powerfully in my direction. It emitted something like an arrow of sharp light.

Dammit! I raised my shield and felt it reverberate with the heavy, dull shock. My whole body ached.

I'd taken damage, straight through the shield.

"Ugh . . ."

"So you can absorb an attack with that much power? Impressive."

It was hard to stay focused through the pain. But I couldn't lose myself. Not now.

"That was some attack."

It might have been a piercing attack. They showed up in games now and then.

They had a chance of ignoring the defense rating of the target. Some attacks would even deal more damage to targets with higher defense ratings.

Is that what the other heroes had meant when they said that shielders became less useful with time?

Experience points, in online game, tended to get harder and harder to accrue as you leveled up. I don't know what kind of game the other heroes were familiar with, but as for the games I'd played, I could think of some examples of how it could be true.

The first is the simplest. The enemy's attack power would

eventually outrank the defensive capabilities of the shield.

The next was based on dodging because as you leveled up there were more and more enemies that could kill quickly with one hit.

The last was firepower-type games, as the defense abilities of the shielders were not nearly as useful as the ability to quickly overpower the enemy with your attack power.

I'd given a fair amount of thought to everyone's dismissal of the shield class, but none of those options seemed to be the case in this world. I couldn't figure it out, but I had no choice but to keep moving forward.

I cast First Heal on myself to heal my wounds.

"I have discovered the weakness in your attacks."

Glass spoke with extravagant confidence.

"The black flames appear in response to attacks in your immediate vicinity. If you are attacked from a distance, it will not activate. Then you shout to your subordinates to indicate the target."

Damn. She'd figured it all out. She was a real *bushi*. And her powers of observation were sharp.

Two waves back, it was a black beast; then it was a chimera. This time it was intelligent. It was a person.

Just what were these waves? Weren't they just natural disasters?

"So that is all I must do to win. I defeat your party and then attack you from a distance. It would be very easy. But honestly, such strategies aren't even necessary in a fight like this."

"Ugh . . ."

"Come at me with your strongest attack."

It was like she was playing with me. She didn't even look like she was preparing to avoid my attack.

I knew why. It's because she was playing with me.

If she stood up to my strongest attack and took the full force of it without buckling, that was her way of humiliating me.

But I wasn't going to lose that easily. I couldn't!

"Shut up already! Shield Prison! Change Shield (attack)!"

Glass was immediately trapped in the Shield Prison, and the shields quickly turned into shields that would attack her.

And then . . .

"Iron Maiden!"

I used my newest skill—an instant kill.

A massive iron chamber, shaped like a woman, appeared in the sky and pulled the Shield Prison inside. The door slammed, and the shields themselves were pierced through.

"How's that?!"

But . . .

"You're more powerful than I expected."

The door swung open, and Glass was alive and well inside. The Iron Maiden hadn't damaged her much, and it dissolved into small particles and vanished, leaving Glass standing there without a scratch.

Like nothing had happened at all.

"But . . ."

There were no other options.

"Very well then, we will consider this wave ended—and we have emerged victorious. I bare you no hatred. However . . ."

Before she finished her speech, the hourglass countdown icon in the corner of my visions quickly changed.

00:59

A new set of numbers appeared.

"The time? But it's much sooner than . . ."

Now! Raphtalia aligned her breathing with me and quickly chanted a magic spell.

"First Light!"

A ball of light appeared right before Glass—then it exploded in a great flash of light.

Glass was stunned by the flash and stood there motionless for a moment.

I immediately changed to the Chimera Viper Shield and ran over to Filo. She had jumped to her feet, ready to go crazy, but quickly recovered her senses.

"Get us out of here!"

"Wait!"

"Don't doubt her speed. We'll get away just fine."

"You would subvert the rules of the waves? I can't have you making time for yourselves like that!"

"I'm tired! What's going on?!"

I guess she couldn't seriously hope to fight.

If the Iron Maiden didn't work, then I was out of options.

"Very well then. It's disappointing, but we seem to be out of time."

Glass walked off toward a giant rift. Before she entered it, she paused, then turned.

What? What did she want to say?

"I will withdraw for now, but you will not be so lucky next time. Do not allow yourself to forget that it is WE who will emerge from the waves victorious. If that was your true strength, it is only a matter of time."

What did she mean "we"? She was making it sound like some kind of competition.

I didn't understand. I thought that the waves were natural and were going to destroy the world.

Thinking further though, I realized that nobody seemed to know anything at all about the waves. We had to figure out what they were. At the very least, we'd realized that the enemy was intelligent and a force to be reckoned with.

Trash and his Bitch were really holding me back. We just

THE RISING OF THE SHIELD HERO 3

figured out who our real enemy was, who the heroes needed to be fighting.

Geez . . . enemies. Everywhere I looked, more enemies!

"Naofumi. I will remember your name. Lick your wounds and await my return."

"Don't bother learning my name. We aren't planning on losing to you."

She nodded, satisfied. Then she killed a Soul Eater that had been hiding near the rift before stepping inside and vanishing.

Did she just kill her ally? Glass was a human, so was she not on the Soul Eater's side?

At Glass's retreat the rifts closed, and at the same time the hourglass countdown vanished from my vision.

"Whew . . ."

"We made it out of that alive, but who was that woman?"

"Who knows?"

"Wheeeeew!"

Filo was out of energy, and she lay sprawled on the ground. For a second, I wanted to join her.

"Well, we managed to close the wave."

"We did."

"I'm tired!"

"Me too. Let's leave the heroes where they are and pick up the pieces."

Honestly, it had been a terrible loss. How could we have

known the enemy was so strong? If we couldn't win despite knowing all the secrets of the game, what hope did we have?

And what was that countdown that appeared at the end?

Regardless, we needed to get stronger before the next wave arrived.

It was clear as day. If we didn't class up, we'd never survive the next wave.

But still, the others must have classed up—and they were still defeated. We needed something else, some kind of decisive advantage.

And so the third wave of destruction came to an end, and we made it out alive.

Chapter Thirteen: Parting Ways

We went back to the ghost ship where we'd fought the inter-dimensional Soul Eater. Perhaps because the enemy had been defeated, the ship was lying on its side on the ground. The heroes and their parties were there too, unconscious.

The volunteer soldiers and villagers were standing around them; apparently they'd been protecting them. They shouldn't have had to do that.

Finally, it was time for the best part of this whole disaster: adding the materials to my shield's repertoire. Unfortunately, the Goblin Assault Shadows and Lizard-Man Shadows were just that: shadows. Therefore, there were no materials left for me to absorb. Well, there was a little clump of shadowy material, but I was only able to unlock one new shield with it.

Shadow Shield: ability locked: equip bonus: shadow resistance (small)

There were some other things, but they just unlocked status boosts, so I'll just ignore them for now.

All that was left was the inter-dimensional Soul Eater.

"Oooh. Yummy!"

"Don't eat it."

Filo had grabbed it and was about to put it in her mouth when I stopped her. It was clear enough what had caused her to go crazy and violent. Any way you looked at it, it must have been because she'd eaten the dragon core.

"Come on!"

I reached out and took the material from Filo, but for some reason it instantly ran through my fingers and fell to the ground.

"How did you hold onto it?"

"I cast wind magic on my hands."

"Really?"

So you couldn't hold the fish in your bare hands? That was weird.

"Is everything okay?"

The volunteer soldiers saw the confused face I was making and came over to help.

"Oh yeah. I was just asking Filo how she was able to hold onto the monster here."

"These monsters don't have physical bodies. To get a grip on them you need to use something that has magical properties."

"What?"

"It's pretty well known. Did you not know about it, Shield Hero?"

"No."

"Oh, well, monsters without physical bodies are a pretty

rare thing, so you've probably just never run into one."

"Then do any of you have a weapon with magical properties I could use? I'd like to butcher this thing."

The soldier went around the group, asking if anyone had a weapon like that, and he found one person whose weapon had some cheap magical materials in it. They let me borrow it, and I butchered the fish.

Filo told me how she'd gotten the magic into her hands, and I copied her. I picked up the tail and let the shield absorb it.

Soul Eater Shield: ability locked: equip bonus: skill "Second Shield" spirit resistance (medium): Spiritual Attack Resistance (medium): SP up:
Special effect: Soul Eat, SP recovery (weak)

The shield unlocked with just the tail, and it didn't reference any other parts—which probably meant that further butchering the Soul Eater wouldn't do me any good. I tried letting the shield absorb other parts, but nothing changed.

But what was this Second Shield thing? Spirit resistance probably meant that I could hold off spiritual attacks.

The special effect Soul Eat sounded kind of interesting. I hope it didn't mean that I could eat souls. That didn't sound so good to me.

I slowly changed the shape of the shield. It was like the

whole thing was made from the monster, from the Soul Eater's head. It was a strange design.

And the Chimera Viper Shield had a higher defense rating.

If the special effect Soul Eat meant that I could eat souls, then I should be able to hold the Soul Eater. So I reached for it. But my fingers weren't able to actually touch its flesh.

I guess I was wrong. Good. I wasn't interested in eating any souls.

It was probably a counter-attack of some kind. Maybe it "ate the enemy's soul" in the sense that I absorbed their SP.

Okay, next. What was this Second Shield skill? I tried it out.

"Second Shield."

Air Strike Shield to Second Shield.

That's what the icon flashing in my field of vision said.

"Air Strike Shield!"

I waited to make sure that the Air Strike Shield appeared in the air before continuing.

"Second Shield!"

Another shield appeared.

So that's what it meant. Up until now I could only use one Air Strike Shield at a time. But now I could apparently summon two. There were probably a lot of different ways to use it, but it didn't excite me all that much.

I looked back at the remaining inter-dimensional Soul Eaters.

"I kind of want to absorb them all and leave nothing for the others."

But they would never let me live that down.

Besides, if they didn't get stronger, it wouldn't be good for anyone, let alone for me. If I was going to have to fight with them, they would have to be strong too. Sure, in this fight I was definitely the MVP. Still, I decided to leave materials for the others.

"Master, let me eat the leftovers!"

Filo shouted, a long trail of spittle dangling from her beak.

"Can't fight nature."

I cut through the spine and tossed a tail over to Filo. She gobbled it up.

"The bones are so slimy!"

"Wait. Did we run into any slimes?"

"Um . . ."

The rest of the conversation wasn't interesting, so I'll just cut it off there. Let's just say that I ended up angry because I didn't get to use them to unlock any shields.

"All right! Let's head for the next village and see if we can help them rebuild."

We had finished what we had come to do. So the volunteer soldiers and I started to help with cleaning up the bodies and making repairs in the next village.

We obviously weren't going to be able to help with all the jobs that needed to be done, so we focused on feeding the survivors and treating their wounds.

"Thank you so much! We'll do all we can!"

The volunteer soldiers listened to my orders and obeyed them without issue. I guess it meant that I didn't need to doubt their sincerity anymore.

A day had passed since our long and trying battle—finally, the knights arrived.

The leader of the knights was very upset that I had summoned the volunteer soldiers to the wave with me.

"You bastard! You think you can steal my subordinates and use them to form a private army?!"

"It's not the hero's fault! We came to him and offered to lend out services. He merely accepted our offer."

"What? And you call yourselves soldiers for the great land of Melromarc?! You'd sell yourselves to the Shield?!"

"You fool. Are you really going to focus on scolding your subordinates when you are surrounded by all this tragedy? Do you have any idea how bad the damages would have been had they not been here?"

The villagers had gathered around to hear what was going on. They all nodded in agreement with me.

"And just so you know, those other heroes that you depend on so much—they were defeated along with their parties during the wave, and now they're relaxing in that building over there."

No one had asked them to do it, but the villagers had gathered together and brought the unconscious heroes back to town so they could nurse them back to health. They had the medicine they needed, but it would still be a few days before they were back on their feet. Still, they were recovering quickly, and they'd probably wake up before the day was over.

"Hurry and bring the heroes to me! I will send them to an excellent hospital!"

"Their wounds aren't as bad as the others around here. There are villagers in much worse shape. You should prioritize them!"

"We must prioritize the heroes for the sake of our great country. No, for the world!"

This guy sure was impressed with himself.

Regardless, I'd assumed they would behave that way, so we'd been prioritizing the villagers' treatment anyway.

"Yeah, yeah. Anyway, hurry up and get them out of here! The rest of us have things to do."

"Wait, Shield."

I waved them away, but the knights had been talking about the situation with the volunteer soldiers, and now they called out to me.

"What is it now?"

"Your presence is requested at the castle."

"No thanks. You're a pain."

"You WILL come with us."

I'd like to see them try to force me. We had more important matters to attend to. Why were they always in my way?

I ignored them and turned to leave, but the volunteer soldiers stepped forward, petitioning. They bowed to me.

"Please, Shield Hero. Please come with us."

They had done everything I asked and obeyed all my orders. It didn't seem right to ignore them now. Besides, I did have that new carriage that I needed to pick up from the guy at the weapon shop.

"Geez."

I scratched at my head and slowly turned around.

"Fine. All I have to do is go with you, right? I owe these soldiers, so that's the only reason I'll do it."

"Thank you so much!"

They were all clearly thankful that I was going with them. I slowly nodded.

And so we all made for the castle.

We arrived the next day and entered the castle.

"We'd like for your companions to wait in the other room."

"You'd bring us all this way and then send them off?"

These people drove me crazy.

"Mind if I just get out of here?"

It wasn't like they were going to do anything nice for me. All this was a waste of time.

"You may not leave. We have a great deal of information we need to learn from you."

"I told you everything on the way here."

I'd already told them about how the heroes were defeated and we were left to face the final enemy alone. The volunteer soldiers had seen it all happen, albeit from a distance, so there was no room for them to doubt what I was saying.

Trash might try to make something up, but if he did, I would just run away.

I was strong enough to get away now, and if Raphtalia and Filo were with me, then I should be able to outrun anyone who tried to pursue us.

"Silence! You are before the king!"

The door hinges squealed as the door opened, and we were led to the thrones, where Trash sat and looked down severely at us.

I'm sure he'd already been told everything. He was obviously irritated at how successful I had been during the wave.

"It is incredible to think it, but I hear you were able to fight back the wave, Shield. As for myself, I don't believe a word of it."

"Is that how you express your gratitude?"

"Insolence! I have a question for you—not that I can trust your words."

"What?"

How awful was this guy? Did he need to indicate his distrust after every single sentence he spoke?

"Shield, I hear that you have discovered a strength that has made you more powerful than the other heroes. I don't believe it, but you have an obligation to tell me if it is true. Speak now. Not that I believe you."

He was so transparent, the fool. He was wondering if I was stronger than the other heroes, but he wasn't honest enough to ask me directly. He made me sick, the Trash.

Honestly though, I had no idea why Glass retreated after she defeated the other heroes.

She'd mistakenly thought that I was the strongest hero, and so we started fighting. But then a counter indicating a time limit appeared, and she retreated.

I could tell that the hourglass timer had something to do with what happened, but the rest of it was a mystery. What would have happened if the counter had run out?

There were too many questions remaining. Eventually, we would have to find the answers. But I didn't have time for that now.

But still. I could tell what was going on here. I turned to Trash and smiled, jabbing my finger at the ground before me.

"If you really want to know, crawl down here and bow to me."

Trash was so shocked he froze up for a moment. His face was hilarious. I wished I could have taken a picture.

"Did I stutter? Are your ears plugged up? If you really want to know, come down here and put your nose on the floor!"

"Uh . . . Uh . . . Uh . . ."

"What are you grunting like a monkey for? Or do you only aspire to be as wise as a monkey? The king is trash! Not that I would believe the words of a monkey anyway."

As I parodied and mocked him, his face grew red and stiff. His eyes glared at me, full of hate. You know what? It felt great.

"You bastard!"

Trash roared. His shout echoed through the halls.

The first enemy was the wave, and the second was Trash. But I wasn't going to lose to Trash.

"Don't you ever show your face here again!"

"You're the one who asked me to come! You don't have to ask me to stay away!"

And so I said my final farewell to Trash.

Chapter Fourteen: On the Road Again

"I'll have your head!"

Trash wasn't happy with my behavior.

"Uh-oh! How are you going to get me to the guillotine?"

There was a clatter of armor as knights began inching toward me from their posts around the throne.

"Are you guys forgetting? I'm the one that defeated the enemy—the one strong enough to take down all the other heroes."

I readied my shield and faced the knights. They all stopped moving.

I was a hero, after all. They did all know that I'd survived the wave where others had fallen, so why would they risk drawing close?

Even if I was half faking it . . .

"What are you doing?! Kill this insolent fool!"

"Hey now."

I turned back to him and spoke threateningly.

"Don't you understand? I'm strong enough to march into this castle, kill you, and make it out of here unscathed. You see that, right?"

"Uh . . ."

Trash looked very upset.

"If you don't believe me, I can demonstrate."

I'd learned that some tricks and threats were necessary to negotiate effectively in this place.

I had to use the tools available to me if I was going to restrain Trash.

"Those heroes you depend on were defeated by the enemy—an enemy I then defeated! Now you want to make me into your enemy?"

"Ughhhhh . . ."

He was so angry he was grinding his teeth.

"The only reason you can speak that way . . ."

"I'll kill you if you touch my party members."

I thought it best to tell him how that would play out.

Iron Maiden was a very powerful skill. It had defeated the Soul Eater, so I knew it was capable of killing someone. At the very least, I could use self curse burning and give them all some serious burns.

Trash's face was pale. Apparently he finally understood his place.

"Don't ever summon or speak to me again, Trash. When the waves are over, I'm out of here. Until then, I will do what I have to. But don't get in my way."

I couldn't pull any punches when I threatened him—and I couldn't use my trump card either. I had to save that for when I didn't have any other options left. If I killed him here and now, nothing would change. Whoever was pulling the strings behind the scenes would just pop up and take his place.

Still, if I had to fight the other heroes directly, I didn't know if that was a fight I could win.

And if I had to fight them all at once, I was sure to lose.

"Later."

I turned and left the throne behind.

"I won't forgive you! I won't forgive you, Shield!!!!!!!!"

His screams echoed through the castle.

"That makes two of ussssss!!!!"

I shouted on my way out of the chamber.

I left the castle and was walking down the stairs when I passed a woman who looked like she was from the nobility.

She hid her mouth with a fan, and she was wearing an expensive-looking dress. I couldn't see her whole face, but I could tell she was pretty. I wonder how old she was. She was probably in her early twenties. Her hair was purple. That was a rare color.

"Zank you for all your hard work, Zir."

Zir? Crap, I almost turned to look.

Huh? The woman was followed by the younger princess.

"Ah."

I ignored her and kept walking. I didn't have anything to say to Bitch's younger sister.

"Mz. Melty . . ."

"I understand, thank you!"

Yes, at the time I thought nothing of it and kept walking.

At the time, I wouldn't have thought, not even in my wildest dreams, that the younger princess would be the key that unlocked the door to dramatic change.

By the way, Raphtalia and Filo were waiting for me back in the room. Apparently they had thought that I might cause a ruckus and had been planning to come after me. I didn't know if I should be happy they understood me so well—or if I should be bothered by it.

I left the castle, and the first thing I did was stop by the weapon shop to see if the carriage I'd ordered was ready.

"Hey, kid. The carriage is all ready to go."

"Well that was fast. Old guy, you sure do work with metal quickly. You manage everything I ask of you so fast."

"I just organize it all. I have friends that help out with the actual work. I didn't actually make the carriage!"

Yeah, I suppose it only made sense that he'd get a local blacksmith to help him out.

"I was just thinking that you're one of those guys that can make anything happen for the right price."

"Kid, I swear it's depressing to hear you talk like that. I'm not young and skilled like you are."

"I'm not skilled."

What kind of person did he think I was?

"It's parked out back. Come have a look."

"Right on, can't wait to see it. By the way, I was thinking about Raphtalia's . . ."

Before I could finish my sentence, Raphtalia reached out and grabbed my hand.

"What is it?"

"You don't need to mention the sword. I have a backup sword anyway. So let's save whatever money we can for now."

"Hmm . . . Well, if you really think so, then I guess we can."

Filo's attack had gotten so powerful that she was doing most of the damage anyway. If Raphtalia could take on a support role, that should be fine. And she was probably thinking that we might find a better sword than the old guy could make for us.

We made our way out to the back of the shop, and sure enough, a large metal carriage was waiting for us.

The carriage was metal. Even the roof was metal. It reminded me of a little tin wagon my parents had bought for me in the past—only this one was life-sized.

"Wow!"

Filo's eyes were wide and sparkling. I'd never seen her look so excited.

She tottered over to the front of it and slowly reached for the reins.

"I'm allowed to pull it, aren't I?"

"Sure."

"Yay!!"

Her eyes were fluttering, and she readied her grip on the reins. She was so excited, she looked like she might explode.

"Let's load it up first."

"Understood."

"Okaaay!"

We went to the old carriage, took all of the luggage out of it, and then moved everything to the new carriage.

I couldn't help but notice that we were spending more and more of our time moving things and carrying luggage around.

"What do you think, kid?"

The old guy poked his head out to see how it was going. I gave him a "good job" thumbs-up.

"It's just what I wanted."

"Great, though I have to say, it looks pretty heavy. Think the bird-girl can handle it?"

"Yeah!"

"No problem. She was pulling the last carriage with three carts linked to the back."

"Impressive."

"She might even start whining that it's not heavy enough."

"You know what I like? Hard ones!"

Maybe it was a Filolial thing. Did they compete to see who got to carry the heaviest, hardest objects?

"Ahahaha. You can do it! Hey, that has me wondering. Where are you off to now?"

"What do you mean?"

"I heard all about it. You did something crazy at the castle?" The old guy looked a little worried.

"Well that was fast."

"Rumor is the spice of life."

"Whatever. Trash was acting crazy again, so I had to make sure he knew his place."

"I was sure you'd do something someday, kid."

"Glad I didn't disappoint."

"I could have used a little disappointment, actually."

"Great. Well, to answer your question, I'm thinking of heading for Siltvelt or Shieldfreeden so that we can class up."

Sure, I could have gone and threatened Trash to get permission to use the Dragon Hourglass in the castle town, but I needed to class up Filo and Raphtalia, and I didn't want to put them in any unnecessary danger.

I still didn't have a very good understanding of what the class-up process entailed, but the people who managed the Dragon Hourglass were apparently so concerned with it that they had invented all these rules and regulations to control our access to it. If it was going to be such a pain, then it seemed like the best idea would be to just head to another country where it seemed like we would have a free pass to do whatever we wanted.

"You know, kid. I've been thinking you'd head in that direction for a while now."

"Really?"

He was nodding at us in approval. I wonder what it meant.

"I'd suggest Shieldfreeden. Siltvelt can get a little . . . crazy."

"What do you mean?"

"Well, they are demi-human supremacists, and they turn humans into slaves there. Kinda the opposite of Melromarc."

I see now. Considering I was human, it probably wasn't the best option.

"And yet . . ."

"Thanks for the advice. We'll head for Shieldfreeden."

We finished loading the carriage and climbed aboard.

"All right. Well, I look forward to seeing you the next time you're in town."

"Sure. The next time I see you I'll probably be looking for equipment that is good against ghosts and spirit-type monsters."

"I see. Sounds like you've advanced enough to worry about monsters like that. I'll make sure I have the things you need."

"I'd like to gather materials to keep costs down."

"You can do what you want, kid. Just do me a favor and don't show up needing everything within twenty-four hours. I'll tell you where you can get the materials, if you want."

"Got it. I'll make sure you have enough time. Okay, we're out of here. Later, old guy."

"Later."

Filo started tugging at the reins.

Our immediate goal was to class up. With Filo pulling us, we could get there in two weeks. It would be a long trip, but it would be for the best.

"That's it!"

There was a loud voice coming from outside the gates. As we left the castle town, we were suddenly overwhelmed by the sound of someone banging against the sides of the metal carriage.

"Found you!"

"Huh? Mel!"

"What?"

I had Filo stop and turned to look outside. The younger princess was there. Her eyebrows arched, and she pointed a finger at me. Behind her stood a crowd of knights. It was the knights whose voices we'd heard.

"Please return to the castle!"

"What? Just like that?"

"I'm asking you to return and have a real conversation with my father!"

The little brat was getting obnoxious. I didn't have anything to discuss with Trash.

"Your father is wrong about everything. I'm not wrong. So at least we figured that out."

"What was that?!"

Did it take her so long to figure all this out? She was Bitch's younger sister. Why should I spend any time talking to her?

"Tell your father this: I can kill him at any time. Tell him to always be afraid."

"Why? Why do you have to say such horrible things? Please tell me!"

"Because your father is a piece of trash! I won't waste my time talking to Trash. Your parents are the WORST!"

"Y . . . You . . . I won't forgive you! My mother was wrong! The Shield Hero is a jerk!"

One of the knights behind her stepped forward.

"Heh. You want to fight me? Filo . . ."

"What?"

"Let's go."

"But . . . I want to play with Mel!"

"You can't."

"But . . ."

"Let's GO!"

"Fine . . . Bye Mel!"

Filo nodded, turned back to the road, and took off running.

"Hey. Waaaaaaaaaiiiiiiiit!"

The shouts of the younger princess faded away. The castle town really was filled with garbage. Other than shopping, there was no other reason to go there.

Chapter Fifteen: The Shield Demon

"Mr. Naofumi, don't you think you should have spoken with her?"

"That's easy to say, but think about it. She's Trash's daughter and Bitch's sister! I can't imagine her as a reasonable person."

"That's true. But she did help us once. And before that, she was our travel companion for a time."

Hmm . . . Raphtalia was right. She had helped us once, back when Motoyasu was running wild in town.

But still, that was probably a strategy to steal Filo from us. If we'd let her keep talking, she probably would have had Filo seized. Filo was already pretty attached to her.

"Fine. If they chase after us, I'll hear her out."

"That's a good idea. She is Filo's friend, after all."

"Mel is nice!"

"She pretends to be. Anyway, focus on the task at hand."

"We'll sell things along the way, right?"

"Yeah. I mean, we have to pay for the travel and for all our equipment, not to mention Filo's appetite."

Filo would help us get there, but we'd have to keep her belly full if we wanted to keep the speed up, and that would cost plenty. I'd been letting her eat the monsters we happened upon, but that wouldn't be enough to cover her whole diet. I don't know where all the money went, but I knew that we had to raise money while we had the chance. We could just set up shop in the villages and towns we stayed in on the road.

"Huh?"

In the back corner of the carriage there was a large bag I'd never seen before.

Wondering what it was, I opened the bag to find a single letter mixed in with a whole pile of items.

Dear Kid,

I was too embarrassed to give you these directly. I went ahead and made you all some tools I thought might be useful. Use them if you like.

The old guy from the weapon shop! It was so kind, so considerate.

I reached for the item on top.

It was a long sword. It was the same sword that Raphtalia had been using, the one that had broken.

The old guy must have been inspecting us closely. He was very observant. I was honestly touched. I thought I might cry.

"Raphtalia."

"What?"

"The old guy made you a present."

"But this is worth a small fortune. I don't know what to say."

Raphtalia accepted the sword, her eyes welling up with tears. That guy really did seem to care about us.

"What else is in there?"

The bag was stuffed with things, and all of them were labeled with our names.

The letter also included short descriptions of the items. He must have rushed to write it all out, as the handwriting was quick and hasty.

So the first one was for me. It was an item for the jewel in my shield. It sat over the jewel like a lid of some kind.

According to his note, it would help me look up information about the shield.

Well, the shield was the whole reason I couldn't really fight for myself. Anything he did to make it easier to understand was a good idea in my book.

It clicked into place over the jewel.

The next one was for Raphtalia. It was another short sword. But why? I passed it to her.

"He says this one is for you too."

"Another sword?"

She quickly slid it from its scabbard. There was a soft pop, and it turned out that there was no blade on the handle.

What was it for?

"Is it a stage prop or something?"

"I . . . I don't know."

The memo indicated that it was an experiment of his: a magic sword. He said it would work against shadow monsters with no physical body.

He wrote the memo is if he expected us to know what he meant. Normally he would have explained it to us, but he must have been embarrassed because he forgot to write how it was used. Where was the blade? Did it mean that only shadow monsters would be able to see it?

"There must be a reason it is missing the blade. I'll try to look it up later."

"Yeah, I don't think he'd give us anything we couldn't use."

All right. Raphtalia would do all the research about the magic sword.

"Next up . . ."

I thought it would be for Filo, but it was for me.

"Is it a glove?"

It looked like a glove with a jewel affixed to it. It was pretty cool-looking.

Let's see here. Yup, there was a memo explaining it.

Reading it made me tense up.

It was supposed to help out if we were ever in a situation in which Filo couldn't pull the carriage. Apparently if I put on the glove, I'd be able to pull the carriage too.

The effect was somehow linked to my current magic power rating. So I guess it was some kind of power glove. Not that I wanted to pull a big, heavy carriage around. If he wanted to be nice, he was going about it in the wrong way.

"Filo. This one's for you."

I figured it was best to leave the pulling and tugging to Filo. After all, she was the one who liked it.

"My hands won't fit in those!"

I guess it wouldn't work when she was in her Filolial Queen form. Well, that only made sense.

"You can wear them when you are in human form. Use them to play or something."

Even in the worst-case scenario, I could use them to craft something.

"Okaaay!"

Seriously, I was surrounded by jerks left and right, but just knowing that there were people like the weapon shop owner out there . . . Well, it made me want to keep moving forward.

There was a good chance we'd run into Glass during the next wave. We would have to get strong enough to face her before that happened.

Which meant that we would probably need the old guy to make us some weapons before the next wave. I felt like my efforts wouldn't be futile—like I had to get stronger for him too.

"Let's go!"

"Yes."

"Yay! Here we gooooooo!"

We were back on the road.

The next morning, after a light breakfast, we left the inn early. It was that kind of town.

"Waiiiiiiiit! Please talk to my father!"

I sighed and slapped my palms to my forehead. I figured they'd chase us, but I didn't think they'd catch up so quickly.

If they were capable of keeping up with Filo, they must have been moving quickly. And to think, I'd purposefully steered Filo in the wrong direction to throw them off.

"We finally caught up with you!"

"Ah, Mel."

Filo had stopped, so I climbed down from the carriage and faced the little brat.

"Apologize and speak with me!"

She'd been so polite at first. Now I guess she thought she could order us around. And so the monster sheds its skin. I knew she was after Filo.

"Sorry. Here I am."

"Don't apologize to me. Apologize to my father!"

Ugh, shut up already. I couldn't handle talking to the little brat.

"If you don't, my mother will make him pay."

"What are you talking about?"

I considered jumping back into the carriage and running. But Raphtalia had already told me off about that kind of behavior. I guess I needed to hear her out, just this once.

To be fair, this girl hadn't actually done anything bad to us. As for stealing Filo, that was just my guess. She'd never been anything but nice to us. And yet here she was, begging me to speak with Trash. I couldn't imagine anything I'd rather do less.

What did she mean that her mother would make him pay? Was Trash in for a spanking?

"What do you want me to do?"

"That's what I've been trying to say! I'm trying to create a space for the Shield Hero and the king to make amends."

The group of knights behind her ignored our conversation and drew their swords.

What's that? One of the knights in the back was pointing a crystal ball at us.

Huh? What was that supposed to be? Then I noticed.

None of them were looking at me.

I suddenly had a really bad feeling. A shiver went up my spine.

It was a feeling similar to how I felt when I realized Bitch had betrayed me. Tension, with a lot of dread. It was a feeling I'd spent the last few months trying to forget. That sense of betrayal—the air was thick with it.

Without stopping to think, I quickly ran toward the

knights. The reason for my growing dread became immediately apparent.

The knights turned their swords on the younger princess.

"Ahhhhhh!"

"Air Strike Shield!"

The little brat let out a shrill scream. The Air Strike Shield appeared before her just in time.

"What are you doing?"

In a flash, I was in front of the brat, glaring at the knights.

"You—Shield! You would use the princess as a hostage?!"

"Huh?"

They were the ones moving to attack her! What were they talking about?

It looked like the younger princess understood that just fine—her face was pale.

"The Shield is our enemy! We've known it from the beginning!"

The knights shouted and came running to attack me.

I readied my shield to protect the younger princess. The air was soon filled with the clang of sword on shield.

"Ugh . . ."

The knights in the back were busy casting a spell. It started to rain fire.

There was no time. I threw my cape over the princess and we waited for the fire to burn out.

"You . . . You Shield Demon!"

"Filo! Raphtalia!"

"Understood."

"Okaaay!"

They knew what I meant, and they were both attacking the enemy in a flash.

The knights knew a counter-attack was coming. They jumped on their horses and fled.

"Fools."

Filo was way faster than any horse. In less than a second, she'd knocked one of the knights from his horse.

"AHHHHHHHH!"

"No! A demon!"

We'd already taken care of one of them, but as we chased down another, then another, the other knights were able to get away.

"What the hell was that about?"

Weren't they here to protect the younger princess? How would we get to the bottom of this? We tied one of the knights up with a rope and questioned him.

"Okay, jerk. Why did you all just try to kill the princess in front of me? Better speak up."

"I don't have lips for talking to demons."

Ha! So I'm a demon now? It's been a while since people had been so rude to my face. There were plenty of people who said that the Shield Hero was a demon without knowing that I was that person. I'd wondered what they'd meant, but I had never gotten a chance to ask.

And then here was this guy, saying he didn't have lips to speak with a demon.

"You do understand the position you're in, don't you?"

I called out to Filo.

"Lunchtime?"

The knight went pale. But he recovered his sense and spoke.

"Even if I die, I would be a martyr for a holy cause. God will lead me."

So he was religious. Threats probably wouldn't work against this sort of fanatic.

"Hey, Princess, you have any ideas?"

The princess was trembling with fear. She shook her head.

"Huh, you don't say? What religion are you talking about? Some stupid cult, I'm sure."

"The Church of the Three Heroes! You demon! You would blaspheme our god?!"

Of course. Fanatics can't stand it when you start to make fun of their beliefs.

I could use that to wring information out of him.

"That's the major religion here."

Raphtalia whispered to me.

"You know it?"

"Well, most people are part of the church here. My village was a different religion, so I'm not part of it. Mr. Naofumi, you mean you've never heard of it?"

"Never."

"I thought that you knew."

"Why didn't the weapon shop owner tell me anything about it?"

"He was probably just trying to protect your feelings."

Maybe he'd thought I would do something reckless if I'd found out the real reason that everyone had been treating me so poorly. There really had been a time that I would have done pretty much anything. The last time I saw him I'd rushed the conversation too, so I don't know if he had actually been trying to tell me. I'd have to make an effort to listen to people more.

"Fine. Go through their belongings and see if you can find anything relating to the religion."

"Oh, okay."

Raphtalia rooted through their things and came back with a rosary.

From what I could tell, it was just a normal item, made from normal materials, and without any special properties.

"Put it on the ground."

". . ."

What a strange symbol. There were three weapons all folded into one design. Sword, Spear, and Bow. It was a weird selection of violent weapons.

That reminds me, the church we'd visited to buy the holy water had the same symbol hanging up. I guess I'd entered the church without saying anything, so Raphtalia had assumed I already knew about the church.

"All right, guy, if you don't start talking, I'm going to stomp on this thing."

"No! Nooooo!"

The veins on the guy's head stood out as he screamed.

He sure was quick to anger. Was this little string of beads really that important?

Back in my own world, there were religious groups that were fanatical enough to go to war. These guys must have been like that.

"Well, well."

I slowly lowered my foot until it was almost touching the rosary, and then I raised it again. Then I pretended to step on it again, raising my foot at the last moment. I did it over and over.

"You demon! Our god will never forgive your behavior!"

"What do I care what your god does? Now tell me why you tried to kill the princess. No? Are your beliefs so flimsy?"

"Ugh . . ."

"Are you just going to let me, a DEMON, stomp on your precious little rosary? Your god must be very understanding."

It was the reverse of the Japanese *fumie*. If they really believed I was a demon, they had no choice but to stop me.

"If you tell me the truth, I won't step on it."

"I won't be manipulated by you!"

"Too bad."

I ground the rosary under my heel, crushing it into the ground.

"Noooooooooooo!"

Hmm, what's he going to do? I should probably clear up the first misunderstanding.

"Hey, Princess? Who are these guys? Are they knights?"

"I . . . Um . . ."

She was still visibly shaken by the attempt on her life. Her face was pale, and she was trembling.

"Mel! Master and me are here so it's okay!"

"Filo."

Mel recovered her senses and turned to me, whispering.

"Um . . . These men are Father's knights."

"Trash . . . You mean he wanted to kill me so badly he would sacrifice his own daughter?"

Unbelievable. Did he really hate me that much?

"I . . . Um . . . I don't think so."

"Why not?"

"I don't think my father knows about this. When he plays strategy games, he's super smart—my mother can't even beat him. If this were his plan, it would be perfect. This plan, honestly, my mother wouldn't approve of it."

"I think you've got that backwards."

From where I was standing, it all looked pretty bad. I guess we couldn't expect much from the mother either.

"This seems like something my sister would think of. It's just like Mother said. We'll have to keep an eye on her."

Hmm . . . I might have been reading too much into it, but it sounded like there was some bad blood between these sisters.

"So you think it was your sister?"

She was an heiress to the throne, so there was a motive for her to try and get rid of her sister—the younger one was apparently first in line. Bitch would know that, and a plan like this certainly wasn't below her.

"She might want the throne. She'd have to get rid of me to get it."

"That does sound like something she would do."

"I wouldn't put it past her."

"My sister, from a young age, has loved bringing ruin to people. My mother has said that she would do anything to get what she wants."

It sounded like, at the very least, she had a handle on the basics.

"But Father doesn't understand that. He keeps saying that she's serious—and good."

So Trash trusted her. The younger princess wasn't taking his words at face value.

"Maybe the king just doesn't want you to inherit everything."

"That's not it."

"Why not?"

"Because Mother is in charge of choosing a successor. And Mother does not trust my sister."

"Mother . . . Your mother . . . Is that the woman with the purple hair, the one who walked with you and said 'zir'?"

"That was a double—they pretend to be her in public."

"A double? So I guess she looked like that."

I couldn't forget how purple her hair had been.

"Yeah. Well, the double looks just like her but talks kind of strangely."

"Huh."

"Because she's the queen, way more powerful than the king."

There she was again, whispering big news like it was nothing.

"What was that?"

"Her mother is more powerful than her father."

"Huh?"

"Mr. Naofumi, Melromarc is a matrilineal country. I just found out recently myself."

Raphtalia jumped in, adding more information as if it were the most obvious thing in the world.

What did this mean? It meant Trash had married into the royal family!

"What are you laughing for, Mr. Naofumi?"

"How could I not laugh? That Trash had to marry into the royal family! Ahaha!"

"Master, you look like you are having a good time."

"Don't speak ill of my father!"

"Why not? He hung you out to dry."

"He did not! Wahhhhhh!"

Uh oh, the younger princess burst into tears and started battering me with her little fists.

Ha! She'd been acting like an adult this whole time. But now she let her guard down. She was just a little kid.

I mean, when we first met her, I knew she was a kid. But now I knew that she really did act her age.

And yet she was speaking differently than she had when we first met. If she were a princess, she'd have to conduct herself with honor when she was in public. I guess what I'm saying is that this whining, crying little girl was the REAL younger princess.

"It's not right to laugh at a crying child."

"She's basically the same age you are!"

Had Raphtalia forgotten that she had behaved the same way only two months ago?

That explained her relationship with Filo then—it was her chance to be the big sister.

It also explained why she was giving Trash more than his fair share of the benefit of the doubt. It would be easy to get a bunch of religious fanatics to kill me—they already had the motive, and he could easily deny involvement. Even if he wasn't involved, the explanation of Bitch trying to secure the throne for herself made perfect sense.

"Mr. Naofumi . . ."

"I know!"

Raphtalia was starting to get angry, so I decided to behave more seriously.

"Is there some way for us to clear our names and also to protect the life of the younger princess?"

Honestly, I don't see why I needed to protect the progeny of Trash and or his Bitch daughter's sister. I didn't like the fact that they shared blood. But I couldn't just leave her there, and I couldn't kill her.

Even still, I could sympathize with her plight. Betrayed by her own family and left to die in a pit of despair. I knew how that felt. Hm . . . There must be some way . . .

"The queen . . . Do you know where your mother is?"

That was my first idea. If the queen didn't know what Trash was up to, we could find her and explain the situation.

She had more power than he did, so if we could get her on our side, then that would solve the issue.

If we went that route, the younger princess would be an important bargaining chip.

If we could just keep her alive, she would be of use to us. She seemed intelligent enough for decent conversation. The only problem would be if the queen were just as stupid as the king. If so, she wouldn't believe anything I said.

"I don't know where she is. But . . . but Mother said that she wanted me to be friends with the Shield Hero."

"And you know that she wasn't involved in this?"

That was a possibility we couldn't rule out. Giving her youngest daughter the right of succession might have been part of her plan to find and kill me.

"Uh . . ."

"Don't cry, Mel! Imma help you! I promise!"

The princess had started crying again, so Filo comforted her.

"Hey, don't you promise her anything!"

"But Master . . . I . . . I want to help her!"

"No."

"But I want to help! I want to help!"

"Ugh! Shut up already!"

Dammit. I was getting a bad feeling about all this. What was happening?

We went back and forth a few times before I noticed that the knights were laughing.

"Looks like the demon has finally learned his place."

"Shut up. I don't have time to deal with you losers right now."

"That's not true. This means we have fulfilled our purpose."

"What's that supposed to mean?"

"The death of the princess would guarantee the public's opinion of you, demon, but even without her death, there is no major problem. There must be a huge price on your head by now."

Yeah, well. I suppose I should have expected that much.

"You can assassinate a member of the royal family and flee to another country, but don't think that you won't be followed!"

"Wait. I don't understand why you had to murder the princess before my eyes."

If they were trying to frame me for her death, why bother with all this? Bitch framed me just by pointing at me, and everyone believed her. But they wanted to bring the younger princess out into the middle of nowhere, kill her, and then frame me for it? Why did they bother actually catching up with us when they could have killed her any time?

Then I remembered the knight in the back with the crystal ball. Most of the knights in the back row had managed to escape. What if . . . What if that ball had functioned as some sort of camera?

"Shield Demon, your murder of the young princess is now well known all throughout the land. You have nowhere to hide, nowhere to run."

I was starting to get it. The last time, they tried to frame me in their own country, but they went too far and weren't able to make it stick. If I had run to another country, they wouldn't be able to call for my forced removal. What it would lead to is my exile in another country—and that would give me an opportunity to recruit sympathizers.

But this time was different.

They had a crystal ball that contained a scene of me leaping at the princess. That would be all the proof they were likely to need. They could easily show it to any neighboring countries, and it would put an end to any domestic revolts they might face.

Wow, honestly, I was pretty impressed. So that brings me to my main options.

Option 1

Leave the princess and be on my way.

The knights that Trash sends after her will kill her, and that will give the Crown all the cause it needs to go after me. The queen would put a huge bounty on my head. The word would spread to neighboring countries, and someone would always be after me.

I'd be in real danger when the next wave came. They'd arrest me when I teleported to the scene.

Option 2

Take the princess back to Trash and explain the situation to him.

It would save the life of the princess, but then we'd have to deal with Trash. I wonder if he would try to charge me with kidnapping. Basically, it would save the princess, but I couldn't guarantee my innocence would be accepted.

The queen might step in to save me—but we didn't know where she was, so we couldn't go meet her. We would have to wait for her to come to us. We certainly had no obligation to put ourselves in that kind of situation. And if the queen was the one pulling the strings this whole time, then that would be the end of us all.

Option 3

We run back to the castle and kill Trash ourselves.

My crime and sins would be absolute and known to all, so the church and knights would hunt me down and kill me.

Considering the possibility of failure, the risk was probably too high.

"Whatever we do, I can't prove my innocence!"

Why did Trash and his family have to go so far out of their way to make me miserable?

"Ahaha! This will be the end of the Shield Demon. Now you will suffer for threatening our church."

"Shut up!"

I ordered Filo to eat them, and they finally learned to shut up. I could have killed them, but it wouldn't matter—some of them had already escaped. With that crystal ball as evidence, I was soon to be charged with murder. Even still, the Church of the Three Heroes . . .

The Church of the Three Heroes is a church with three heroes. So that must be what the name meant.

The symbol of the three weapons showed how much they valued their afterlives.

But something didn't make sense.

There were supposed to be four legendary weapons: the sword, spear, bow, AND shield.

Not only were the knights trying to frame me every chance they got, but apparently the church was against the shield as well.

That must explain why, when I first found myself in this world, none of the assembled adventurers volunteered to travel with me.

If the Crown had gathered the adventurers, then it was safe to assume they picked people they felt they could trust.

Thinking back on the large church in town and the behavior of the knights here, it was evident that the church held a lot of power in Melromarc. If the church said that the shield was a demon, the people were sure to go along with it.

Why would anyone, of their own free will, volunteer to team up with a demon? It didn't matter if they knew me or had all the information or not. Any little push would do it.

If all this were true, it would explain the nasty looks I got everywhere I went.

The fanatical zealotry of these knights made sense in that context, as they were under control of both the Crown and the church.

Thinking back on it all, I thought they had been acting strangely toward me even before Bitch had me framed for rape. They intentionally ignored me and then convicted me without a shred of evidence, both of which would be easier with the power of a church behind you. The people didn't need evidence when it came to me. If I were accused of something bad, they'd accept the accusation because I was already a demon in their eyes.

When I'd gone to see the Dragon Hourglass, the sisters had been cold, treating me like an enemy from the get-go. That was all the proof I needed.

I was starting to understand what Trash was up to.

If he wanted to keep his position, he would have to treat the Shield Hero differently than he treated the other heroes. Over the last month or so, the public was starting to think that maybe the Shield Hero wasn't actually all that bad. I'd acted as the bird-god saint and traveled all over the place. I'd saved people. Lately, even in the castle town, people had been more polite to me than they had been.

It had to do with the teaching of the church—it just had to.

All they had to say was that the three heroes had been threatened, and that wouldn't exactly be a lie. That was why they used their trump card: the princess next in line for the throne.

All this was just a guess. And it wasn't going to clear my name.

Still, running to another country . . .

Then I remembered what the guy from the weapon shop had said.

I think he'd said that the citizens of Siltvelt were demi-human supremacists. That would mean that they probably didn't have close relations with Melromarc. If we took the princess, the heiress of Melromarc, there to force negotiations, the queen would have to show her face.

Sure, I was a human, so I wasn't likely to receive a very warm welcome. But Raphtalia was with us. It might be the perfect hideout.

By the way, Siltvelt was to the northeast, and Shieldfreeden was to the southeast. But I would have to cross through two other countries to get there. Like I'd learned earlier, they were pretty far away. I'd just have to press forward and hope that something turned up.

"All right, we're going to go to Siltvelt for now. There might be a way for us to set all this straight—if we can get there."

"That's the demi-human country, right?"

Raphtalia nodded.

"Um . . ."

The younger princess muttered, unsure of what to say.

"What is it?"

"Oh . . . nothing."

"Fine. Raphtalia, once we arrive, I'm leaving all the negotiations up to you."

"Understood!"

"All right, Princess—you should come with us, for your own good. I promise to protect you, so relax. If you don't want to die, come with us."

"Okay."

The princess slowly climbed up into our carriage, but she didn't look very happy. I had no problem with good kids that couldn't understand what was going on. Just like this. But it might be a good opportunity to teach her about Trash and Bitch, to teach her about how dirty and fallen the world really was. She would have to live or die with us, so if our fates were linked, she'd better learn about the world.

She was still a kid. If I could teach her the truth, slowly, then she'd come to see things my way.

"Yay! Mel and me are together again!"

"Yes. Thank you, Filo."

Filo was thrilled that she was getting the chance to travel with her friend.

"So what is the queen up to? Why did she leave the kingdom?"

"She's always traveling to maintain our diplomatic relations. I used to go with her."

"Really . . . Diplomacy, huh? And what about us?"

"Mother said she wanted me to go meet with Father and to look for the Shield Hero and to befriend him. She works so hard every day to keep us from going to war. She said the waves have made the world crazy and that I needed to be home to protect Melromarc."

From the way Mel described her, she seemed way more reasonable than Trash—that is, if she wasn't secretly behind all of it. Even still, all this was based on the word of a child, one who came to us for a fight to protect Trash.

We hid the fainted knights in a nearby grove and cautiously turned our sights on Siltvelt.

Chapter Sixteen: Appointment Arrangements

"Hm . . ."

I was hiding in the shrubs, observing the situation.

It had been a few hours since we picked up the young princess. We went to a nearby village, and now we were hiding out to see what would happen. The village wasn't far from the village where we had fought with the Zombie Dragon.

Turns out, those knights were telling the truth.

"The Shield Demon, Naofumi Iwatani, has savagely murdered a group of royal guards, abducted the princess, and is running loose. He is wanted dead or alive. A reward . . ."

There were already bulletins pasted around town detailing my crimes and the promised rewards for my capture. There were soldiers walking through town and shouting about it.

It had only been a few hours, so it was impressive that they had managed to pull all this off.

They had said that everything had been set up from the beginning. People that came after us were volunteer soldiers, and they did so thinking they would be captured or killed. Back in my own world, I'd heard there were people who would wrap themselves around bombs and attack people—thinking they would go to heaven for it. So this world didn't have a monopoly on crazy fanatics.

"What became of those knights is recorded in a crystal ball, taken at the end of their lives. The soldiers that brought this recording to the castle died from their wounds shortly after delivery."

And that wasn't all. The recording they spoke of worked something like a hologram.

They'd manipulated my face into an aggressive frown, made it look like I was covered in blood, and paused the scene at one particular moment so that it looked like I had my arm hooked around the princess's neck.

They were capable of some impressive forgeries.

Even though they had scampered off like rabbits with that crystal ball, here they were making it sound like I'd butchered them.

They looked pretty healthy last I saw.

Still, it wasn't like they could completely fabricate the data. If you looked close, the princess's face didn't look like I was choking her—more just that, she was surprised by something. But still—if they could make up a forgery like this, why did they go through all the trouble of trying to kill her in front of me? I didn't get it.

"He is moving with a large carriage, which he has pulled by an evil, strange bird-demon. If you see him, immediately contact the nearest official guards."

Filo was in the hologram too. They'd manipulated her face

so she looked like an angry hawk, and they'd made it look like she was spitting poison. Well good for her. In this forgery, she could spit poison—just like she'd always wanted.

But if people were looking out for Filo, that would make it harder to get around. On second thought though, maybe I could use Filo to draw the attention away from the rest of us.

"Understand what I mean, Filo? We're traveling separately from here on out."

"No!!"

I finished checking out the village and went back to see everyone. I told Filo that she stood out too much, so we were going to have to split up. Filo would pull the carriage and draw everyone's attention while the rest of us snuck away. Then Filo could ditch the carriage and catch up with us at her natural speed. She wouldn't have a carriage or any luggage, so she'd be able to run pretty fast.

I explained my plan to her, but all she did was complain.

"There's no other way. You stand out too much."

All I meant was that she was a pretty rare kind of monster. She was known around the country as the bird-god, so she was practically a target.

"I just have to look different when people are around, right? I can do that!"

"How are you . . ."

But before I could finish speaking Filo started to glow and she began to transform.

Why did she bother? She was just going to have some stupid idea, like pulling the carriage in her human form. That's what I was thinking anyway, but her neck and legs started stretching.

"Gweh!"

She looked something like a large ostrich—or actually, she just looked like an ordinary Filolial.

Though she was still larger than a normal Filolial.

"So you can turn into one of them?"

"Gweh!"

She gave a heavy nod.

"Why are you clucking like a bird?"

"Gweh!"

"I guess she can't talk when she's in that form."

Hm . . . I guess that meant she didn't like being stuck in a normal Filolial body.

"Wow, Filo! That's amazing!"

The princess was very excited, and she and Filo were practically jumping up and down.

"Gweh."

You know, if she was spitting poison, maybe it meant that I wouldn't have to listen to her shrill cries anymore.

"Stay like that from now on. Then we can enjoy the quiet."

"Gweh!"

Slam! She raised a foot and wrapped her claws around my head. Filo and Raphtalia basically never broke any of my rules, so I'd forgotten all about them, but attacking me was definitely breaking a rule. Before I could even move or think, the monster control spell on her began to activate.

"Gweh?!"

"Filo?!"

"Oh, come on, what is it now?"

"Don't be mean to Filo!"

"I'm not. She attacked me, so the monster spell activated. That's it."

In a way, it was much cuter than having to listen to her whine as a human. I don't know what Filo wanted, but I would have to say I preferred her new form. The reason pets help people relax is because they don't talk. If that pet turned into a person and never shut up, well—I don't think many people would keep pets.

"But it's hurting her!"

"You reap what you sow."

"Uh . . ."

The princess had taken a weird interest in Filo. Was it really just because they could talk as friends?

"Anyway, stay in that form at least for a little while. At least until we can be sure we are safe."

I'd been able to keep her hidden up until now, pretending

to be a saint and all that. I'm sure it would work itself out.

"Raphtalia, as for you, maybe you could mess up your clothes and, I don't know . . . rip your hat or something?"

And so we all hid in the carriage that Filo pulled. Raphtalia changed her clothes, Filo changed her body, and Mel and I stayed hidden.

The carriage rattled down the road, and our straw-laden carriage began its journey to the northeast.

Chapter Seventeen: The Princess's True Strength

A few days had passed. We spent the days traveling, having Filo in her Filolial form pull the carriage, and we did the best we could to avoid towns and villages on our way to the northeast. We usually slept in the fields or forests. Finally, we were nearing the border.

"Gweh!"

Filo's cry came shrill and sharp.

Was it an enemy?! Mel and I peeked out from the bundles of straw to get a look.

"Heh, heh, heh . . . Leave your valuables and be on your way."

I'd heard that voice before. Sure enough, it was the same group of bandits that attacked us back when we'd traveled with the accessory merchant.

"Can't you hear? I said LEAVE YOUR VALUABLES! Wait now. What's this? She's kind of pretty . . ."

They were looking at Raphtalia in her new, dirty clothes. But once they got closer to see her, their faces went white.

"You guys never learn, do you?"

There was no point in hiding anymore. I jumped out of the carriage.

Filo, sensing it was okay for her to show her true form, morphed back into the Filolial Queen.

"Are you going to fight?"

The young princess looked very worried.

"We'll be fine."

"What? What's wrong with you guys?"

About two-thirds of the bandit group hadn't been there the last time we met up. They were looking around at their pale friends and wondering what all the fuss was about.

"Uh . . . uh . . . uh . . . This guy has a bounty . . . on his head. If we kill him . . . we'll . . . be heroes."

The man at the front of the group was trembling and muttering in falsetto.

He looked very shaken, very uncertain.

"Back on your feet already? Considering you lost all your equipment, you've really made a quick comeback."

After hearing what I had to say, the curious members of the group started checking their footing and getting ready for battle.

"You . . . You just shut up! This is all your fault! We're working for someone else now, and we're at the bottom of the barrel!"

"What a shame. Your little group was absorbed into a big, bad bandit group?"

"Our boss went back to the countryside!"

"Good for him. He managed to wash his hands of your dirty profession."

"Shut up! We'll take care of you!"

Everyone readied their weapons and ran at us.

"Filo! Raphtalia!"

"Yes!"

"Okaaay!"

I fell back to protect the princess.

Neither Filo nor Raphtalia was weak enough to be actually threatened by a group of mere bandits.

"Take that!"

A bandit brandished his sword at Filo.

"Filo!"

The princess jumped from the carriage, threw her hands out before her, and began chanting.

What? Could she fight?

"I am the source of all power. Hear my words and heed them! Shoot a ball of water at them!"

"All Zweite Aqua Shot!"

A large ball of water materialized before her and then split into a number of balls before flying into the enemy. They were all knocked back.

Zweite . . . I think that meant it was a medium-level spell, and the "all" must mean it was plural.

"Ugh!"

"Uwa!"

"Huff . . ."

All the enemies that were preparing to attack fell to the ground. The attack must have been very strong.

"I am the source of all power. Hear my words and head them! Attack them with a blade of water!"

"Zweite Aqua Slash!"

The princess immediately cast another spell. A ball of water appeared, then elongated into a sharp blade that flew through the air and sliced through the group of men with a satisfying swish. The men didn't fall, but a tree behind them split in two and fell with a loud crash.

"I'll make sure it hits you next time."

She was breathing hard. It must be difficult to cast magic in succession like that.

"They . . . They have a witch with them! And she's powerful!"

"Filo!"

"Okaaaay!"

The bandits were momentarily stunned by Mel's display, and Filo took the opportunity to rush over and kick them.

"I'm done over here."

"Not yet!"

I turned to see a pale-faced bandit had snuck behind us in the confusion. He'd climbed onto the roof of our carriage and was about to leap down onto the princess.

"Air Strike Shield!"

"Ugh!"

He jumped, but the shield appeared below him in mid-air, and he fell right into it.

"One more!"

The last bandit standing, probably the weakest among them, ran for the princess.

"Second Shield! Change Shield!"

I called for another shield to appear, used them to stop the running bandit, and then used Change Shield to turn them into Bee Needle Shields. They had a poison effect, which wouldn't kill the bandit but would paralyze him.

"Ugh . . . Uh . . ."

He fell to the ground, twitching.

"They're still coming."

Bandits were crawling toward the princess for a surprise attack.

"Nope, we're done here."

"Ah . . ."

Filo's large shadow fell over the bandits. They must have noticed too. They started crying.

In their hearts, they were probably thinking of their last words or waving white flags.

"I'll save you, Mel!"

Filo plopped down heavily on the bandits.

"The sun is starting to go down. Perfect timing, guys. Tell us where your hideout is."

We tied them all up for questioning.

"If we talk, then we'll . . ."

"Filo."

"Over here!"

"Hey! What are you doing?! Don't tell them!"

Apparently there were still bandits that didn't understand the situation they were in.

One of the bandits among them, one who we'd run into last time, started furiously trying to explain the situation.

"If you don't tell them what they want to know, they'll feed you to the bird!"

"You're . . . You're not serious!"

"You think he looks like he's joking?"

One of them jerked his head in my direction and asked, "What's with that one over there? What was with that magic?"

"You don't know!? That's the Shield!"

"What?!"

Once they all understood who I was, the whole lot of them turned pale.

"The one with the human-eating demon bird?!"

"Yes! That thing eats you—starting with the head. If it goes after you, you're as good as dead!"

"Think of your lives! Just give him what he wants!"

I guess the rumors were building on each other now.

Raphtalia, flabbergasted, put her hands against her forehead and sighed.

"If you lie . . ."

"I know! Please, just let us live!"

They led us to their hideout. Obviously, we took it over.

We stayed the night in their hideout and entertained ourselves with all their stolen valuables.

Most of it was food. Since we'd been on the road and sleeping in the wild, our meals had consisted of monster meat—and I was getting tired of it.

When we first entered the hideout, the princess had looked pretty scared. But she warmed up soon enough. We found their gold and valuables, which was mostly money. We took that, rounded up the rest of their stuff, and burned it.

If we had done a less-than-thorough job of disposing of their equipment, they would just take it all back and come after us. The very thought annoyed me, though to be honest, I sort of enjoyed the look of disappointment on the bandits' faces.

"Hey, Princess. I didn't know you could use magic."

"I can. I learned it to protect myself."

"How good are you?"

If Mel was able to fend for herself in battle, it would probably be a good idea to go ahead and add her to the party.

"And what level are you?"

"I'm at level . . . 18. As for magic, I can use pretty much all the mid-level water magic."

Well that was lower than I had expected. She was a princess, after all. I'd hoped for a higher level.

But she could use mid-level magic.

"And you're good with water magic?"

"Yes."

Probably because her hair was blue—that must have something to do with it.

"And I can use a little earth magic too."

"Really?"

She had a pretty wide repertoire.

"That reminds me—your sister could use wind magic, couldn't she?"

I didn't want to remember it. But I couldn't forget how she'd attacked me from behind during my duel with Motoyasu.

Ugh, just thinking about it put me on edge. Better think about something else.

"My sister? She's good with fire magic, but she knows a little wind magic too."

I guess that made sense. She had red hair after all.

"Mother is good at both fire and water magic."

"Huh . . . Interesting. Anyway, I'm going to invite you to join the party. Accept it."

"Okay."

I wasn't planning on depending on her in battle or anything. But she would be good insurance to have around. If she was capable of fighting, there was no reason NOT to add her to the party. Even still, I didn't want to use her in battle if I didn't have to.

"Um? I was wondering what you did to make Father so angry?"

"I guess we never talked about it. It all started when your sister framed me for a crime . . ."

Over the course of the evening, I explained all the things that Trash and Bitch had done to me.

For some reason Filo sat next to me when I talked and followed the whole story as if I was putting on a play. I didn't mention any of the mistakes we had made.

I didn't lie about anything either. I just told her exactly what had happened.

I suppose a little of my hatred and irritation found its way into my telling, but I was fine with that. I considered it part of her education.

"Father and sister are terrible! How could they complain about you after treating you that way?!"

"Right? I feel the same way."

"Mother always told me to be as nice to you as I could."

"Huh?"

What was she talking about? Wasn't the Shield Hero considered a demon by the church? The queen wasn't part of the religion?

"What's wrong, Mr. Shield Hero?"

"Nothing. I was just wondering what your mother thinks of me."

"Hmm . . . I don't really know. But she did send a letter to Father, asking him to treat the Shield Hero the same way he treats the other heroes."

I honestly didn't know what to make of what she was saying, but it seemed like it was safe to assume that the queen was looking out for me in some way. Regardless, she didn't actually end up protecting me at all, so in my eyes she was just as bad as Trash.

"Master . . . A bunch of stuff happened before I was born, huh?"

"Yeah."

"Huh?"

The young princess suddenly looked very put out.

"Um . . . Filo? How old are you?"

"A month and three weeks!"

"What?!"

It was only natural that she'd be surprised. Monsters grew up fast.

"You've grown so quickly!"

"Oh, he, he . . . Stop flattering me."

"I don't think that's flattery."

"Then I guess I'm the big sister here."

"If you're talking about age, then yes. You and Raphtalia are actually about the same age."

"Raphtalia is . . ."

Filo looked over at Raphtalia, a slight look of disappointment on her face. Raphtalia just looked confused. Filo could be really abrupt. It was only natural to be confused.

"Wh . . . What?"

"She's a demi-human. So even though we're the same age, she looks older."

Melty looked at Raphtalia as she spoke. Something about it all made me feel sympathy for Raphtalia.

"I don't know . . . I feel like I've lost something . . . I don't know why."

"Well just because we all know how old everyone is, people are going to think I am some kind of pervert."

They'd say I had a Lolita complex. Both Filo and the princess were little kids. With Raphtalia being a kid herself, it meant I was surrounded by young girls.

"Well, it is what it is. You're fine the way you are, Raphtalia."

"Mr. Naofumi . . ."

With three little girls around me, people would say I had a Lolita harem going. I could only imagine what the other heroes would say.

"Anyway, let's rest here for the night. We're crossing the border soon."

"Okay."

"Yay!"

"Whoa . . ."

I looked at the checkpoints lining the border crossing and muttered in amazement.

What was so amazing was there were lines of knights so long it would be impossible to count them.

There were so many it looked like the whole army was there. Could they afford to all be here? What if another country attacked?

No, it couldn't be the entirety of the army—but it sure looked like it could be.

"The Shield Demon is, without a doubt, aiming to cross the border into Siltvelt! Do not let him over this border!"

"Yes, sir!"

They looked . . . rowdy.

The border was so heavily watched it didn't look like an ant could get over it without being noticed. Had I been alone, I could have just run through the ranks, but with Raphtalia and the princess in tow, that would be tough.

I could have run through by myself and they could follow later—but if the other heroes were there, then they'd be spotted.

Not to mention that with so many knights in one spot, I wasn't sure that I'd even be able to outrun them all.

Besides, how did they know that I was heading for Siltvelt?

Granted, they might just want to stop me from entering Siltvelt because their relationship with that country wasn't the best. Even still, they were more prepared to stop me than I would have anticipated.

"What do you think? Could we avoid the checkpoint and cross somewhere else? Somewhere off-road?"

"I don't think so."

The young princess whispered.

"Why not?"

"It looks like they have emergency checks set up. If you cross the border, an alarm will sound, and they will chase you down."

"Damn . . ."

I pictured some kind of infrared beam. They had something like that over the border. With so many guards, they would eventually hunt down anything that illegally crossed the line. It would only be a matter of time.

"You don't think Filo could outrun them?"

"They'd cut you off. The alarm would alert them before you even made it to the other side."

"Hm . . . You sure know a lot about the border."

"Mother said I should memorize these things in case of an

emergency. The system is expensive to maintain, but everyone agreed to keep it for emergencies."

"Excellent foresight."

I could have killed someone. These people would stop at nothing to get in my way.

"Then I guess our only option is to go to a different country that neighbors Siltvelt, then enter from that shared border."

This was the closest country by far, but we didn't seem to have any other option.

Just then some villagers passed by with a loaded cart, and we accidentally bumped into them.

We were in disguise, so we should have been fine. The princess and I were hiding in the straw too.

"Um . . ."

For some reason, a mysterious silence fell between the villagers and Raphtalia.

"Shield Hero."

They found us?! Could we get away?!

"Do not be concerned. You are okay. You once gave us a plant seed, and because of it, prosperity has returned to our country. Thank you very much. We will not do anything to indicate your location to the soldiers."

I looked closer. Sure enough, they weren't villagers but people from the neighboring country. And they were apparently traveling merchants. They passed me some old clothes.

"The people with you could stand to look a little dirtier, especially that pretty raccoon-type demi-human girl. She'll give you away."

I couldn't deny that. Among raccoon demi-humans, Raphtalia was exceptionally pretty. She'd met all the villagers while we were traveling merchants too, so she might have developed a reputation for herself.

Back when I first bought Raphtalia, the slave trader had said that raccoon-types were not popular with humans. But Raphtalia was exceptionally pretty, so she was sure to be noticed. And if any one of them had seen her before, they'd probably recognize her instantly.

I couldn't leave Raphtalia behind though, so we'd have to find a disguise for her.

"If you plan to run from them, that carriage will stand out too much. You can use our cart. Move your stuff into it."

"Thank you. And you're right. This big metal thing does stand out. We probably need to get rid of it."

"Gweh?!"

Filo was in her Filolial form, but she shook her head and grunted in protest.

"Gweh! Gweh!"

"We don't have a choice! Do you want us to be caught? Want to go to jail? They'll kill the princess, you know?!"

"Gweh . . ."

Once Filo realized that Mel would be in danger, she reluctantly stopped protesting.

She'd really loved that carriage, but I guess she valued her friend more.

"Good girl, Filo. You had to pick between an object and a person, and you chose to value the person."

I rubbed her head. Even if she didn't understand the reasons why, she was making the right choice.

"Gweh?"

"Once we're done, we'll come back for the carriage."

"Gweh!"

She knew I was promising.

"Please accept out cart."

"We will. Thank you."

"It's all right. We will leave it with a nearby village."

"We'll make it up to you."

"You already have."

"Oh yeah. Okay, Princess. It's time for you to change. If you don't, they will catch us for sure."

"Oh . . . All right . . ."

I gave a few silver pieces to the villagers to thank them for their help.

The only remaining problem was how to feed Filo. Since we'd been on the road, she had thrown a fit whenever she got hungry.

And the worst thing that could happen now would be if she slowed down. At the moment, our only strengths were our disguises and Filo's speed. After all, there were more dangerous things that we could run into than bounty hunters or adventurers.

The princess looked like she was not happy about having to wear dirty, old clothes, but she agreed to do it, understanding the situation.

The clothes they provided her with were very worn-in. After she changed, she looked like a messy little girl. Sure, she was still a princess, but I felt like she could pass for a villager.

But she clearly had a good diet. She looked very healthy, and when she spoke she was obviously educated—not to mention her bright blue hair suggested a royal bearing. No one would know from a distance, but if they inspected her closely . . . Whatever, leaving her behind was not an option.

We were going to need luck on our side.

"Get a bag and stuff it with things."

We collected things that we could reasonably carry and then covered them with a cloth. Anything we couldn't carry we gave to the villagers. Even if we made good progress, it would take more than two weeks.

"Um, are you a merchant? I have a little shopping list."

Dammit! A soldier was walking up to the foreign villagers to shop.

"Shield Hero?"

Dammit! He spotted us! I turned to Filo to run.

"It's me. Remember? We fought together in the wave?"

I looked him over. Sure enough, he was one of the volunteer soldiers that had fought with us.

Yeah, we parted at the wave, and I hadn't been able to follow up with them since we'd parted ways with Trash.

I was relieved, but then I realized that he was probably sent out here specifically because he had helped us.

Back then I hadn't known anything about this "Shield Demon" business. Thinking back on it with what I know now, it must have taken enormous stores of willpower to overcome their beliefs and help me. They must have paid for it too. Society would shun them.

"Were you demoted?"

"No, there was no punishment."

"Oh, good. So you weren't assigned to this post as a demotion?"

"Apparently not. Almost half of our knights are here."

All that, just for me?

Hey now. Wasn't that a bit of an overkill? Just how bad did Trash want to keep me out of Siltvelt?

I couldn't understand it anymore. What did he really want?

Could it be that there was something in Siltvelt, something I didn't know about yet?

I had to go. If the enemy was this upset about it, then it had to mean something good for me.

I didn't know why they were so upset, but I had to go find out.

"Anyway, it's too dangerous for you to be here. Run away."

"Thank you."

"It's not just knights; the other heroes are here too. I was afraid you might bump into them."

He was right. I had to admit that they were all considerably stronger than I was.

When we were fighting Glass, they'd fallen when I hadn't, but she'd appeared randomly and hit them with a finishing move before they had a chance to fight back. So they never got to show off their true powers.

And they had all gone through the class-up, whereas none of us had.

It would be foolish to think I could beat them in a fight. If we ran into them unprepared, I might end up dead.

"Let's get going."

"I am praying that you are cleared of these charges and suspicions."

We parted with the foreign merchants and volunteer soldier, heading to the south for a long detour.

Chapter Eighteen: Persuasion

We'd made some progress when we saw them.

Motoyasu and Itsuki were there with their parties, watching the carriages on the road. The soldier had been right.

I peeked out from my hiding place. There were wizards around. They were chanting spells.

"There he is! He's in that cart!"

I had a suspicion, a fear—and apparently I'd been right.

Motoyasu and Itsuki took off running in our direction.

Damn! How did they know?!

It must have been those wizards. I don't know what they did, but it must have been them.

I threw off the cloth I'd been hiding under and jumped out of the cart. Filo knew something was happening, and she quickly transformed into her Filolial Queen form.

"I knew it! There he is!"

He must have been nearby, because Ren was running for us too.

Dammit. It was the worst situation I could think of.

"We found you! Release Princess Melty!"

Itsuki was shoving a sanctimonious finger in my direction and calling out in a self-satisfied voice.

"I can't release her because she's not my prisoner! She's not tied up, is she?!"

"Say what you want. We have proof! Justice is not on your side."

"Justice? Ha!"

This was from the guy who left the lives of innocent villagers up to the knights during the wave? And he was telling me about justice.

These guys really only thought about fulfilling their own ideas of justice.

Wait a second. There was one option. I could try telling them about all that had happened. I remember that Ren felt bad about the village he abandoned to sickness, and there were certainly holes in Itsuki's theory of justice. Maybe I could use that.

Still, they had obviously made up their minds not to believe anything I said.

But I had to try. I had to make them understand. I needed to get them to focus their justice on something else. They needed an evil conspiracy to fight against. It was a situation that any gamer would love. I'd need them to believe me, though, or at the very least I'd need them to start doubting the Crown.

"Are you all so sure that you are right? Are you so sure that you are on the side of justice?"

"What's that supposed to mean?"

"The princess, as you can see, is perfectly unharmed."

I readied my shield and showed off the princess. An attack could come from any direction at any time.

She looked worried, but she looked up at me and nodded.

"Sword Hero, Bow Hero, Spear Hero—The Shield Hero is innocent. He actually saved my life."

She wasn't speaking like a child anymore. She spoke with a regal tone.

They listened to her, and I could see a shadow of doubt creep over their faces.

Could there be a shred of evil on their side of things? If there were, their inflated egos and sense of justice certainly wouldn't be able to tolerate that.

"Please believe me. There is a great conspiracy behind all of this."

"But, Princess Melty, isn't that man taking you all around the country in secret?"

"Yes, but he is doing it to save my life. I asked him to do so."

Mel explained the situation, and Itsuki flinched, confused.

"Does it not seem odd? What would the Shield Hero stand to gain by my abduction?"

"Well . . . That's . . ."

Was he trying to think of an answer? He looked lost.

"But . . . But this guy . . ."

"Did you ever think that Melromarc has been treating the Shield Hero, and ONLY the Shield Hero, poorly?"

"It's true, but . . ."

"My mother told me that it was time for us all to join hands and fight back the coming disaster. This country simply does not have the time or resources to allow its heroes to dally about with such things. Please, put away your weapons."

The three heroes might have been listening. They loosened their grip on their weapons.

They were starting to come around. After all, they had lost the last battle during the wave.

And the young princess was right. We really did need to spend our time on leveling and strengthening our weapons. If they were serious about following through on the purpose of being a hero, they would realize that any time not spent on leveling or strengthening their weapons was a waste.

"Do you get it? This is a conspiracy. Now I'm going to tell you everything I know. Can you decide to fight me after you hear me out?"

Bitch stepped forward from the crowd.

"Why should we listen to the words of a demon?"

What did she want? Was she trying to get points for pretending to be concerned about her sister?

"Didn't his actions speak loud enough? He must be using the Brain Washing Shield!"

"Sister?!"

Mel was absolutely shocked. She glared at Bitch.

Really, there was only so much I could stand to listen to.

What the hell was a Brain Washing Shield? If I had something like that, none of this would have ever started to begin with. It was so easy to ignore the fruits of someone's labor if you just threw out a phrase like "brain washing!" Besides, brain washing and religion tend to go hand in hand. Ha! Brain washing, give me a break.

"The Brain Washing Shield is a shield imbued with very powerful magic. Of course your story sounded fishy."

"I don't know when you found the Shield, but the church thinks it must have been around a month ago."

That was around the time I started my peddling business. It was back when I had to prioritize making medicine for that village over my business. That was when people started calling me a holy saint of the bird-god.

I get it now. It fit, time-wise. From the church's perspective it was a perfect explanation—a perfect lie.

"I feel like the situation explains itself perfectly. You've traveled a long way and gotten all mixed up. And here you are, practically working with Naofumi! Every normal citizen knows that he is a criminal, and yet here you are, helping him? Why would you do that?"

"Everyone is crazy. I'm saying that the Shield Hero

wouldn't do the things he's accused of—and I've met old ladies that practically worship him."

"That old lady . . ." I had a pretty good idea who she was referring to.

Even still, what the hell were they talking about?

It was just a fact that I had helped and saved a lot of people. But most of what I'd done was clean up the messes that THEY had left.

Did they really think that anything they didn't know meant some kind of enemy strategy? Seriously, what was in their heads?

"It very well may be that simply standing near him and talking to him will allow him to brainwash you. At this very moment the church members among us are pooling their resources to break his spell over you."

"You freaking idiot! Who has that kind of power?!"

No one responded to my outburst.

Actually Raphtalia, then Filo and Mel, were stunned.

What they meant was that they had traveled around looking for me, and instead of listening to what people said and actually processing the good things people had to say, they just invented this idea of the Brain Washing Shield, and Bitch used that to convince the other heroes.

It was an amazing lie. She really outdid herself.

"Does the Shield Hero really have that kind of power?"

The young princess looked up at me, worried.

"Does it look like I do?"

"Um . . . no."

"You didn't have to hesitate."

If I had a shield with powers like that, my life would be a lot easier. If I had a shield like that, I could have brainwashed soldiers, knights, and wizards. I could have taken over the whole kingdom. Basically, if I had that kind of power, I wouldn't be in this position.

In other words, the very fact that people were chasing after me was a good reason to doubt the efficacy of any supposed Brain Washing Shield.

Couldn't the stupid heroes understand something so simple?

"So that means that Raphtalia and Filo are brainwashed by him!"

"That's not true! We are not brainwashed!"

"Don't worry. We're going to save you two."

"I'm with Master because I want to be!"

Motoyasu still hadn't given up on chasing after Raphtalia and Filo?! How obsessed can a guy be?

"Okay, enough of your stupid theories. Listen up. Depending on your reaction, I'll give you the princess."

"What?!"

The young princess let out a surprised yelp.

"We're listening."

Ren took the initiative. I had to answer quickly and concisely. I couldn't afford to misspeak.

"Okay, first of all there is no such thing as brainwashing. Next . . ."

"I don't believe you!"

"Shut up! I'm not talking to YOU, General Commander."

Before I could finish speaking, Itsuki butt in and I had to shut him up.

I didn't have any use for the sort of hypocrite that would decide the veracity of a claim only one sentence in.

"Anyway . . . This is a conspiracy. Whether it was the king, that woman, or the church—I don't know. But someone wanted this princess dead, and they wanted to pin it on me."

"Understood. Now then, we will tie you up and you will come with us. In exchange for your acceptance, we promise that no harm will come to you. We need time to investigate your claims."

"You would believe him?! This evil cretin?! He brainwashed Filo!"

"Yeah! I don't believe him!"

"Sword Hero! You must not listen to what the demon says!"

Ren was just on the verge of listening and believing me when Bitch and the others jumped in.

"If we can end this without a fight, it's worth it, no? We can investigate his claims later."

Ren was acting as cool as you'd expect—but at least he was trying to calmly assess the situation.

Was it safe to assume he understood?

"No."

The princess reached up and squeezed my hand. She was shaking, and her face was pale.

"I think . . . I think they will kill us."

She might be right. I took a second to think it through. There was a good chance that she would be treated differently than the rest of us.

To keep their theory looking plausible, they'd probably hand the princess to some wizards so that they could cast spells to clear her of the brainwashing. But then what would happen? They would probably have to pretend that, just when they cleared her from my influence, a powerful curse activated and killed her—but of course they would just assassinate her in secret.

It seemed like a likely scenario.

If that was the plan, then Ren, who appeared to believe what I said, was absolutely lying. He must have truly believed I was a criminal.

If the plan was to try and pin another crime on me, then it followed that Bitch most definitely had a hand in it. But to think that she would act against her own sister . . .

"Help . . ."

Her plea was nearly silent. Her voice was hoarse. And to think, I was so close to gaining their sympathies.

Oh well . . .

"You promised, remember?"

"What?"

Back then. Back on the day they framed me for rape. Back when there wasn't a single person that believed in me.

And now, the young princess was standing on the verge of life and death.

Brainwashing. They'd use a simple, convenient word to tie it all up. Then they'd have her killed.

Seriously, the plan was so transparent. Even I could see through it.

If the princess died, that would be the end of us. Who would stand up for me—no one even believed me.

"Sorry, I just can't believe you. If I gave you the princess, I don't think you'd be able to protect her. And that's what I promised her: protection."

I put Mel onto Filo's back and then called to Raphtalia to climb on too.

"Filo, I know you don't want to hear this, but we're abandoning the cart. Let's leave these guys in the dust!"

"Okaaaay!"

"Later."

Filo was ready and waiting. The second she realized that we were all on her back, she took off running.

"Wait!"

"Haikuikku!"

"We won't let you!"

"Wh . . ."

Motoyasu produced a hoop of some kind and tossed it at Filo's legs.

It spun around her, tripping her up. We crashed into the ground.

"Ugh!"

"Ahhh!"

Raphtalia, Mel, and I were all launched forward with Filo's momentum.

"Ouch . . ."

There were already two soldiers flying at us. I jumped to my feet just in time to block their attack.

Motoyasu had been expecting Filo's "Haikuikku," and he interfered just before she could finish it. I really couldn't stand him.

"Ugh . . . Hrm . . . I can't get it off, Master! I can't get it off!"

Filo was feverishly tugging at the hoop her legs were entangled in, but it showed no signs of loosening its grip on her.

The hoop itself looked like it was made from black iron, but it must have had some kind of special effect. If it had been normal iron, Filo should have been more than powerful enough to remove it.

"You're not getting away, so don't bother. Now then, give us the princess."

"Why would I?!"

It was as clear as day. The smiling Bitch standing next to him was behind all of this.

If they killed the princess, I'd never be able to prove my innocence!

"Filo!"

"Y . . . Yes! Ah . . ."

Filo struggled to her feet, but then all her strength gave out and she fell to the ground again, her legs just as entangled as before.

"I don't . . . I can't . . . I can't get up! I have no energy!"

Filo started glowing and turned into her human form.

"What are you doing?!"

"I'm not doing it! I transformed automatically!"

What? How could that be? The only idea I had involved Motoyasu's hoop . . .

"Check it out. I had an alchemist make it. It will make it so that Filo will be a little angel forever. As long as she's in that hoop, I don't think she'll be able to attack me anymore."

"Ugh! Let me go!"

Motoyasu walked over to Filo, where she was struggling to stand. He pulled her to her feet and showed her to us.

"That alchemist did a good job. He was even able to seal away her magical powers."

Damn, I'd thought that Filo could get us out of there with her speed. That wasn't looking likely anymore.

How was I supposed to know that they had the power to transform Filo and then suppress all her power?

And what was with that stupid hoop?! Did he really want Filo that badly? But yeah, I guess he was going on and on about "little angels" back in town. He must have had that hoop made specifically so that he could catch Filo. And to think he'd get a chance to use it so quickly and in a situation like this? What the hell was going on?

Regardless, Filo's legs were out of commission, so we weren't going to be escaping on them.

"Filo!"

"Mel!"

The two girls were yelling and reaching for each other. But their fingers were not able to touch.

"I kind of like rambunctious little princesses. Don't worry. If you come with us, you can be with Filo."

"Ugh!"

He really thought he was on top of things, didn't he? What an idiot! Why didn't he understand that he was basically sentencing both of them to death?

"Hey . . ."

"Um . . ."

"What are you doing? Sword and Bow Heroes! Hurry and arrest the Shield Hero!"

"But . . ."

Ren and Itsuki hadn't responded to what was happening yet. They were frozen in place. If they jumped in and attacked now, it would all be over.

The whole lot of them were obsessed with their own ideas of justice. They'd just seen us try to flee, only to be stopped by Motoyasu. On top of that, Motoyasu had taken a hostage to control our actions. That wasn't the sort of situation they would throw themselves into. But what would they do? I couldn't begin to venture a guess.

What should we do? They had Filo, so I couldn't try running.

Bitch was standing just behind Motoyasu. Who knew what she was capable of?

"Wait! I'm going to save you, Filo!"

"You idiot!"

"I am the source of all power. Hear my words and heed them! Slice the enemy with a blade of water!"

"Zweite Aqua Shot!"

Mel ran straight for Motoyasu and cast the spell as she ran.

"Ha!"

Motoyasu jumped to the side just in time to dodge the blade of water.

"Ugh! Let me go!"

When Motoyasu jumped to dodge Mel's attack, Filo managed to wiggle free from his grip.

Yes! I was thrilled when Filo wiggled free, but just then, as if to make up for his loss, Motoyasu's hand shot out and closed around Mel's neck, taking her hostage instead. He passed her over to Bitch.

"Myne! That's your precious sister. You better protect her!"

"Mel!"

"Filo! Let me go! Sister!"

Filo reached for Mel, but before she could reach her, Motoyasu made to grab Filo's hand again. I pulled Filo back just in time.

"I can't let you go, Melty. The Shield Demon is manipulating you. I'll clear you of that brainwashing influence."

Now!

"Shield Prison!"

I immediately switched to the Shield of Rage II and used the skill on Motoyasu.

"Wh . . ."

Not yet . . . I had to control my anger . . .

"Change Shield (attack)!"

I changed the Shield Prison into my best attacking shield, the Bee Needle Shield.

"That's as far as this is going! Take this! Iron Maiden!"

I used all my SP in a last attempt to turn the tide and take Motoyasu down. Honestly, I would have preferred to use it against Bitch, but I couldn't. If I could stop Motoyasu with the skill, it would be worth it. It might be strong enough.

"It won't be that easy! Shooting Star Sword!"

"I knew you were evil! Shooting Star Bow!"

Whoa! Ren and Itsuki both turned and used their strongest skills against the Iron Maiden.

There was a loud crack, and a fissure appeared in the Iron Maiden. The closing door slowed down.

"Everyone! Now! Break it now!"

"Yes! Ren!"

"Understood, Itsuki!"

"Motoyasu, we'll save you!"

Ren, Itsuki, and Motoyasu's party members all sent their strongest attacks and spells flying at the Iron Maiden. There was a loud, dull clang. And then the Iron Maiden crumbled to dust.

Damn. I was out of SP from my last attack.

"Th . . . Thank you, everyone!"

Motoyasu had taken some damage from the Bee Needle Shield attack, but he smiled now, discovering himself free from the Iron Maiden.

"Can't have you forgetting about us."

"Yes. We've saved the princess. The citizens of our country

will want her brainwashing removed as soon as possible."

Ren and Itsuki had jumped to Motoyasu's aid. On top of that, Bitch had taken Mel hostage. If we didn't free her immediately, they would have her killed.

I'd forgotten. Whenever I switched to the Shield of Rage II, Filo went crazy.

But with Filo in human form, nothing had happened.

Why? I suddenly noticed my shield emitting a red . . . something. It flew at Filo but bounced off of her. I wonder if that hoop was somehow deflecting any assist spells or stat boosts.

Her movement was probably restricted by protective magic, which had the side effect of blocking my spell.

If Filo went wild, we wouldn't be able to control her, and that would make fighting with the Shield of Rage II difficult.

"Raphtalia! Can you get rid of that hoop around Filo?"

If we were able to get it off, I planned to switch to another shield as soon as possible.

"I'm working on it now! It's tough!"

Raphtalia was striking the hoop with her sword, it clanged and it filled the area with sparks. She didn't seem to be making much progress.

How strong did they really need to make that hoop? She was hitting it really hard.

What to do? I was out of SP, so I couldn't use any skills. Filo was stuck in human form.

All that was left was Raphtalia, but with her sword and magic alone, she wouldn't be able to turn the tide of battle.

"Master!"

"What?!"

"They won't catch me again!"

"That's easy to say—they already caught you once!"

"I'm fine!"

Filo reached under one of her little wings and pulled out the present that the weapon shop owner had intended for me: the power gloves.

That's right; they were convenient tools for harnessing superhuman strength.

Filo pulled both of the gloves onto her hands and then crossed her arms. I could tell that she was concentrating.

"It's MY turn to save YOU, Mel!"

"What are those gloves? You think you can overpower me with gloves? Oh, Filo, you're so cute! Better just put them away."

"I'm not losing!"

"Ah, Filo!"

I threw out an arm to stop her, but she had already swung a solid punch at Motoyasu.

"Ugh . . ."

Motoyasu had his arms out, reaching to grab Filo again, but that left his stomach wide open, and she slammed her fist into it.

He doubled over and fell to his knees.

"This . . . This isn't . . . nothing."

"Hiya! Let Mel go! Hiya!"

"I . . . I won't . . ."

He stumbled to his feet and backed away.

"Filo! Calm down and get back here!"

"Okay!"

Filo came back over to us after she pummeled Motoyasu.

"Do you think you can take those guys out?"

"Watch me!"

"Great. You take Motoyasu. Raphtalia and I will take care of the other two. If anyone has a chance to free the princess—take it."

At the end of the day, Motoyasu was a feminist—so he wouldn't raise a hand against Filo, even if she was crazy.

"Mr. Naofumi."

"What is it?"

"I have an idea. Do you think you can draw the attention of the enemy?"

"You have a plan?"

"Yes . . ."

Hm . . . So Raphtalia wanted to try something, but what?

Got it. She wanted to hide and then sneak around behind them. She was good at that.

That must be what she was after.

"Okay. I'll do what I can. Let's go!"

"Let's do it."

"Okaaay!"

"Here we go!"

Even still, there was no way we could win against the three heroes. But that wasn't my plan anyway. There was still a way for us to escape.

"Raphtalia, keep your distance."

"Okay."

"Let's go!"

"HIYAAAAAAAAAAA!"

Filo led the charge. Just like I'd told her, she ran straight for Motoyasu. But this time he knew she was coming, and he readied his spear. I was sure he wouldn't stab her with it.

"Now then, Melty, I'm going to ask you to take a little nap."

Bitch pulled out a small package of medicine and made the younger princess smell it.

Anyone from another world who had experience with Japanese anime or dramas would recognize it as a medicine that knocks you out.

But I had been here for a while. I knew what Bitch was like, so that medicine was more likely to just kill Mel.

"Filo! Help!"

"Mel!"

I could feel, physically feel, Filo gathering her magical power into the gloves.

"Haikuikku!"

She looked like she blurred for a second, and then, in a flash, she was right in front of Motoyasu, and she was swinging her fist. The gloves looked different. She'd filled them with so much magic that they were glowing pale and had magical claws growing from them.

How did that happen? Did the magic somehow crystalize and harden?

"Ugh! What was that?! Her attack is so high! Stop it! Filo, stop it!"

Motoyasu was forced to defend. The claws on the power gloves were hitting their mark each time she swung a fist.

If she could beat Motoyasu back like that, her attack power must have been through the roof.

"Hiya! Take that! Hiya!"

Filo was strongest in her Filolial Queen form, but with the way she was fighting now, in those gloves, she must have had nearly the same attack power or more.

Because she had someone to fight for, she would fight with all her magical power. Her legs were constrained by the hoop, but she could still harness her magic.

I was concentrating on Ren and Itsuki but stealing glances at Motoyasu.

Even though I was their target, they knew their attacks wouldn't be really effective against me, and it looked like they weren't making much of an effort.

Ren, actually, had his head cocked to the side as he considered the situation. He was just watching.

Itsuki was convinced that I was his enemy, but he wasn't rushing over to attack me. I thought for sure he would fire some volleys to protect Motoyasu—but thinking over it now, both of them had a strong sense of justice.

They won't want to intrude on one-on-one combat. That wouldn't feel just to them.

They must have decided to jump in and stop my Iron Maiden because of the risk that it might have killed Motoyasu or something like that.

There must have been a way to use the situation to our advantage.

I had to keep them focused on me, not Raphtalia. I made sure not to look in her direction and slowly backed away to keep them following me.

The time for escape was still a ways off.

But if I could get them to focus on me . . .

"I figured out how to use these!"

Filo held the claws out and crossed them.

"Torna . . ."

"Sorry! You left me no choice, Filo. This will hurt a little."

Motoyasu readied his spear, pointed it at Filo, and prepared to use a skill.

"Chaos Spear!"

"Ugh!"

Filo kept her claws out and flew at the enemy. When she had almost reached him, she started to spin and ran right into him.

"Wh . . ."

Filo had spun right through his rain of spears, connected with her claws, and sent him flying. Now she was heading for Bitch.

"Yaaaaaaahh!"

Bitch was desperately trying to make Mel sniff the medicine before Filo could get to them. But she was too slow. As Filo approached, she let go of Mel in an effort to protect herself.

"Mel!"

Filo stopped spinning and scooped up Mel's hand in one motion, and then the two of them took off running.

"Ugh . . ."

Motoyasu had fallen heavily to the ground. Now he struggled to his feet and looked over at Filo and Mel.

"Back away, Mel. I'm going to take out this spear guy. Then you and me are running."

"Okay."

Filo turned back to Motoyasu and readied her claws.

This was the start of a new fight. Where it had been a one-on-one between Filo and Motoyasu, now Bitch helped Motoyasu and Mel helped Filo.

The rest of us were watching, and suddenly the fight was on.

"You can do it, Filo! All Zweite Aqua Shot!"

"We don't need a baby who thinks she is better than her older sister! Zweite Hellfire!"

Bitch and Mel were flinging spells at each other.

Stupid Bitch. What was she talking about? She was last in line for the throne but messing with her sister?

Fine then, if this was a fight for succession, I knew who I was backing. That Bitch wasn't fit to sit on a throne.

"Zweite Earth Hammer!"

"Zweite Fire Arrow!"

But the other party members of the heroes were worse than we could have expected. Instead of aiming their attacks at Filo, they were heading for Mel.

"What are you doing?!"

Ren jumped in and beat back the magic that was flying at Mel.

"Are you trying to kill the princess we've been charged to protect?! Even if she is brainwashed, we still need to protect her! Think about her level!"

That's right. The younger princess was whom Ren, Itsuki, and Motoyasu were supposed to protect.

Bitch might have wanted to murder her little sister, but the heroes wouldn't want that to happen.

This was our chance. I could win them over to our side.

"But the princess has already been brainwashed by the Shield Hero. She won't be able to control herself."

"Even still, if you don't hold back, you'll kill her! She's obviously not trying to attack us!"

The princess's magic was clearly a threat and nothing more, as every spell slipped right between Filo and Motoyasu. There was plenty of room for them to avoid it.

It actually looked like Bitch and her friends were using their magic directly against the princess—like they were trying to kill her. It was so obvious that even Ren had seen through it.

"You know that her level isn't very high! If you hit her with that magic, she will die!"

I feel like Bitch was probably well aware of Mel's level. Didn't they understand that she was TRYING to kill her?

"That . . . That's true . . ."

Bitch turned away in frustration. She sighed, then nodded.

"Ren, Itsuki. She wants the princess dead. Can't you see that?"

"What?!"

"Myne is second in line for the throne. The younger princess is the current heiress. I'm sure you can figure the rest out."

"Don't listen to his lies! Bow Hero! Sword Hero!"

"What are you rushing for? You know it's true. Just ask your party members."

Ren and Itsuki were visibly shaken. Bitch was acting so crazy it should have been apparent to anyone. Maybe they were swayed by my confidence. Whatever. It actually was TRUE—if they looked into it, they'd figure it out soon enough.

"That's how he brainwashes people! Don't listen to him!"

What an annoying excuse.

"She's right! Die! Shield Hero!"

One of Itsuki's party members was clad in gaudy armor. He swung an axe at me.

That's just what I was waiting for!

"Hiyaaaaaa!"

"Take that! Die! Shield Demon!"

I used my shield to stop his attack.

"Now! Attack while his guard is down!"

"Okay!"

"Don't attack!"

"Yes, don't! You must be careful. They are dangerous!"

Ren and Itsuki's party members ignored their order to stop, and they all rushed us at once.

They formed a large group and came at us all at once—but they weren't used to fighting together.

This was our chance! The lot of them thought that I had no way to counter-attack—but they were wrong.

I used self curse burning, centered on myself, and burned the whole area.

"ARGH!!!!"

"Hiyaaaa!"

"Wh . . . What?!"

Itsuki was stunned to silence. He was staring at us.

Ren jumped in and bat away a magical attack that had been aimed at the princess. He tried to counter-attack, but he was too slow and ended up missing.

"Ugh . . . My body . . ."

Everyone, including the guy in the armor, had fallen to the ground. They couldn't get to their feet.

"Don't think I can't fight back. This shield has plenty of power."

"Ugh . . ."

Ren sheathed his sword and groaned. Itsuki did the same.

They turned to their party members and started casting healing magic on them. Too bad. The self curse burning had cursed them—that would make it hard to heal them.

But watching their parties suffer hadn't won me Ren or Itsuki's sympathies. Further negotiations would be difficult.

"Hand Red Sword!"

"Arrow Rain!"

Ren and Itsuki both turned and sent attacks flying at me.

When Ren called Hand Red Sword, a number of swords appeared in the sky; then they began to fall on me. At the same time, Itsuki drew the string on his bow and aimed it high into the sky. When he released the string, arrows of light began to fall all around us.

Both were ranged attacks.

"Ugh . . ."

I quickly covered my head with the shield and blocked the falling swords and arrows.

Damn. It really hurt. I could feel my nerves tense with pain.

"That must be it."

"Yeah, I think so too. That power of his wasn't in the game, but it only makes sense that it would work that way."

"Melee attack counter."

They were right. Self curse burning looked like the perfect attack, but it only activated in response to melee attacks. Once they figured that out, the Shield of Rage II was only half as useful.

Just knowing that I had an automatic counter-attack that would hurt them was enough to prevent them from attacking us. But if they had figured out how to get around it, then they could just attack me from a distance until I fell.

If they'd figured it out, then the battle had just gotten even worse.

I couldn't just keep the Shield of Rage II equipped and hope to win.

If the situation was going to continue worsening, then I would have to switch to another shield.

Which meant that they should just wait for the time to . . . No. I didn't know how long I could keep the Shield of Rage II equipped, so there was no need to follow that train of thought.

I didn't have to lay my cards out on the table—tricking them was a good strategy.

"What's wrong? You guys realize that I can handle any attacks you throw at me, right?"

"I bet you're lying."

"Yeah, if we all attack at once, I'm sure it will be effective. Not to mention all the knights gathering just down the road."

Damn! It wasn't looking like they would fall for it.

But that's not what I was really after.

"He can't counter any of my attacks! Eagle Piercing Shot!"

Itsuki fired an arrow at me, and as it flew, it changed shape to resemble an eagle.

I focused on the eagle-shaped energy shot and was able to see the arrows inside of it. It was flying straight and fast—very fast.

Based on the name of the attack, it seemed safe to assume it was a piercing attack. I'd played my share of online RPGs, so I was pretty familiar with bow attacks. Piercing meant that it would shoot straight through, leaving a hole. If his skill was an arrow that was capable of a piercing attack, it probably meant that I wasn't going to be able to stop it with my shield, which meant that if I was going to respond, I'd have to either run out of its range or find some way to snatch it out of the air before it hit me. Could I do it? It would be dangerous.

I concentrated.

I focused on the flying eagle of energy, reached out, and brushed its head. Then my fingers found its neck. I closed my fist around the neck and stopped it.

"What?! He just grabbed my Eagle Piercing Shot?!"

Itsuki shouted. He was clearly surprised by my response.

The energy eagle, surprisingly enough, wasn't very strong. I squeezed it and it crumbled.

"There, I stopped it. Ren, think about it. You know this fight isn't right."

"How so?"

"All these people are overly antagonistic toward me. And they are using an imaginary brainwashing shield to justify their actions. If the Shield Hero had a weapon like that, then you should all have one too, no?"

". . ."

Yes. I'd talk them down and then have them leave.

As for Bitch—if the heroes weren't backing her up, she'd have no choice but to retreat.

Or so I thought. Bitch quickly summoned a ball of light and sent it rocketing skyward.

"I've called for reinforcements! The country's soldiers will be here any minute!"

Damn. They were really closing in now.

"Hiya! Take that!" Boom!

"Ugh . . ."

Filo threw a flurry of punches at Motoyasu. She almost looked like she was dancing.

She was spinning in tight circles and hitting him with her spinning claws. He was completely at her mercy.

I was surprised at how well she could fight in her human form.

I had been hoping to win Ren and Itsuki over to our side, but was that even possible anymore?

I didn't have time to worry about it. The soldiers had arrived.

"Finally! Here is the Shield Hero that abducted the princess! Kill him!"

"Yes!"

The soldiers readied their bows and attacked from a distance.

"Wait! I'm not done explaining."

Before I could finish, the arrows began to rain down around us. There were magical fire arrows among them.

I was standing off on my own. I don't know if they manipulated the arrows with wind magic or something, but they were all flying straight for me.

The soldiers were not as powerful as the heroes, but they were still plenty dangerous.

"Myne! We're still talking!"

"No, Mr. Ren. You should not listen to the Shield! He'll use the Brain Washing Shield to control you!"

That Bitch, she never gave up!

She could say whatever she wanted, but she wasn't fooling me. Even now she was trying to shoot spells at Mel. It was all as clear as day.

The party members were acting strange. It was like they were being held in place by magic.

What was going on? I could feel a powerful, oppressive force nearby—something much more powerful than everyday magic.

"Take this! This will end it!"

Bitch and the soldiers around her finished chanting a spell, but she didn't send it flying at me. She attacked the princess.

"Group Magic."

A huge ball of fire appeared in the sky. If it fell on the princess, she'd die for sure!

But then . . .

"I'm sorry. I cannot allow that."

From behind, and right through Bitch's shoulder, the blade of a sword appeared.

Chapter Nineteen: The Tools

Bitch swayed, and Raphtalia stepped out from behind her. As I distracted them, she had apparently used magic.

Her timing was perfect. We were in the middle of a crisis. Did this fix it?

"Y . . . You! Do you have any idea who you just stabbed?"

Bitch was inflamed. Demon-like, she shouted at Raphtalia.

"Ms. Myne! Are you all right?!"

"Wait. Ren! Ugh!"

Ren flew over to Bitch and locked swords with Raphtalia.

I tried to run over also, but the rain of arrows and magic kept me back.

The sword was still stuck in Bitch. It must have gone in the wrong way, as Raphtalia couldn't pull it out. Once she realized it wasn't coming out, Raphtalia immediately switched to her backup sword.

"What are you doing?!"

"You are all teaming up to attack Mr. Naofumi! I have to stop you!"

"That doesn't matter!"

The clattering of the swords against one another filled the area. Ren had more experience with the sword. He parried and knocked Raphtalia back.

This wasn't good. She was practically unarmed.

Filo was still fighting with Motoyasu, and the princess was busy supporting her.

Little by little, Ren and Itsuki's party members were sneaking closer to the princess.

This wasn't good at all. Desperate, Raphtalia reached for the magic sword the weapon shop guy had given her. She pulled it from the sheath and it released with a pop. The hilt was empty—there was no blade.

"Ahaha! What do you have there? How cute!"

Bitch had been healed with magic by now. She pointed a finger at Raphtalia and laughed. But Ren and Itsuki had a very different reaction.

"The sword doesn't have a blade? Everyone, be careful!"

"Okay!"

"Wh . . . What's happening?!"

Ren's party members were confused.

"That might be a magic sword. It can form a blade from the user's magic power. It might be very dangerous."

"He's right. I don't know where she could have come across such a thing . . ."

Thinking back on it, the old guy at the weapon shop had given us a note that said something similar.

"After we read his note, I couldn't just ignore what he'd said. It had to mean something. So I did a little experimenting."

Raphtalia whispered, and she wrapped her fingers around the hilt, holding it tight. When she clamped down on the handle, a blinding light shot from it.

Bitch looked upset.

"Here I come!"

Raphtalia pointed the sword forward, then ran for Ren and Bitch.

"Damn! Shooting Star Sword!"

Ren used his best skill.

Shooting Star Sword was a skill that shot stars from the arc of his sword swing. I imagine that if it hit the target directly, it was very strong. Even still, Ren wasn't fighting with all his strength. He was fighting to stop us. He would probably hold back.

Even if he held back, if he connected with Raphtalia, it would probably do fatal damage.

What could I do?!

If I went over to help, I'd draw the soldiers' attacks toward Raphtalia.

But Raphtalia dodged the stream of stars and moved in.

"Your moves lack conviction!"

"Ugh . . ."

Ren wasn't sure where he stood in the fight, and it was affecting his attack strategy. Raphtalia dodged his sword, and her own sword flashed.

Ren looked suddenly dizzy. He held his head in his hands and stumbled toward Raphtalia. Then he fell to his knees.

"Now I understand. He gave me this sword to cut things that aren't physical. So when you cut a person with it, this is what happens."

Raphtalia seemed to understand something. She turned from the fallen Ren and ran for Bitch.

"You think a criminal like you can stand before the likes of me?!"

Bitch readied her sword and swung it at Raphtalia.

"Please be QUIET!"

Raphtalia's blade disappeared just in time to avoid clashing with Bitch's. It would not be a duel. Raphtalia pivoted, turned, and let Bitch's sword skirt by her, missing her by a hair.

The magic sword's blade reappeared and slid forward effortlessly, straight through Bitch's chest.

"AHHHHHHHHHHHH!"

Bitch screamed.

Then, as if she had fainted, she dropped her sword and fell forward against Raphtalia.

Raphtalia used her foot to flick her own sword up into her hand. Then, using Bitch as a shield, she turned toward Ren.

"Myne!"

"Myne!"

Ren and Itsuki, then Motoyasu, all shouted.

"Sword Hero? I'm sure you realize this, but she is not dead. I've simply put her to sleep for a moment."

Raphtalia held her sword against Bitch as a threat.

"Do you think you could listen to all Mr. Naofumi has to say?"

"B . . . But . . ."

"Release your hostage! If you do not, you will be in danger. You had better stay back from Naofumi!"

Itsuki screamed, but Raphtalia regarded him coldly.

"You'd say that after taking Filo hostage? He took Melty hostage too. And you'd believe all that on a flimsy story about a supposed Brain Washing Shield?"

"Um . . ."

"And besides, can't you see? Mr. Naofumi can't move right now."

With Bitch unconscious, the tables seemed to have turned. I still couldn't risk getting too close to Raphtalia though.

The reason was the relentless rain of arrows and magic falling all around me.

"Stop that right now!"

Ren shouted to the soldiers, but they didn't seem to be listening.

"Please stop! Commander, please!"

"No! You call yourself soldiers of Melromarc?! Oh, hey! You're the one that fought with the Shield Demon!"

The soldier that had called out for the Commander to stop was one of the soldiers who'd helped me during the last wave.

"Take your punishment now!"

Everything happened in slow motion.

Slowly but absolutely, a sword was slicing through the air straight at the soldier that spoke up for me.

It was just like with the younger princess.

I was lucky enough to have saved her, but this time I was too far away. I couldn't make it in time.

"Stop!"

The Commander swinging his sword at a subordinate set me off. I couldn't control my emotions anymore. I felt like I might explode.

Just then, the little tool the weapon shop owner had given me, the cover for my shield's jewel, cracked and fell.

"Whoa!"

I didn't know what was happening, but I was aware of a great volume of light expanding around me.

What was it? It was a circle of light centered on me, about three meters across. It was pretty big.

What . . .

The attacks raining down from the soldiers could not penetrate the light. They clattered off of it and broke, ricocheting.

"Whoa!"

The sparks and flying ricocheted attacks rained down on Ren and the other heroes—including their parties. Luckily, the sparks avoided anyone associated with my party. Raphtalia, Filo, the princess, and the soldiers were not harmed.

The broken shards fell on the enemies as blackened chunks. But then they began to burn. There were so many of them, scattered so randomly, that no one could get away from them.

The tool the old guy had given me must have reacted to my shield. The black flames suggested that it had instilled my shield with a counter-attack based on the Shield of Rage II. That was the only explanation I could think of anyway.

"Wh . . ."

"U . . ."

Ren and Itsuki were both suffering from the flames. The only one who could still fight was Motoyasu, and he was locked in combat with Filo.

"Hiya!"

"Everyone!"

"Damn! Naofumi! Don't you run!"

Motoyasu understood that the situation had turned against him. He stepped away from Filo.

"Everyone regroup!"

"Okay! C'mon, Mel!"

"Okay!"

What unexpected good luck. This was our chance to escape.

But Motoyasu was still up and kicking. How could we get away from him?

Filo was still stuck in human form because of that hoop. We couldn't get away on her. And it wasn't like Ren and Itsuki weren't capable of fighting anymore. The black flames had burned them, but that was just a surface wound.

"Let Myne go!"

Motoyasu threw a spear at Raphtalia, who was still using Myne as a shield.

"I don't think so."

"Mr. Naofumi."

I was in front of Motoyasu in a flash, but just before Raphtalia could swing back and maneuver behind me, she lost her grip on Bitch.

Motoyasu's gaze immediately went to Bitch.

She'd been our major advantage, and now we'd lost that.

I reached out to see if I could grab her again . . .

"Myne!"

But Motoyasu had already swept her into his arms.

Damn. She was out of our hands.

Our situation had grown steadily worse since we ran into everyone. We couldn't fight much longer.

Honestly, if we tried, we'd lose.

I was thinking it over when something rolled up against my foot.

A bomb? I immediately raised my shield to block the blast, but the bomb just emitted a stream of smoke with a soft hiss.

"Uh . . ."

"Wh . . ."

The whole area filled with smoke, and we couldn't see anything. I took a single step and couldn't tell anyone apart anymore.

With everyone in such close quarters, how were we supposed to tell friend from foe?

"This way, Zir."

"That voice! Shield Hero, follow the voice."

Mel called out to me.

"Is it okay?"

"I think so. Just in case, have Raphtalia use her illusion magic!"

"All right!"

Mel was leading me along, and I ran behind her.

"Wait! Where did you go?!"

Before we escaped, I called out to Ren.

"Ren, I'm sure you understand all this. After using all this force, can you really say that I'm the criminal here?"

". . ."

"I'm using wind magic! Anyone else who can use it—help me!"

"Wait, Itsuki."

"What is it?"

"Now we should . . ."

Itsuki was about to use wind magic to clear away the smoke. It sounded like Ren was trying to stop him.

Would we make it? I didn't know, but we all ran after the voice.

When the smoke cleared, we had put a lot of distance between us and Ren. And just in case, Raphtalia had cast magic back there. They were still looking for us.

That meant . . .

"Zir, better use this cloak too."

The mystery voice spoke and threw a cloth over me.

"Will we make it?"

"Quiet . . . Let's get moving—quietly."

Mel took Filo's hand and ran of silently. We followed after them. And so we were able to escape from the heroes. A short while later, the force field around me vanished. In the end it was clear that we had only been able to escape because of the gifts the old guy had left us.

This wouldn't be the last time though. How would we escape next time? The heroes weren't stupid. They would learn from this and come up with a new plan.

And yet it looked like Ren was starting to suspect that things weren't as they'd seemed. I had to hold out hope for that.

Anyway, it wasn't any time to dwell on things. We needed to focus on running.

Chapter Twenty: Shadow

"Zir. We've made it this far. We should be zafe for now."

I flung off the cloak and got a look at the owner of the mystery voice. And it was one of the villagers from the neighboring kingdom that we'd spoken to at the border. It was one of the people that hadn't spoken.

"You . . . ?"

I felt like it couldn't be the same person.

"Remember how we talked about the doppelgänger that had dressed as my mother?"

"Um . . . yeah . . ."

"This is that person."

"This is our first meeting, Zir. Have you recognized me because of Princess Melty's explanation? I hope so, Zir. Otherwise, I have failed as a shadow."

"I think you're saying that wrong."

"It is a command of the princess, so I have no choice, Zir."

"Let's end the inside jokes already—speak up. Why did you save us? Who are you? What do you want?"

"I am a member of Melromarc's zecret zervice. I am a 'shadow.' That is why I helped you. Also, I have no name of my own. If you must call me something, Zir, please call me Shadow."

Shadow . . . Was he trying to look cool? I remembered meeting one of them before. It was back in Riyute, when I'd raced Motoyasu.

There must have been some difference between the way I thought, having come from another world, and the way natives of this world thought.

If I started to number them all, the list would be huge—so I just put that out of mind for the time being.

"Why did you save us?"

That was what I wanted to know the most. I could think of a few reasons, but none of them stood out as most likely.

"I cannot answer that, Zir."

"How secretive."

"If I must explain, I can zay that it is my job to protect Princess Melty."

"That doesn't explain much."

If that had been the reason, he would have jumped in to help when Melty started fighting.

"I knew that the Shield Hero would protect her then—that is why I didn't appear."

"You . . ."

"That battle was looking quite dangerous near the end, but we were able to escape safely. I believe this is because the other heroes harbored doubts about their own missions."

So basically, he knew what was going on and just watched

as it all happened. He must have been very capable.

"Furthermore, I have arrived so that I might deliver news of the queen's whereabouts to the princess and to the Shield Hero."

Shadow showed us a map, and he pointed to a country in the southwest corner.

It was in the exact opposite direction of Siltvelt.

"The queen is presently in this country. It is in the opposite direction of the demi-human country where you wish to find zanctuary. It is very far, and therefore, your preparations are not enough to get you there. You will need protection."

"Well . . ."

I had started to suspect it, but now it was clear that everyone had guessed where we were going.

The only reason I could think of was that the demi-humans believed in the Shield Hero—the opposite of the church in Melromarc. Had I managed to escape and get sanctuary there, it would have been very bad for the church and Trash.

Naturally, I would have loved to piss them off by getting into the demi-human kingdom, but considering the heavy patrol of the border, that option was now essentially impossible. It would take Filo two weeks to get there, and if the other heroes cut us off and got there first, then we would never get through. Not to mention that they had even anticipated Filo and her power—they even made a special loop to keep her out of the fight.

Still, even if it required a long detour, I still wanted to go.

"The motives for your current troubles are deep-rooted. If it is possible, I'd like the other heroes to assist us."

"What's that supposed to mean?"

"The Church of the Three Heroes is clearly weakened by all that you've been doing, Zir. That is why they are going to such lengths."

"Weakened? They sure don't seem weakened to me."

"Just wait to see what happens when the public finds out about the plan to kill Princess Melty."

It was true that we'd managed to get as far as we had because many people had stepped forward to help us.

Did it mean that the populace was losing faith in the church's teachings?

"See? Father wasn't behind this."

"This shadow might be lying to us. Don't just believe whatever he says."

I had to warn her, but I was still interested in hearing whatever he could tell us.

"Let's just say that I believe you for the moment. That would explain why they are trying to force this ridiculous brainwashing story on everyone."

What could I have done to bother them? Selling medicine, helping villagers here and there. Could that really be it? Ironically, the biggest problem for them might be that I was cleaning up the messes the other heroes had left behind.

If they had a faith built on worshiping all the heroes besides the shield, then my actions actually might cause them trouble. It would shake the people's faith. If they could convince everyone that I'd pulled all this off through manipulation and brainwashing, then they could restore people's faith in their teachings. On the other hand, if I was able to prove my innocence, that would strike a fatal blow to their good reputation among the people.

"What will you do, Zir? Do you want to continue on to Siltvelt and gain zanctuary there?"

"Well . . ."

I couldn't just hand the responsibility over to somewhere else and live out my days in peace. If Siltvelt and Melromarc went to war, it wouldn't save me either—the next wave would come, and I'd just end up teleported into the midst of my enemies again. That wouldn't be good at all.

And think about it—these were the people that had put me in this position in the first place. Bitch was probably working for the church. According to the young princess, Trash wasn't though.

That meant that I probably shouldn't just run for sanctuary, ask for help, and launch a counter-attack. It would make more sense to use the people that had already proven they believed in me. If everything went well, we'd save a few days too.

And yet . . .

"Let's say I meet with the queen. What's in it for you? We might end up destroying the church."

"I cannot tell you that, Zir."

So the shadow would only give me information about the queen. He didn't plan on telling me what to do after that.

But there was no doubt in my mind that he worked for the queen.

He was connected with the princess and worked for the queen. So it was safe to assume he was acting on behalf of the queen. That meant that the queen must think that meeting me would help her somehow.

Honestly, I couldn't figure out what the queen wanted.

From what the princess had said, it seemed like her highest priority was avoiding war with the neighboring kingdoms. Furthermore, if she wanted to go out of her way to help me even though her own country had deeply-rooted beliefs against the Shield Demon, she must have taken the threat of the waves very seriously.

Shadow had said that she wanted their "assistance."

The queen's plans were not in line with the church's.

Well, one thing I felt safe to assume was that the queen was not my enemy. Whether or not she was my friend, I didn't know. But she might be our best option in this situation.

"Just once."

"What do you mean, Zir?"

"You saved us back there. So I'll believe you, just this once. We just need to meet with the queen?"

If she could put an end to this whole debacle, I'd have to trust her.

"I really don't like the idea of being led around—but it's probably our best option here. If you betray us . . ."

"I understand. Very well, I bid you farewell. After all, we don't know when the church's shadows will arrive."

"The church has them too?"

"We are not a monolithic organization. So please be careful."

"How can I do that?"

"Shield Hero, you are full of doubts—they will save you. Say you meet someone who speaks as I do. Would you just believe them?"

He was right. I'd still be suspicious if we met again.

"Now then, farewell."

He said goodbye and vanished in an instant.

He talked weird, but he seemed to be good at his job.

"Think we can trust him?"

Honestly, I didn't know.

"Yes. Mother trusts him."

"I don't know much about the queen."

The queen apparently thought very differently than Trash or Bitch—but I didn't know what she was actually thinking. Everything that Mel and Shadow had said made her look like my friend, but I still couldn't figure out her goal. The worst part was that I couldn't ignore the possibility that she was in league with the church in the plan to assassinate the princess.

If it was all part of the queen's plan to have me killed, then I was already out of options.

If we all turned back and headed away from Siltvelt, then she'd have us all rounded up. I didn't want to believe it, but she might be after the princess's life too. I had to find out what she was after. If I could just figure out where she stood in all this, I'd know what I needed to do also.

"Anyway, at least we know where we are going."

"Yes. Let's go."

"Yes. Let's get going. Filo."

At the very least, we knew what to do now. That put us one step ahead of where we'd been when we were trying to figure out how to cross the border. We turned to the southwest and started walking.

"Yeah, but I'm kinda tired. My hands hurt, and I used up all my magic."

Filo sat down, exhausted. She needed to rest.

"She's right. And besides, we left our carriage and all our things back there."

"We didn't have a choice."

All we had left was our money, a few goods, and a knife I could use for cooking.

But we'd even lost Raphtalia's equipment.

Even worse, Filo was stuck in human form. How were we supposed to get rid of that hoop?

"Raphtalia, can you think of a way to get that hoop off?"

"I can try."

Raphtalia wrapped her fingers around the hoop and tried to pry it off. But it didn't show any signs of budging.

"It's pretty tough."

I was getting worried. I couldn't let that show on my face.

"I'll try too."

The princess stepped forward.

"I wonder if magic would work."

I remembered that my own world had something called a water cutter. It was a machine that used water pressure to cut through things. I was thinking about it, trying to remember how it worked. Mel was fidgeting with the hoop.

"I can't do it—it's too tough. I think we'd need an alchemist or an item-maker to take it off."

"No!"

Filo made a grumpy face.

That was fair. She probably hated being stuck in human form. She couldn't use all her powers that way.

"An item-maker?"

"Yes. I think it might be sealed with magic—in which case no key would take it off."

"An item-maker . . ."

Raphtalia looked over at me. What did she want? I guess I could do a little, basic item work.

"Mr. Naofumi, you're good with handicrafts. Would you mind trying?"

"I can do a little, but I don't know how to unlock things."

I had a little wire for working with items. I could try.

Turning the hoop in my hands, I found a small hole that looked like it might be a lock. I stuck the wire into it. If I managed to unlock it, I wonder if it would open up some handicraft skill.

I decided to try to focus my magic power on it. Huh? Something was responding to the magic.

The item-dealer we'd traveled with had taught me a trick about using both at the same time. I flicked the wire back and forth. It seemed to be locked with a sophisticated mechanism— though I felt like I could break it with force. Or if I just broke it, I might not be able to ever get it off. But if I could lower the quality of it, I might be able to render its inhibiting effect on Filo null.

I went ahead and applied magic to the wire and then rattled the wire inside the hoop. There was a loud click, and the hoop began to degrade. It was like an anime in which they used electric stun guns to break an electric lock.

"Ah."

With a dramatic puff, Filo transformed back into her Filolial Queen form.

"Think you can just do the rest by force?"

"Sure!"

Filo used her free leg and one wing to get a grip on the hoop. Pulling with a lot of strength, she began to stretch the hoop.

"That is one violent way to get it off."

"Oh, shut up. You can't get it off with a dainty touch."

"Thank you, Master!"

"Be careful from now on. Motoyasu will be better prepared next time."

It took a lot of intricate work to get the hoop off. We wouldn't be able to do it in the middle of battle.

"Okay!"

And so we headed to the southeast as secretly as possible.

I don't know if I'd managed to convince them, but there was no sign that Ren or Itsuki were following us. Either that or they might be on the lookout for us somewhere down the road.

Even still—brainwashing? They couldn't be that stupid. I probably had more to worry about from Motoyasu.

Regardless, it was nice that the strongest hero, Ren, and the range-attacking Itsuki weren't around. Filo could take care of Motoyasu, and as long as the princess was with us, they wouldn't attack directly.

Even still, we had a mountain of problems to tackle.

"What to do . . ."

We started discussing our options.

Epilogue: Name

We were progressing on our journey to the southwest.

We didn't have a carriage, so we all had to ride on Filo. It got old really fast.

"Should we steal a carriage somewhere?"

We already had bounty hunters after us. What was one little carriage?

"NO!"

Filo shouted in disagreement.

"If we have to steal a carriage, I don't want to pull it!"

I guess Filo was developing quite a sense of justice.

"Well, I don't want to steal one either, but riding on you all the time gets tiring."

"What do you think, Princess?"

"Hmm . . ."

The princess looked perplexed by my question.

What was bothering her?

"It might be a little dangerous, but it might be best to send Raphtalia to a nearby village to buy one."

That was probably a good idea. Or should we have asked Shadow for help?

"The sun is getting low in the sky. Let's stop for a rest, shall we?"

"Yeah! Oh . . ."

I'd agreed with her idea, but the princess was still looking at me with a scowl.

What was wrong with her?

Filo's stomach was audibly rumbling.

"I'm hungry!"

"You eat so much, Filo!"

Mel poked Filo with her index finger.

"Heh, heh."

I'm glad they were friends and all, but they were starting to act like a stupid couple. It was annoying.

I finished making the campfire and moved on to dinner.

"Here you go, Princess."

I finished making dinner and was handing a plate of it to the princess—but she was still scowling at me.

What was wrong with her?

"Mel, aren't you going to eat too?"

"Yes, but . . ."

She stole a glance at me, then flicked her gaze away. She was worried about something.

But what?

"What's wrong?"

"It's nothing."

When Raphtalia asked her what was wrong, she reached out and snatched the plate of dinner I'd been offering.

"What's wrong with you, Mel?"

"Um . . ."

Mel was acting strange enough that even Filo was concerned now.

"You know I don't have brainwashing powers, right?"

"I know that!"

She quickly turned and looked away, though honestly, she wasn't acting so weird—all things considered. She was playing with Fil, and smiling and talking with Raphtalia.

She was only acting upset with me. She ignored me.

I had no idea what the problem was.

"Don't say that."

"Huh? What is it, Princess?"

She was shaking, and she had muttered something.

"What did I say?"

"Don't call me 'Princess' anymore!"

She shouted. Her eyes were filled with tears.

"Why are you so upset?"

"I have a name, you know! It's Melty!"

"What? Why are you stating the obvious?"

"I'm upset, Shield Hero, that you won't call me by my name! You used to call me Mel!"

The princess must just be venting the stress from our long journey. She was scratching her head and acting hysterical.

Filo and Raphtalia were watching the princess freak out.

They were clearly just as surprised as I was.

"I'll tell you again! I have a name. It's Melty. But the Shield Hero keeps calling me 'the younger princess!' That's my title, not my name!"

"What? You wanted me to call you by your name?"

"That's not why I'm upset! Why do you treat me differently than everyone else does?!"

"Treat you differently? It's not like you've been part of my party for very long!"

"But I'm sharing in your successes and trials, aren't I? Don't call me by my title!"

"And yet you call me the 'Shield Hero.'"

The princess seemed to understand.

"Shield Hero" isn't my name, after all.

"Fine, I'm going to call you Naofumi then. I'll call you Naofumi, so I expect you to call me Melty!"

"Oh man . . ."

"See?! Say it, Naofumi! Call me Melty!"

I didn't like the idea of acting all familiar.

She was very polite with Raphtalia, but we have to act like we are really close all of a sudden?

Still, I didn't want her calling me "Mister" or anything. That would remind me of my time with Bitch. She used to call me "Mr. Shield Hero."

If I tried to disagree now, she was sure to cause more trouble, and besides, she had helped us protect Filo in the last fight.

As far as I knew, she hadn't lied to us either—and she had tried to reconcile Trash with me, at least until the knights jumped in and messed it all up. Thinking back even further, she'd saved us way back when Motoyasu had caused a scene in the middle of town.

She hadn't lied, and apparently she hadn't been trying to steal Filo from us either.

I had my doubts about believing anyone from this world, but if I was going to believe anyone, I guess I could believe in her.

Filo was naive and innocent, but she was a good judge of character. If Filo believed in her, I guess I could try believing in her too.

"Okay, fine. Melty. Is that better?"

"Yeah! You better stick to it!"

"Okay, okay."

So she was going to freak out anytime I called her "Princess"? That could get annoying really fast.

"That was surprising."

Sure, Filo was crazy and loud, but she wasn't hysterical. She only went nuts in a childish kind of way.

Mel and Filo were similar in that way, probably because they were around the same age.

"Oh, Princess Melty, I didn't know that you were so upset."

"Raphtalia, please stop calling me 'Princess'!"

"Very well, Ms. Melty."

"That's better!"

I wonder how Raphtalia felt about that. She had started calling me by my name back when we fought the two-headed dog. I guess when we used our names, it was kind of proof that we'd grown close.

"Raphtalia, I'm glad you aren't so picky."

She was only a real handful in the beginning, but she had eventually come around.

Unlike Filo, she fought traditionally, with a sword. Since I was the Shield, we were really compatible. When we were selling things, she could run the shop. When we were on the run, she wore a disguise. She was always a big help.

"Is that a compliment?"

"Sure."

"And I guess you're being serious?" she huffed.

"What's wrong, Master?"

Filo now?

I didn't like the idea of Filo calling me by my name . . .

"Filo, don't use my name."

"Why?!"

"He, he . . . Filo is the odd one out!"

"But why? Why? How come I'm the only one that can't use your name?!"

"Go ahead and try."

"Naofumi!"

I didn't even get a "Mister?" And she over-pronounced every syllable. It didn't feel right.

"Yeah, I don't think so. And can't I get an honorific?"

"Nanny, nanny, booboo!"

"Okay, Filo, relax."

"But!"

"Melty's right. Filo, you just call me 'Master.' You could call that 'being left out,' but on the flip side, it makes you special!"

"Boo!"

"Fine. I raised you, so how about 'Papa?' 'Dad?' 'Father?'"

"Um . . . I don't like that!"

"Why?"

Fair enough. I didn't like the idea of such a big thing calling me "Papa," anyway.

"I'd rather call you 'Master' than 'Father'!"

"Right? Okay, then stick with that."

I wonder if she had some kind of motivation for preferring one word to another. Whatever.

"Naofumi."

"What?"

Melty turned to me.

"Say my name again."

"Huh? Why, Melty?"

She closed her eyes and listened closely when I said her name.

"It's nothing."

"Weirdo."

I was positively surrounded by crazy people.

Even if she had thrown a fit, I decided to just chalk it up to a mood.

"What do you say we get to sleep early and get a fresh start tomorrow?"

These last few days, really ever since we met Melty at the diseased village, it's all been so busy. So much had happened.

We'd almost died a few times. Lots of bad things had happened, but if our current travels were successful, then it would all be worth it.

Plus, I had another party member who believed in me. Honestly, I was glad.

I was still shocked that I'd been able to trust Bitch's sister, though.

If we trusted each other, we could prove my innocence. At the end of my journey, I felt like there was a little spark of hope.

As for tonight, I would sleep soundly.

I had to—I had friends that were relying on me.

Extra Chapter: Before I Met My Best Friend

My name is Melty Melromarc. I am the second princess of Melromarc, and I am first in the line of succession.

In order to see more of the world, I've been traveling with my mother.

My mother's job is to travel around the world meeting with people to make sure that Melromarc never has to go to war.

I'm supposed to learn how to do that job, so that is why I have been traveling with her.

One day I was really excited because my mother was going to teach me something new about her job.

A letter had arrived from my father, and when my mother opened it, I had a pretty good idea of what kind of job she was going to give me.

To be honest, I don't hate my father at all—but I think he is kind of gross. I'd heard all sorts of legends about what a strong warrior he had been, but I grew up watching him fawn over my older sister. He gave her whatever she wanted, and it was hard to respect him after that.

It was hard to believe the kind of man he had become.

Still, he had a great military mind. You could tell when he played strategy games with mother. My mother would sit there scratching her head in thought, and he would just yawn—and win. My mother was not a weak player by any means. I'd never seen her lose to anyone besides him. No matter how hard I studied, I could never compare to the skills of my mother. Yet my father beat her easily.

I loved my father. He cared about his family—but I simply cannot understand why he was always caving in and giving my sister whatever she wants.

Speaking of strategy games—my sister was the least skilled among us. My father would hold back to let her win, which is fine. But when she played against others, she would lie, cheat, and steal—anything to win.

The strategy games have different names all around the world. The one we played was actually brought to Melromarc in the past by a hero from another world. My mother said he called it "chess."

I wasn't good at using pressure or cheating. So what did my sister do to me?

"Whenever this piece is in trouble, there is a rule that lets me shuffle the position of the other pieces on the board."

Then she reached out and moved all the pieces into more advantageous positions.

Even after that, I won. She flipped the board over in anger.

"It's a special move! All the piece affiliations switch! And the same special move makes it my turn!"

I even let her do that. But then when it was my turn and I reached for a piece . . .

"This one can jump all the other pieces and go straight for the king!" she said, slamming down a random piece where my king was.

"Okay, then it's my turn to use that special move."

Did she think that I wasn't going to follow her own rules?

"Well . . ."

"It's my turn, isn't it? Now then . . ."

I reached for the piece she said had the power, declared that I used the power, and then took the piece off of the board.

". . ."

She was glaring at me with burning hatred. Did she think I was going to ignore the rules she made up?

"I'm the only one who can do that! I'm putting the piece back."

"Then this game is not fair. If you want to play that way, play with Father."

I stood up and left, and she picked up the board and threw it across the room. What was she thinking? The idea of the country falling into her hands was enough to make anyone nervous.

Okay, back to my story.

About two months ago, our world was visited by a strange phenomenon called the waves of destruction. The first time it happened, I was out traveling with my mother. Before we could go home, we were first supposed to attend an international conference about the waves. We were on our way to a country called Faubrey for the conference. We were supposed to attend a panel about defending the country.

Our ability to summon the heroes gave us authority, and that was very useful in a diplomatic setting. So we discussed the ceremony for summoning the heroes.

In order to see how the ceremony was performed in different places, representatives of each country were to gather together and watch.

The first summoning was to occur in Faubrey. But it ended in failure. The heroes never arrived.

"Mother, why don't they hold the conference after the heroes have arrived?"

"Some things are too difficult to decide simply pragmatically, whether they be between people or between countries."

All the countries would attempt the ceremony, and we were to participate, even if just a little.

In the end, it became clear that our own country, Melromarc, had performed the ceremony without notifying the other nations.

The world was complicated and hostile enough before this happened. When Melromarc summoned the heroes, it started a serious international dispute.

Things were hard after that. Assassins were sent after my mother, and the conference fell into chaos.

I thought it was clear that my father and some church associates were to blame, but maybe my sister had a hand in it too.

"You Melromarc weasels! You want sole control over the heroes, is that it?!"

Someone was thrusting an accusatory finger at my mother. She did not retreat but covered her mouth with a folding fan. I was shocked when she calmly responded.

"Would you like me to say that we aim to take over the world?"

"What was that?!"

"Perhaps you mean to declare war against my country, which processes all of the four holy warriors. Think carefully about that."

"Ugh . . ."

I knew her well enough to know that she was actually very troubled.

Soon, she fell sick. She had a fever, and it was difficult for her to swallow. But she hid her discomfort. She participated in the meetings and said that we summoned the heroes for our own protection. My mother had willpower like no other. I respect her very much.

"However, depending on the conditions you propose, we are not opposed to sharing the heroes—depending on the conditions, naturally."

"We can't trust you!"

"Is that so? The world is in a deep crisis, and you would accuse my country of only protecting itself? Are there no other countries here that wish to pull ahead of the others?"

The accusatory speaker swallowed his response.

My mother produced a report gathered confidentially by her spies.

"King Faubrey? What do you think?"

My mother turned the conversation on the king.

To be honest, King Faubrey was a very disturbing man.

He was like a writhing ball of flesh. He was like a monster pig you didn't want to be around.

"Ahahaha . . . Queen Melromarc, you know very well what it is I desire."

"Yes. All I need to do is agree to your conditions?"

The delegates were all shocked by the conditions he proposed.

I know that my mother had to make a very difficult decision in order to satisfy those demands. She had walked a very difficult path to get to these negotiations.

"Very well then. All of your great nations will send envoys to Melromarc. They will meet with the heroes, respect the wishes of the heroes, and the heroes will accompany them back to your lands."

The delegates all nodded along with my mother.

All this happened a few days after Melromarc summoned the heroes.

A week later and the outcome surprised all of us, including me. All four of the heroes had declined to meet with the envoys.

"That's not what we agreed to!"

The various countries had all been making preparations for the heroes' visits. Now they were upset and blamed my mother.

Apparently, the main problem was that the proposed treatment of the Shield Hero was too awful.

In my mother's absence, it appeared that Melromarc had rebuked and chastised the Shield Hero and was doing all that it could to oppress him. It was going out of its way to discriminate against him.

"It seems that the heroes have discovered a disease within our kingdom, and they are currently making efforts to expunge it. They need a little more time."

"You liar!"

A representative of Siltvelt jumped up on his table in anger. The demi-humans of Siltvelt worshiped the Shield Hero.

"Really? Have you heard that the Shield Hero has asked to be left alone?"

"Mmmm . . ."

"Ahaha . . . very well then. Let's let them do as they wish. Apparently they are still dedicating their efforts to accruing strength."

King Faubrey laughed and spoke in support of my mother.

"To the representative of Siltvelt—do you think there are no records of just how long the last Shield Hero spent within your borders?"

The Siltvelt delegate curled his fingers into a fist.

The heroes must be treated with respect—that was how it has always been.

But the last time the heroes had been summoned, the Shield Hero remained in Siltvelt for a few months before mysteriously dying.

Whether it was an accident or a conspiracy or if the Shield Hero himself was simply weak—no one knows, but it was an incident that Siltvelt found difficult to ignore.

"All we can do is wait until the appropriate time. If you would like to prepare, then all I can say is that it will happen once the filth has been expunged from the kingdom."

"Ugh . . ."

The delegates looked upset. They were glaring at us as we took our seats.

And so Melromarc earned the suspicion of its neighboring nations—it felt like war could break out at any moment.

My mother argued passionately and justly in an attempt to stave off the coming war. Two months passed.

I don't know why the Shield Hero refused to meet with the envoys when the conditions had been so favorable.

Especially considering how poorly he was being treated in Melromarc . . .

When my mother heard of his refusal, she looked very concerned.

"Melty, I have a job for you."

"Okay! What is it?"

"I would like you to, very secretly now, sneak back into Melromarc and convince Aultcray to stop this unfair treatment of the Shield Hero."

I'd heard a little about what was happening back home.

I'd heard that Father and Sister were conspiring against the Shield Hero and that they had many plans to keep him handicapped.

The number of things they'd prevented him from doing was nearly uncountable.

Mother had already sent a number of soldiers to speak with my father, but they had all been ignored. My father listened to me and respected my opinion, and therefore she wanted to send me to reason with him.

At night, my mother found a few painted portraits of my father and burned them with magic.

If things continued this way, with my father acting crazy back home, their relationship could not bear the strain. My mother would run out of patience.

I couldn't let that happen.

"Leave it to me!"

I stood up straight and announced that I would see to it.

"Thank you, Melty."

"Yes, Mother!"

And so I boarded a carriage bound for Melromarc.

We stopped to rest often.

We needed to let the Filolials rest, and it gave me a chance to send reports to Mother.

"Now I will deliver this report. It will only take me a little while, but while I am gone, you must not move, Princess Melty."

"Understood."

A shadow had been provided for my protection.

The shadow was from the secret service, which was entrusted with classified jobs like protection.

Normally a group of them takes turns being on watch, but there was so much happening these days that only one of them was available.

So I was left to my own devices while the shadow delivered my reports.

I sighed.

It wasn't that I didn't like traveling by carriage, but it did get a little boring.

I didn't have anything to do while he was gone. I caught myself yawning.

I was bored and looking out the window when I spotted an interesting creature.

"Ah!"

"Wh . . . What's wrong?"

I startled my attendant when I shouted.

I jumped out of the carriage and walked off into a nearby field, parting the grass as I went.

"Gah! Gah!"

There were wild Filolials there, pulling an empty carriage.

Filolials are large bird-like monsters that pull carriages. They were famous for pulling the heroes' carriages and were revered as holy creatures here and there. They could still be found living in the wild like this.

I'd heard all the legends about the heroes from my mother, but I'd always been drawn to the Filolial characters. I loved them!

Apparently all Filolials shared the desire to pull carriages. I don't really understand it all, but apparently they feel anxious without something heavy to pull.

Over the course of my carriage trip back to Melromarc, I started to really enjoy playing with Filolials. That was when I realized that I really loved these creatures.

"What kind is that one? I've never seen that kind before."

I was hiding in the grass and looking at a strange Filolial.

Its wings were blue like the sky.

At a glance, you could tell it was a Filolial, but I'd never seen one colored that way.

The wings looked different too, and the body shape was strange.

The most obvious difference was a single feather that stood out from the top of its head like a crown.

Could I make friends with it? It was must have been a very rare type.

I want to ride on the back of a rare Filolial!

Wild Filolials were quite timid around humans.

But they were also very hungry things, and you could win them over with some jerky or grass.

That's why I'd taken to carrying some jerky around in my pocket.

I pulled some from my pocket, and the Filolial stepped out of the grove.

"Gah?"

The Filolial noticed.

I didn't want to scare it off, so I held the jerky out in front of me and slowly inched forward.

"Come on, Filolial."

The bird was obviously still cautious, but it started to come over in my direction.

I could tell it was sniffing the air for the jerky.

But . . .

"Gah!"

Nonono! The Filolial ran off through the grass.

"Wait!"

I really wanted to be friends with such a rare creature.

I also knew that there were kinds of Filolials that would only respect you if you ran after them (because Filolials love to run).

I ran back to the carriage and quickly told my attendant what to do.

"Follow that Filolial!"

"B . . . But!"

"Please!"

The attended hesitated for a moment, then nodded and gripped the reins.

Our carriage was also pulled by a Filolial.

"Gah!"

With a lurch, we were running after the strange blue Filolial.

"Wait!"

We were still chasing after the blue Filolial.

The road had grown steeper in the forest, though, and was beginning to wind deeper into the mountains.

"Wait! Please wait!"

The blue Filolial was running its heart out. It looked like it was having fun.

It was so fast. Our own Filolial was tiring out.

"Stop."

"Huh? Um . . . Okay!"

"Gah . . . Gah . . ."

I climbed down and let our Filolial drink water, and then I cast a water spell on her to cool her off.

"Are you okay?"

"Gah!"

I had pushed her too hard. I probably should have given up the chase.

I was thinking on that while I watched the blue Filolial run away.

But then it stopped and looked back at us, as if it wanted us to chase it.

I don't know if it was a game, but it looked like it was having fun.

"You want to keep going?"

"Gah!"

She seemed chipper and eager.

"Then let's go!"

I got back into the carriage, and the chase was back on.

The blue Filolial was running and seemed to be enjoying itself.

It was hard to keep up. It was amazing that such a rare bird would be so fast too.

"Oh no!"

I remembered something I'd forgotten. We were running down switchbacks now. Each curve led to a steeper dip ahead.

The blue Filolial was running near the bottom of the mountain. But she was heading for a place humans should avoid. It was populated with dangerous monsters and dragons.

Filolials and dragons never got along. And the blue Filolial was running right for the dragon's land. It was so focused on the chase that it must not have realized.

"We have to stop it!"

It was kind of cheating, but I jumped down from the carriage, went over the cliff face of the switchback, and jumped down toward the Filolial below.

It was dangerous, but I could use magic to keep myself safe.

"Ms. Melty!"

I heard the attendant call after me, but it was too late.

I fell straight down onto the blue Filolial.

"Gah?!"

"I'm sorry! But you are about to run into dragon territory!"

"Gah!"

The Filolial was agitatedly flapping its wings.

But I was too late.

"GROOOAAAAR!"

A dragon was descending on us from above.

It was much bigger than my carriage had been.

The forest was filled with the dragon's roar and the Filolial's cries.

The Filolial was preparing to defend itself.

Dragons are large, vicious monsters covered in hard scales. They could fly, and it was hard to hurt them with a sword. They had long claws and fangs.

They could also use magic, but it was different than the magic humans used.

One of those very powerful dragons was now right there before us.

What should I do? I didn't want the Filolial to end up hurt. I stepped forward.

"I . . . I'll fight you."

I was only level 18, but I could use powerful water magic.

If I used my strongest spell, I might be able to scare the beast off.

The attendant was nearby too, and there was a tool in the carriage for times like these.

If I didn't time my attack right, I'd leave myself wide open for the dragon's counter. I had to relax, then take care of the dragon.

"Wa . . . Wahhh!"

The attendant took off running.

Terrible. Without him there, who was going to get me the tool from the carriage?

"Gah!"

The Filolial from the carriage ran over to protect me from the dragon.

I'd become pretty close friends with that Filolial during our journey back to Melromarc. I was glad to know that I hadn't imagined our friendship.

To think that the Filolial would protect me . . .

"Gah . . . a . . ."

The dragon thrust its fangs through the neck of my Filolial . . . No . . . my Filolial!

"Stop that!"

It took all my discipline to control myself, but I steadied my breathing and cast a spell.

"I am the source of all power. Hear my words and heed them! Attack him with a blade of water!"

"Zweite Aqua Slash!"

The blade of water flew from my hands and hit the dragon.

It scratched the dragon but was not a fatal blow.

All I'd done was scratch one of its scales.

Was I so powerless?

"Gah!"

The blue Filolial kicked the dragon. But because the dragon had locked its jaws onto my carriage Filolial, the blue Filolial had to hold back.

I turned to the dragon and started to cast another spell.

"I am the root of all power . . ."

"GRAOOOAAAR!"

"AH!"

The dragon whipped its tail and knocked me down.

"Ah!"

It had only felt like a light touch, but before I realized it, I was flying backward and crumpled to the ground. A large blue bruise appeared where the tail had hit me.

"Ugh . . . U . . ?"

I climbed to my feet but found it difficult to stand.

"Gah . . ."

The blue Filolial kicked the dragon again, and this time it hurt enough that the dragon stumbled, releasing its grip on the other Filolial.

"GRAOOOOAR!"

The dragon was so focused on chasing the blue Filolial that it seemed to have forgotten about me. I ran over to the Filolial the dragon had bitten. It was collapsed on the ground. The wounds were deep and serious—the poor thing could die at any moment.

We needed to get back to the carriage . . .

"GRAOOOAR!"

Another dragon appeared and tried to claw at the collapsed Filolial.

If this kept up any longer, the poor bird was sure to die.

All I could think of was saving the Filolial. I focused on chanting a spell.

"I won't let you!"

I ran forward to protect the Filolial, but the dragon flapped its wings, producing so much wind that I was knocked back.

"Ahhh!"

I slammed into a tree and felt my consciousness slipping. The wind slammed into the carriage, and it flew through the air and broke. If I stayed put, I might have been able to avoid the battle. If they ignored me, I could escape later. But I just couldn't leave the Filolial there.

Ever since I was a child, I traveled with my busy mother, and I'd spent all that time becoming friends with these Filolials. I couldn't abandon them.

"Ug . . . Uh . . ."

My creaking body and fuzzy consciousness were straining. I reached out my hand.

"I am the . . . source of all . . . power. Hear my words and . . . heed them. Attack him with a . . . blade of water."

"Zweite Aqua Slash!"

I focused all my magic power into the attack and sent the blade flying at the dragon.

I'd used all my remaining strength, and I fell forward, exhausted.

"Groaaar . . ."

From somewhere in the dim distance, I heard the dragon scream.

I hope . . . I hope that my last attack had managed to drive it off.

"Thank you for protecting me."

I heard a voice, but I don't know whose it was.

I felt something like a strong breeze . . . kindness blowing . . . and then I drifted into darkness.

"Gah!"

"Oh . . . Ah?"

When I opened my eyes, I saw the blue Filolial standing over me.

The hurt Filolial was resting inside of the carriage. It was alive.

I looked around, but we weren't in the mountains anymore. We were in some kind of field.

"Did you save me?"

"Gah!"

The blue Filolial nodded.

I don't know how it did it, but the blue Filolial apparently saved both me and the other Filolial from the dragons and managed to bring us far away to safety.

"Thank you."

"Gah!"

The blue Filolial happily chirped, then licked me.

I rubbed the bird's head in return.

I looked my body over to see if I had any wounds.

The Filolial was squinting and looked very comfortable.

I didn't have any large cuts or anything. My clothes were fine too. I was a little worried that I might have some bruises . . . but I seemed to be okay. I looked over to see that the blue Filolial had covered the other Filolial's wounds with her wings and was healing them.

So she could use healing magic too? Amazing.

In gratitude, I gave all my jerky to the two Filolials.

Later, the blue Filolial let me ride her around a little bit. That was when I noticed . . .

"Oh yeah . . . I . . ."

The shadow had told me to wait for him where he'd left me.

What should I do? The carriage was broken. And the Filolial was too hurt to pull it anyway. I hadn't applied the monster control seal, and I couldn't make her work when she was hurt anyway.

"Gah?"

"I'm sorry. I have to go soon."

I'd taken a bit of a detour, but I'd have to meet up with the shadow and make my way back to Melromarc soon.

"Gaaah!"

My Filolial called out to the blue Filolial.

"Gaaah!"

After nodding a few times, the blue Filolial called back.

Then, all of a sudden, we were surrounded by a whole group of Filolials.

There were so many—I'd never seen anything like it.

Three Filolials came walking over to the blue Filolial.

It looked like they were all listening to her, and I know I wasn't just imagining it. She was like their mother and clearly the leader of the group.

"Gah!"

"Gah!"

The blue Filolial raised a wing and motioned for me to approach the other three Filolials.

"Um . . ."

I climbed down from the blue Filolial and walked toward the others.

When I approached, all three of them knelt to the ground in what I assumed was a signal to climb up.

"You'll take me there?"

"Gah!"

All three nodded.

"Gah!"

The blue Filolial was waving its wings at me.

"Thank you!"

I yelled my gratitude, and the three Filolials took off running.

I had such a mysterious experience with the Filolials that day. I'd never forget it for as long as I lived.

The three Filolials found the road I'd been on originally and then brought me across the border into Melromarc.

On the way, we got tired and took a rest. I'm pretty sure we were near a village in the east of Melromarc.

"Gah?!"

Someone was approaching us, and the three Filolials were squawking in surprise.

Then, as if they suddenly noticed something, they all ran off.

"Ah . . ."

I guess that was the end of our friendship. This wasn't a very convenient place to be dropped off. But I guess I wasn't so far from Melromarc. I could just get a carriage or something.

"That bird looks delicious! Every time I pass one I can't get over how good they look."

"You're one of those birds."

I heard people talking.

"If you chase them, you can still get them, Master!"

I walked in the direction of the voices.

There was a Filolial there, but she was different than any Filolial I'd seen before.

She was wider than normal, with white and pink fluffy feathers. And she was really big.

She had clear, blue eyes and a very happy and cheerful face. She looked like a very pure, happy Filolial.

The blue Filolial was no doubt rare, but I had never seen anything like this one before.

I was so fascinated that I walked right over to her.

"Wow . . . Are you a Filolial?"

"You mean me?"

"You can talk?"

To meet a Filolial that could talk like a person—it was like a dream!

This is all the mysterious stuff that happened before Filo and I met.

After we met, it took a little while to become best friends. In that time, all sorts of things happened—but that's a story for another day.

End

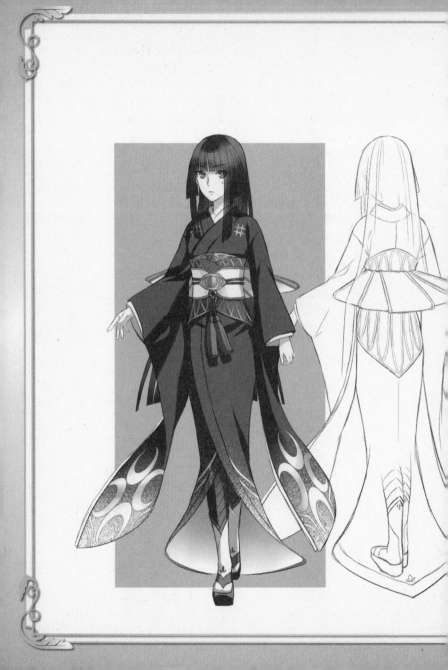

Character Design:
Glass

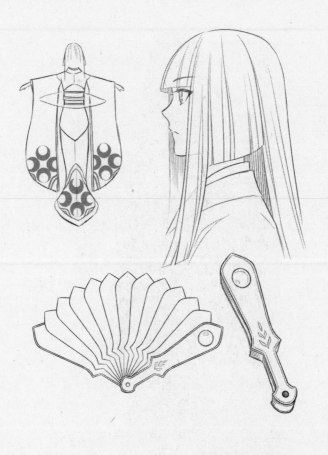

グラス

Character Design:
Melty

Character Design:
Motoyasu Kitamura

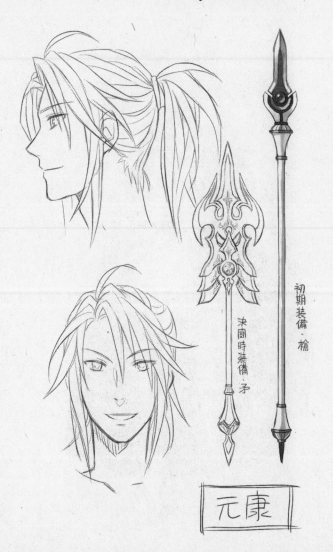

決闘時装備・矛

初期装備・槍

元康

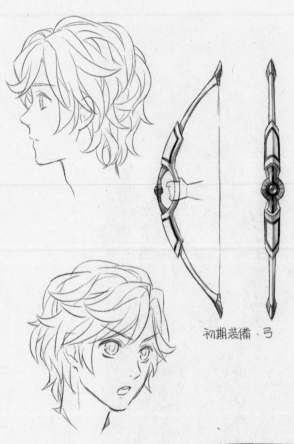

初期装備・弓